Stolen Child

Felicity Pulman

First published by Random House Australia in 2006
This edition published in 2015 by Momentum
Pan Macmillan Australia Pty Ltd
1 Market Street, Sydney 2000

A CIP record for this book is available at the National Library of Australia

Stolen Child: The Janna Chronicles 2

EPUB format: 9781760082888
Mobi format: 9781760082895
Print on Demand format: 9781760300128

Cover design by Raewyn Brack
Edited by Kylie Mason
Proofread by Laurie Ormond

Macmillan Digital Australia: www.macmillandigital.com.au

To report a typographical error, please visit momentumbooks.com.au/contact/

Visit www.momentumbooks.com.au to read more about all our books and to buy
books online. You will also find features, author interviews and news of any
author events.

Felicity Pulman is the award-winning author of numerous novels for children and teenagers, including *A Ring Through Time*, the Shalott trilogy, and *Ghost Boy*, which is now in pre-production for a movie. *I, Morgana* was her first novel for adults, inspired by her early research into Arthurian legend and her journey to the UK and France to 'walk in the footsteps of her characters' before writing the Shalott trilogy–something she loves to do. Her interest in crime and history inspired her medieval crime series, The Janna Mysteries, now repackaged as The Janna Chronicles.

Recently awarded the inaugural Di Yerbury writer's fellowship, Felicity will spend several months in the UK in 2015 researching and writing the sequel to *I, Morgana*. She has many years experience talking about researching and writing her novels both in schools and to adults, as well as conducting creative writing workshops in a wide variety of genres. Felicity is married, with two children and six grandchildren, all of whom help to keep her young and technosavvy–sort of! You can find out more about Felicity on her website and blog: www.felicitypulman.com.au or on Facebook.

Also by Felicity Pulman

Prologue

The scrawny, mud-stained youth froze in his tracks. Someone was coming! He quickly snatched up the snare he'd been about to set and slipped it down the front of his tunic. Should he be seen, he must seem innocent—but he would do all in his power to remain undetected for it could mean the difference between his life or death.

Nervous, needing a hiding place, he scanned the forest. A sheltering screen of holly bushes nearby was his best, his only option. He raced to them and, wincing, eased himself between the prickly leaves, trying not to shake or disturb them in any way, or make any sound that might betray his presence. Once safely inside his thorny cover, he peeped out to see who was on his trail. Sometimes a guide came through the forest, leading a band of pilgrims, or perhaps a cleric or a nobleman, to safety. When that happened, laughter and chatter usually accompanied their passage, for the travelers would have permission to be in the forest and would be passing through on legitimate business. But this traveler moved silently, and therefore must be alone.

If it was the forester who pursued him, he was in deadly danger. Gravelinges was a royal forest and the king's forester patrolled it regularly to protect it from poachers, to make sure that there were always deer and wild boar for the king and his barons to hunt, as well as hares, coneys and even fat doves. Anyone caught red-handed would be hauled to the forest court, where justice was summary and swift: if your life was not forfeit, at the very least your hands could be cut off, so Edwin had heard.

He looked down at his hands. They were dirty but not blood-stained, at least not so far as he could see. To make sure, he wiped them across a patch of damp grass, then turned them over and wiped them again. He inspected them carefully. Cleaner now, but it was perfectly possible that there might still be blood under his fingernails, for he had killed many creatures while hiding in the forest. Hares, coneys and squirrels, voles, mice and birds—anything to fill his empty, aching belly and keep him alive just a little longer. He felt about him for a small twig and quickly began to scrape it under his cracked and broken nails in a vain effort to lift out the ingrained dirt. He listened as the traveler came closer.

If not the forester, then who? The servants of his liege lord? Edwin's heart sank further as he pondered the possibility that he might have been traced here to the forest. He might already have walked into a trap. He cowered in the prickly holly, trying to make himself invisible.

The walker was a youth, and he was alone. Even better, he seemed unarmed. Edwin cautiously eased some leaves aside so he could see the boy more clearly. His eyes narrowed in calculation as he weighed up the choice of staying hidden and taking his chances, or jumping the youth and catching him unawares. Whether he was here on legitimate business or was an outlaw, the boy might have something worth stealing. He might even have brought food and ale along for the journey. Edwin's mouth watered at the thought.

A fallen tree lay close behind him. Edwin reached out and quietly raised a branch that had broken away, testing its strength and weight. It would do. He had the advantage of surprise. A well-placed blow...

Edwin smiled to himself. His muscles tensed, poised, ready to spring, yet something made him hesitate. He watched as the unsuspecting youth passed close to the holly bushes, flushing a bird from its cover. The boy stopped to look about him, his face open to scrutiny.

"Who's there?" he cried.

Edwin's eyes widened in surprise. His fingers relaxed their firm grip on the dead branch and his smile broadened. He settled deeper into his prickly hiding place to wait, to watch, and to make quite sure.

Chapter 1

The first thing she needed, Janna decided, as she followed the faint trail that snaked through the forest, was to find a pool or stream to wash out her filthy, flea-ridden clothes. Her lip curled in disgust as she looked down at the peasant's smock and breeches she wore. Not only were they far too big for her, they were stained with sweat and dirt. In fact, they stank, and therefore so must she. She raised her arm to take a surreptitious sniff under her armpit and nearly swooned from the powerful odor released by her action. Even worse than the smell was the itching. Something—or lots of little somethings—was living in her clothes. Janna felt her skin crawl. She longed to scratch her arms, her legs, her body, but she knew scratching would make the itches much worse. Better by far to find somewhere she could strip off and wash herself as well as the garments she wore. It would also give her a chance to inspect the burns she'd sustained in the fire that had so utterly destroyed her cottage.

If Godric—or even the dashing lord Hugh—could see her now! Janna shook her head as she tried to imagine their reaction. But she must not think of them; she must forget everything about her past life until she had succeeded in her quest to find her father. If he lived—and if she could bring him around to her way of seeing things—then she could think about the past once more, and about the man who had done her and her mother such grievous harm.

Meanwhile these filthy garments were part of her disguise and she would have to endure them until she found somewhere to cleanse herself. She quickened her pace, hoping that she was heading in the right direction. She needed to put as many miles as possible between herself and those who had burned her home and who wanted to harm her, just in case they discovered the truth. She had heard there was a trail that went north through the forest of Gravelinges to Wicheford on the other side; she hoped she was on it. Her journey would not end there, but it would put the barrier of the forest between her and those whom she had once considered allies and friends. The memory of their treachery cast a dark shadow across her heart.

The great canopy of branches high above turned the forest into a cool, green dimness. Only a few rays from the setting sun pierced the leafy shield, pebbling the path with coins of gold. Bright spongy moss coated tree roots, while sticky-footed ivy clung to dead and living trees alike, encasing them in ruffled coats of green. The soft groans and murmurs of wood pigeons gave way to an alarmed rattle of wings as they flew away from the sound of Janna's approach. She felt as if she was walking through an enchanted wonderland, yet loneliness and sorrow walked beside her, step by step.

She scanned the silent forest for signs of water, and licked her dry lips. She'd been walking for a long time. How much further before she reached Wicheford? Everyone knew that Gravelinges was enormous, but how big was enormous? Could she walk through the forest before nightfall, or was she already running out of time? She had no way of knowing where she was. Huge beech and oak trees towered above her, silent watchers in the dark forest, interspersed with birch, ash and hazel too, their summer green brighter than the dark patch of holly ahead. Janna shivered. The forest was a dangerous place, especially at night, when it became the demesne of wolves and other fierce creatures.

Her footsteps quickened, but then slowed again almost immediately. The trail was barely discernible in the dim light. She was further through the forest than she'd ever gone before, so could not rely on familiar landmarks to guide her. She was afraid that, in her hurry, she might misread her way and become truly lost.

A faint rustle ahead froze her into stillness. Her heart thumped with fright. Slowly, her gaze sifted the landscape. There was a tall thicket of weeds in an open space ahead, which might give shelter to anything from a coney or deer to an outlaw. She watched for shaking leaves for any signs of movement, but all was still. Her gaze moved to the clump of holly bushes and then on and over to several huge oak trees.

Nothing moved. Janna turned slowly in a full circle, watching and listening. She took a few steps forward, pressing her feet carefully on grass and weeds so as not to make a noise, for she sensed now that she was not alone.

A silvery trilling set her heart leaping with fear. A pale yellow-gray wood warbler, flushed from cover, flew away. She felt the stir of air from its flight on her cheek. Sweat prickled her shoulder blades. "Who's there?" she cried, her voice high and wavering with fright. Too late, she recalled that she was wearing a man's clothes. "Is anyone there?" she tried again, striving for a deeper tone.

Silence. Janna's ears stretched to hear a noise that wasn't her own. She could feel eyes watching her every move. She whirled abruptly, hoping to catch—what? Something animal...or human? She swallowed hard, feeling again the sweat of fear as she recalled the last time she'd been lost in

Gravelinges in the dark, when she'd stumbled across the path of a wild boar. In her panic to escape she'd run in circles, enraging it to such a degree that it had charged and almost killed her. If Godric hadn't been out poaching that night...

Godric. Janna's mind skittered hastily away from the image of the villein who had been so kind to her, and who had promised her so much more. She *must not* think of him, for although he lay heavily on her conscience there was no way now for her to make amends.

Bringing her mind back to her present predicament, Janna scanned the silent, secret forest, hearing only the frightened thudding of her own heart. She forced her legs to move once more, taking one reluctant step after another while she assessed the situation. Wild animals didn't only come out at night, she reasoned, but if it was a wild animal stalking her now it would not trouble to conceal the noise of its passage. Which meant that the watcher must be human.

Could it be the king's forester? Her mouth twisted in a grimace. She had only her feminine wiles to talk her way around the fact that she was trespassing in the royal forest, and she doubted they would be enough to save her—especially dressed as she was! But if the forester was following her, would he not have shown himself and challenged her as soon as he noticed her?

Not the forester then. Could it even be Godric, who sometimes came through the forest on legitimate business, guiding people to safety on the other side? Briefly, desperately, Janna wished that it might be him. In spite of feeling deeply ashamed of her behavior, she longed to see him, longed for the comfort of his familiar presence. But she dared not call out once more, for it seemed more likely that the silent watcher was an outlaw, and therefore greatly to be feared.

Janna had heard numerous stories about those who fled the king's justice: how they hid in forests and preyed on travelers, seizing whatever they might find and showing no mercy to any who stood in their way. Fear kept her motionless for long moments. God rot it, she thought, wishing she was safely home in her cottage with her mother and Alfred, her cat. She drew in a deep breath to steady herself. Her home, and those she loved, were gone, all gone. She was alone out here, with no kith or kin to comfort her and only her knife for protection. She drew it out of its sheath and, feeling slightly braver with a weapon in her hand, she forced herself to walk on.

Her way became more open, the tree cover now quite sparse. Janna realized she was no longer climbing. She seemed to have reached the high point of the forest, for the open weedy growth ahead lay downhill before being swallowed into darkness under the trees. She walked toward it and looked about the open glade. It must be very late, for the sun, always slow to disappear in the summer months, had now vanished and light was fading fast from the sky. Even if she hurried, Janna knew she could not get through the forest before it was too dark to see her way. Nor could she keep on walking for fear of straying from the path, which was already so faint as to be almost indiscernible. She'd heard tales of travelers who'd been lost in Gravelinges for days, weeks even. If they survived, they were half mad with fear by the time they were rescued. She must not lose her way.

Should she then remain here through the night, and continue her journey in the morning? She shivered with unease as she looked about her. She was sure eyes still watched her, yet although her senses were alert for a betraying signal, she could hear nothing out of the way, nor were there any signs of movement. She tried to comfort herself with the notion that it was only her imagination, for an outlaw would not bother to stalk her when instead he could have taken whatever he wished and, by now, be safely on his way.

She wished she could light a fire. It would bring warmth and a measure of protection from any wild animals that might be lurking nearby, but it might also attract the attention of the king's forester. She couldn't risk it. Nor could she risk making a nest of grass out here in the open, not when she was so deep within the forest. If she slept on the ground she would be in danger from any wild creature, animal or human, large or small, that crossed her path. Better, perhaps, to wedge herself up in a tree for the night, she decided. It would be uncomfortable, but she would be in a position to protect herself; she would be safe.

With her knife, Janna drew a large and careful circle around her feet to mark the faint trail she was following, then cut a long staff of hazel and staked it in the center so that she would be able to see it from a distance. She pulled out her old kirtle, which she'd hidden under her smock, and tied it to the top of the stake. She stepped back and surveyed her handiwork. Her kirtle had been burnt to tatters in the fire and was useless to her, but it made a good beacon. Besides, she no longer needed the disguise of a fat stomach, for anyone who met her from now on would be a stranger to her. Even if, by unlucky chance, she were to come across anyone from her past, she hoped they wouldn't recognize her anyway—she was no longer Janna, daughter of a *wortwyf*, she was now a youth called John.

Janna nodded, satisfied with her arrangements. With frequent glances at her home-made marker to prevent herself from roaming too far, she looked for a tree with a lot of branches to cradle her and keep her fast should she fall asleep and neglect to hold on. She also kept a lookout for any sign of water, or even some juicy berries. Her stomach growled with hunger; her throat was scratchy with thirst. A few creamy white mushrooms caught her eye. She pounced on them, and inspected them carefully before stuffing them into her mouth.

They tasted yeasty, of raw, damp earth; they brought saliva to her mouth and helped to fill her hollow belly.

Janna tried to ignore her discomfort, ignore too the itches that plagued her, and the tickling, biting midges that swarmed around her face. Still she had the uneasy sense that she was not alone. However, if the watcher was human, it seemed he was in no hurry to accost her. Perhaps he intended to wait until she fell asleep? Janna caught her breath at the thought. I'll stay awake all night, she promised herself, and gripped her knife more tightly as she searched for a tree with branches reaching down low enough for her to haul herself up.

There was a thicket of yew ahead, a dark, dense tangle of knitted branches and spindle leaves. Her mother's voice came into her mind: "*Yews are ancient and sacred trees. The druids built their temples nearby them, believing them to be sites of burial and resurrection.*" Janna took a step toward them, then stopped as she recalled her mother's warning. "*The fruits and seeds are highly poisonous, so you must be careful, Janna. Stay away from them, if you can. They're otherworld, and they're dangerous.*" The trees rose before her like a solid wall; she could not penetrate their depths. They would make a perfect hiding place. Should she risk it? It wasn't as if she was planning to eat any part of them!

She recalled what else she'd been told about them: that faeries believed yews had the power to render them invisible, and that they used yew to conjure up a darkness into which they might disappear. Janna, too, sought to disappear; it seemed like an omen. She hurried over and eased herself into their sheltering arms, then pulled herself upward from branch to branch. Climbing was so much easier wearing breeches. In fact, just about everything was so much easier for a man than a woman.

When she could no longer see the ground below, she judged she was high enough to remain unobserved, while being secure enough to defend herself should anyone climb up and attack her. She wedged her body into the interlacing branches and hooked her arms around them for safety. It was almost completely dark now. She couldn't see anything other than her immediate cover, but she knew her beacon was close enough for her to find it in the morning.

With a sigh, she closed her eyes, then quickly snapped them open. She must not go to sleep. She touched the purse at her waist, heard the faint crumple of parchment and the clink of coins. Everything she owned that was of value to her was in her purse, including her journey's purpose: the clues that might lead her to her father.

With the last of the light gone, the night became cold. A soft rain began to fall. Janna pulled the hood of her gorget over her head, and huddled deeper into the prickly shelter in a vain effort to stay dry. The rain kept on, soaking through the gorget as well as her smock and breeches. It was too gentle to cleanse the filthy garments or drown the creatures that tormented her, but it was persistent enough to chill her to the bone. Janna shivered, and debated climbing down from her tree. If she walked about, her blood would flow freely once more and she might get warm.

But if she wandered about in the dark, she left herself open to attack. Almost certainly, she would also get lost. So Janna stayed where she was and continued to shiver as she listened to the sounds of the forest at night: the haunting call of an owl overhead; the scuffle of a scavenging badger below and, in the distance, the anguished howl of a wolf. Secretive rustles betrayed the hunters; squeaks of distress marked their prey.

The night wore on, black and dismal, all trace of moon and stars hidden behind cloud. In spite of her best efforts, Janna's eyes closed. She slept, jerked awake, and slept again. When she next awoke, the sky was beginning to lighten and the birds of the forest were celebrating the birth of a new day with chirps and cheeps, trills of interrogation, whistles and snatches of songs. Janna rested quietly for a moment, listening to their conversations, but her body was numb with cold and she was desperate to get down from her tree.

Her limbs were cramped and stiff and, as she clambered downward, she slipped off a rain-slicked branch and crashed through prickly foliage to land with a thump on the ground. She groaned with the pain of it. A brief vision of her home flashed into her mind: the fire warming and lighting the small cottage, the fragrance of dried herbs, hot griddle cakes and rich vegetable pottage, her mother's busy efficiency, and Alfred's welcoming purr...

Tears came into Janna's eyes as she felt once more the wrenching grief of her mother's death, an aching sense of loss. There was also the added frustration of knowing that her mother had been on the brink of divulging the secret of her father's identity, a secret Janna was sure was contained in the letter her mother had kept hidden from her. But to find it out she must first learn to read, for that was something Eadgyth hadn't taught her. Janna thought about the parchment in her purse with its indecipherable marks. Only the name at the end meant anything to her. John. It was her father's name, she was sure of it. She burned with curiosity to know what he had written to her mother. Eadgyth had loved him, she knew that now, yet his words had caused her mother to pack up and run, and keep his identity forever a secret.

Janna came back to the present, becoming aware of her surroundings once more. She choked back a sob. She was lonely and frightened, but somehow she must find the strength to carry on. So she scrubbed the tears from her cheeks with a grubby hand, eased herself into a sitting position, and carefully massaged the base of her sore spine. She stretched out her legs, rotating first one foot and then another. Satisfied that nothing was broken after her fall, she stood up and walked over to the stake she had left as a marker. She pulled it from the ground, removed her bundled kirtle and threw it into a clump of bushes. The stake she kept, for it gave her an extra weapon to protect herself, should she need it.

Remembering her sense that she was being watched, she glanced around, searching for signs. A sudden crackle of twigs set her heart leaping into her throat. She backed behind a tree, then caught sight of a grazing deer. Fascinated, she stood quietly, watching it. Its belly was swollen, reminding Janna that the fence month might already have begun, the time when the forest was forbidden to everyone so that the does might drop their fawns and nurture them in safety. It was an extra reason to get out of the forest as soon as she could. The doe stepped on delicate feet toward Janna, head bent as it nibbled grass, lulled into a sense of safety. Janna extended a cautious hand toward it. "Tck, tck, tck," she called softly. Startled, it jerked up its head and surveyed her with liquid brown eyes. After a moment, it bent its head once more, and resumed feeding. She smiled at it, feeling a sense of peace as she contemplated the creature's innocence and trust.

She tiptoed past, fighting her reluctance to leave the safety of this open space for the forest that lay ahead of her. She must get through the forest today. Not for anything would she spend another night like the one she'd just passed. She walked on and under the sheltering trees, and stopped, unsure now if she was on a path at all, for the way ahead seemed unmarked and undisturbed. She looked up, hoping to determine her direction by the position of the sun, but the forest had closed over her head and the sky was barely visible. Hastily she retraced her steps, and was relieved when she reached the clearing once more. She tilted back her head to find the sun, but dark clouds banked thick across the sky; there was no trace of golden radiance. Even as Janna glanced about, rain began to fall once more, soaking through her already wet clothes.

"Hell's breath," she muttered miserably, knowing she would give almost anything to anyone if it bought her food and shelter. She longed to be free of the forest. Its silence oppressed her to the point where she could hardly find the strength or courage to keep on going.

But to stand still was to give in to despair. She prowled around the open space, hoping to bring life to her chilled feet and limbs while she tried to find the path that would take her through to the other side of the forest. To fail, she knew, would result in her death.

Fear almost paralyzed Janna. It took all her strength not to scream for help in the hope that someone, be it forester or outlaw, would come to her aid. She curled her hands into fists, feeling her nails dig into her palms. The pain helped to calm her. Breathe, she thought, remembering Eadgyth's instructions to panicky patients. She took a slow, deep breath, feeling time pass as the cold air sucked through her nostrils and down into her chest. Slowly, she expelled her breath through her mouth, blowing it out in a thin stream, like smoke in the chill morning air. After several more breaths, and feeling slightly calmer, she began a careful inspection of the edge of the clearing once more.

A new thought alarmed her now. How would she be able to tell the difference between the track she'd already taken, and the track that would lead her to where she wanted to go? But here was a sign! Trodden leaves marked a faint trail. Abandoning caution, Janna hurried along it, confident this must be a new trail for she could recognize nothing from the night before. Her foot slipped from under her and, unable to break her fall, she slid down into icy cold water. It sucked up around her, filling her boots and making her gasp for breath.

Speechless with shock, Janna flailed about until she found her footing. She realized that the water came only to her thighs.

She looked about her at the great, leaf-filled depression in which she stood; it seemed to be a large and ancient dewpond. She tried to step out, but slimy mud, formed from the detritus of the centuries, held her boots fast. Janna stood on one foot and leaned on her staff to help her balance while she wriggled her other foot until she'd managed to work her boot free. She took off the boot and threw it to safety, then cautiously lowered her bare foot to the bottom of the pond. She shuddered as it sank deep through the icy slime. Maintaining a precarious balance, she worked her other foot free, tugging hard until the sucking mud released it. A second boot joined its companion on the leafy bank.

With a sudden gasp of fear, Janna snatched up her purse and opened it, belatedly understanding the danger if the precious parchment had got wet. The outside of the purse was damp, but its contents were dry. Janna released her breath in a quiet prayer of thanks to whoever might be listening. She flung the staff onto dry ground, and untied her girdle. Purse and girdle followed the staff and boots to safety. Time now to attend to her greatest need: water! She scooped twigs and leaves out of her way, bent her head and began to drink, relishing the icy wetness sliding down her parched throat. She drank until she could drink no more, but now another idea had come into her mind. She was already wet and uncomfortable. She had nothing to lose save the family of biting creatures that inhabited the garments she wore. With a quick glance around her to make sure she really was alone, she waded into the middle of the pond and gingerly lowered her body into the water. Anchoring herself in the freezing mud, she stripped off the stolen gorget and smock, untied her breeches, and gave herself and her garments a good scrub before dressing once more. The gorget came last, but the hood clung cold and wet around her head and water dripped into her eyes. She took it off and cast it out onto the grass.

Remembering her itchy, burnt scalp, she ducked down into the freezing water once more and massaged her fingers through the remnants of her hair. At last, satisfied that every little creature must be drowned, she waded to the bank. A memory teased her: Godric's story of the ancient road built through the forest by the Romans. Could this dewpond have been fashioned to provide water for the soldiers and merchants who had once traversed this land?

Something sharp pierced Janna's foot and she cried out, forgetting the need for silence. She raised her foot out of the water, and frowned as she inspected it. The tender skin of her instep was cut and bleeding. What could have been so sharp that it had pierced her skin like that? Not a flint, surely, but a sword perhaps, or a dagger? Janna knew that such things were sometimes found in water. She'd heard that it was an ancient custom for warriors to throw their weapons into rivers and pools in order to propitiate the gods and seek good fortune. Coming across a pool in a huge forest such as this must in itself have seemed like good fortune to the old ones. They might well have shown their gratitude with costly gifts.

Her own knife was quite small, no match for a wild animal or an outlaw. The staff she'd found was better than nothing, but with a real weapon in her hand she would feel much, much safer. She took a deep breath and ducked down, carefully feeling through the icy mud for something sharp. Janna's lungs were bursting. She shot upwards and gasped for air, greedily sucking it in. Her teeth chattered with cold; she was tempted to get out of the pool but instead forced herself to take another deep breath and duck again into the darkness. She groped about in the slimy mud.

Nothing. She surfaced once more, her whole body shaking in protest. One last time, she promised herself, and filled her lungs with air. This time her search was rewarded. Janna felt the blade bite her hand. She snatched it away, then cautiously stretched out her fingers, feeling inch by careful inch until at last she touched the blade again. Her chest was on fire. She was desperate to take a breath but she stayed down, carefully patting along the flat of the blade until she came to the solid shape of its hilt. She closed both hands around it and tugged, feeling the sword slide free. She shot up, breaking the surface with a triumphant whoosh of escaping air.

She breathed deeply, savoring the air's freshness, and looked down at the muddy object in her hands. It was longer than a dagger, but shorter than the swords worn by noblemen such as Hugh. Part of the hilt was broken off, but there was enough left for her small hand to grasp the weapon. She swished the sword around in the water, carefully breaking off lumps of caked mud and grit and rinsing it clean. The blade was rusty, its sheen dulled from its long immersion in the water. But it was sharp enough to inflict a grievous wound, Janna noted, as she gingerly put her foot to the ground and limped out of the dew pond.

Wiping her injured foot clean, she eased it into her boot. She put on her other boot, picked up the gorget and looked about for her purse and girdle. There was no sign of them. Janna frowned and looked more carefully, unable to understand the significance of their disappearance. Where could they be?

Panic constricted her chest. She began to search frantically, thinking she must have misread the direction in which she'd thrown them. Perhaps they'd slid beneath a bush or were buried among long grass and bracken? She scoured the clearing, poking into banks of tall nettles and patches of flowering weeds as she gradually widened the area of her search. In her heart, she knew that she'd not mistaken the direction and that they were gone. Someone had been watching her all along, waiting for just this opportunity to steal from her the only clues she had that might lead her to her father.

Chapter 2

Janna bowed her head as a wave of grief and loss swept over her. She had so little, yet even this had been taken from her. A few silver pennies—yes, they might be of use to a desperate vagabond, as might the ring and brooch if he could trade them. But, for Janna, the only item of value in her purse was the letter she'd found from her unknown father. She was quite sure it would prove the key to everything, if only she could read it.

Would an outlaw be able to read? Janna doubted it. He'd keep what he could trade, but might he perhaps throw away the piece of parchment, thinking it worthless?

A faint glimmer of hope lifted her spirits. If she could manage to follow the thief's passage through the forest, might she find the parchment discarded along the track? It was a hope worth pursuing. She looked about her once more, this time seeking any sign of a shelter close to the pond. The thief must have hidden somewhere while he watched her and waited to pounce. He might well have left signs of his presence—and the direction of his departure.

A dense thicket of hazel stood close by. Gripping the sword tightly, she marched toward it. She examined the surroundings, looking for signs: a thread snagged on a withy perhaps, or bruised and broken herbage. Her search was rewarded by the sight of a footprint indented in a patch of soft earth. Another print ahead led away from the thicket. Janna followed, on the alert for any further clues to point her way.

Several times she thought she'd come to a dead end, but she trusted her instincts and kept on going, following the most obvious route through the trees. Although she kept a constant watch for it, there was no sign of her father's letter. But scuffed moss, a broken twig, some flattened grass or herbs, a sliver of snagged bark all helped to point the way. She placed her feet lightly, carefully, while she repeated in her mind like a prayer: *Please let him throw away the parchment. Please let me find my father's letter.*

She came to a dense patch of the forest, hazel and holly hedged by a wall of prickly brambles. There seemed no way through. Baffled, Janna stopped and looked around her before bending over for a more careful inspection. Every instinct told her she was close to her quarry, but the brambles barred her way. Or did they? Here they were bent one way, there another, cunningly plaited to disguise a thin and twisting passage through. Quiet as a hunting owl, Janna eased herself to the left then to the right, pushing deeper into the prickly heart of the brambles, until a small clearing opened before her. She stepped forward, then hastily slid behind the trunk of a large beech for concealment.

She could see the thief clearly—he was sitting with his back to her. Janna saw a faint glimmer as he held the gold ring up for inspection. Her other possessions lay on the ground beside him. Clearly, he was gloating over his good fortune. A wave of fierce rage coursed through her, hot as the blazing sun. Without thought, she launched herself at him, arm raised and sword at the ready to strike him flat with the blade and, if necessary, run him through. How dare he take her treasures, how dare he!

Swift and silent as she was, the young man heard her and sprang to his feet. His upraised arm deflected the sword's blow. The blade missed the side of his head and hit him flat against the wrist instead. He grunted with pain but was still able to grab her wrist and wrench the sword from her grasp, flinging it safely out of range. Enraged, Janna swung back her foot and kicked out, aiming for his groin, hoping to cripple him with pain. But she was too slow and he read her mind. Just as her foot came forward he released her, giving her a shove so that she lost her balance and fell. But before he had time to flee, she launched herself at his ankles and tugged, pulling him down on top of her. She rolled free and raked his face with her nails.

"Devil's spawn!" She began to pummel him with her fists. "Dog's droppings! Pond slime!"

She kept up the attack, feeling proud of the fact that she was getting the better of the rogue, until she realized he was making no effort to defend himself. Instead, he'd curled into a ball to present the smallest target to her flailing arms and fists.

"You can stop hitting me, mistress. I won't harm you," he muttered.

As she understood the import of his words, shock stopped Janna mid-blow. Wide-eyed, she jumped to her feet and snatched up the sword, ready now to grab her treasures and run.

"H-how did you know I wasn't a boy?" she stammered.

His face reddened slightly. He grinned at her, but did not answer. Janna felt her own face redden as she worked out how he'd managed to fathom her secret. "You watched me bathe, you...you bastard, damn you to hell!" She closed her eyes as she remembered how she'd stripped off and washed both herself and her clothes. Mortified, she lashed out once more. He took a hasty step out of her reach.

"I turned my back to you as soon as I realized what you were. Who you are!" he protested.

"Liar!"

"By a snake's tits, I swear it!"

An oath not to be trusted then, Janna surmised. Certainly he'd seen enough to know the truth about her. But at least she'd crouched down in the water to wash, and had both undressed and dressed in the pond. How long had he been watching her, waiting to pounce? She eyed the youth warily. He hadn't harmed her—not yet. But that didn't mean he might not try in the future.

"Why are you wearing men's clothes anyway?" he asked, his grin returning. "Certes, they don't become you, nor do they fit you very well!"

"They do well enough." To prove her words, Janna tugged on the cord holding her breeches in place to tighten it, then hitched the breeches higher so she no longer trampled the fabric underfoot. "And don't think to change the subject either!" she said, recalling the reason she had followed him. She bent to snatch up the ring that the young man had dropped in the surprise of her attack, and hastily shoved it into the purse that lay on the ground nearby, hearing the comforting crump of parchment as she did so. The brooch and silver coins had also been dumped on the grass and they swiftly followed the ring to safety. Janna straightened and glared at the thief, ready to protect what was rightfully hers.

He held up his hands in a gesture of peace. "I beg pardon, mistress," he muttered. "I have nothing save the clothes I am wearing, so I was going to use what I stole from you to travel somewhere safe, to find shelter and buy food. But I won't try again; leastways not while you're holding that sword!"

"Why are you here in the forest?" Janna demanded, not in the least mollified by his explanation. "What are you hiding from?"

"Why are *you* here? What are *you* hiding from?"

Janna was silenced, but only for a moment. "I asked first."

A grin stole over his face once more. "I'll make a bargain with you. I'll tell you my story if you'll tell me yours." He waited for her grudging nod before continuing. "I am on the run from my lord. He's a cruel man, cruel as the devil. He beat me." The youth touched his dirty face. Janna saw a jagged scar on his chin, and winced in sympathy. "I ran away. I decided I'd rather live as an outlaw than stay at the mercy of that swine. I've been hiding here in the forest ever since, catching whatever I may to eat, and drinking water from that pool you fell into."

"How long have you been here?" Janna strove to keep any hint of warmth from her voice, lest he believe she might take pity on him and relax her guard.

"I don't know the time in days exactly, but I reached the forest as the trees were just coming into bud from their winter sleep. I think it must be mid-summer by now?"

Janna nodded. "Close enough. The fence month may well have started already. You must certainly leave the forest as soon as possible, as must I."

"Why?"

"'Tis the time when does give birth to their fawns. The forest is forbidden to all at that time so that mothers and their babies are not disturbed. 'Tis a dangerous time to hide here, for the forester will be on constant watch to protect the king's deer for the hunting season to come."

The young man nodded thoughtfully. "I'll have to take my chances. I can't leave until the seasons turn full circle."

"Why so long?"

"If I can stay hidden for a year and a day, I shall have earned my freedom from my lord." The youth grinned ruefully. "It's the winter to come that I dread. I don't know how I shall keep myself alive through the cold."

Janna felt some sympathy for the ruffian. His story touched her. So, too, did the fact that, although he'd stolen her purse, he'd made no effort to harm her, or keep her goods once she'd tracked him down. Besides, she was in no position to judge what anyone might do when pushed to the limit of need for she, too, had stolen something: the clothes she wore, and from a poor peasant who could ill afford to lose them.

"What will you do after a year and a day?" she asked.

The young man shrugged. "I would like to become an apprentice, to learn a trade, but I have not the money for that. So I will do anything at all that might help me earn my bread and keep."

"No-one will give you work and shelter once they know you're a runaway serf," Janna pointed out.

"They will if they think I've come from Wales. That's what I'll tell them. They won't care who my lord was, so long as I show willing and work hard." The youth flexed his muscles. "I am strong," he boasted, "and I can turn my hand to anything I'm asked to do. I'll have no trouble finding someone to take me in."

Janna nodded thoughtfully. If she helped him, might he, in turn, help her? She held out her hand. "My name is Johanna, but I'm known as Janna," she said. "I, too, am in hiding from those who wish me harm. That's why I'm dressed like this. I call myself 'John' after my father—for I believe he was a man of wealth and importance."

The youth nodded. He relaxed his wary stance, sprawling back against the grass. "My name is Edwin."

"If you come from Wales, shouldn't you should call yourself by a Welsh name? Hoel or Gwyn, something like that?"

"Edwin, Hoel, it makes no matter so long as they believe I'm a free man from across the border." He shrugged, and patted the grass beside him. "Sit down," he invited. "I won't hurt you."

Not taking any chances, Janna hooked the purse onto her girdle, and tied the girdle firmly around her waist. Then she sat down as she was bid, sword close at hand, keeping a careful distance from Edwin.

"So where are you bound? And why are you hiding?" he prompted.

Janna hesitated, hardly knowing where her story should start. With the fact that her cottage was burnt to the ground and she was homeless? Or a few days before then, when the nightmare first began?

"I am Janna, daughter of Eadgyth the *wortwyf*," she said, and went on to tell him something of what had forced her to take shelter in the forest. "My mother taught me all she knew, but she is dead," she concluded. "She died in mysterious circumstances, and I have sworn to avenge her death. But I cannot accuse the man responsible, not yet, for he is all-powerful whereas I am a reviled outcast. So now I'm searching for my unknown father to help me in my quest for justice." She patted the purse at her waist. "And I'm hoping that this letter and these pieces of jewelry will help me find him."

"No wonder you took after me in such a fury!" Edwin gave her a rueful smile. "But I still don't understand why you're dressed like a youth and why you travel in such secrecy?"

"The man responsible for my mother's death turned the villagers against me. They burned my cottage to the ground, thinking I was in it. It is safer for me if everyone thinks I died in the blaze, but just in case anyone sees me..." She swept a hand down her body indicating the clothes she wore, and bobbed her head to him.

Edwin's lips pursed in a silent whistle. He regarded Janna thoughtfully for a moment. "It seems to me that, if we can't stay here in the forest, we should journey together. We might be able to help each other."

Janna nodded in quick agreement. "Your lord searches for a lone runaway, while you understood what I was without any trouble." She slid a sideways glance at him

"Yes, well I was in a… a position to see more of you than most," he said, looking somewhat abashed.

"Than any man has ever seen before," Janna said tartly. "Had you not seen what you did, would you say I could pass for a youth?"

He looked her fully in the face now. He was taller than her, and older too. His face was comely rather than handsome, and he had an attractive smile. She took note of the scratches on his dirty brown cheek, freshly made and dappled with beads of blood. She, too, had left her mark on Edwin. "You should wash those scratches," she said. "I'll find some herbs that will help them to heal." She felt sympathy for the mistreated youth, but she would not apologize for attacking him; she wasn't ready yet to forgive him.

He nodded his thanks. "You dress like a man," he told her, "but you walk and talk like a young woman." He jumped to his feet, put a hand on his hip and took a few mincing steps.

Janna was surprised into laughter. "I do not!" she protested.

"You laugh like one, too."

Janna gurgled into silence. "I can't dress as I really am," she pointed out, making her voice purposely deep. "These clothes I'm wearing are all that I own."

"That's better. And if you walk like so…" He began to stride about, his arms loose and swinging freely by his side.

Janna scrambled up and copied his gait, walking first beside him and then in front so that he could watch her. "Like this?"

He nodded. "You fight like a maid, too." He winced as he touched the scratches on his face. Janna kept silent, refusing to feel guilty for protecting what was rightfully hers. "If you're going to live as a boy, you'll need to learn how to defend yourself in a fight," Edwin continued. "You haven't the strength to fight fair, but your instinct was right." He patted his groin. "A hard kick here will cripple your attacker and give you time to run like the devil himself. But you were too slow. I knew exactly what you had in mind." He forked two fingers and, before Janna had a chance to react, he stabbed them toward her eyes. "You could also try to blind your opponent like this, or..." Edwin's fingers closed together. "You can use your hand to break his nose, or his neck." His hand became a blade as he chopped up toward Janna's nostrils and then sideways at her throat. She felt the side of his fingers slam against her skin, and swallowed involuntarily.

"Hit hard, hard as you can. And be quick, you have to take your enemy by surprise," Edwin said. "But what will you do if he comes from behind you?" Giving Janna no time to reply, he ducked behind her and grabbed her, pinning her arms to her side and holding her close to his chest. With a startled cry, she tried to fight him off. "What will you do then?" he whispered. His breath blew against her ear. She felt a deadly fear as she realized she was powerless in his grasp. Still he held her, while she struggled uselessly. He gave a small huff of amusement and tightened his hold. The sound enraged Janna; she increased her efforts, but to the same end. She could not get away from him.

"You stamp down on my foot. Hard," he told her. As Janna's knee came up he released her with a push, and skipped away out of danger. "Don't signal your actions," he warned. "And don't give your enemy any chance to escape."

Janna nodded slowly. Without warning, she sprang toward him. Her fingers stopped a hair's breadth from his eyes.

"Yes, that's it. Now go practice on someone else!"

Janna scowled at him. Her heart was still racing after the fright he'd given her.

Unrepentant, he smiled back. "You'll do, John—so long as you remember who and what you are!"

"I'll remember." She squeezed her fingers together and tried a few practice chops at the air, pretending that she was aiming at an opponent's neck. And his nose. Her fingers formed into a V to stab at unseen eyes. For good measure, she stamped down hard on an imaginary foot.

Edwin craned his head back to look up through the green veil of leaves. "There's not enough sunlight to tell which direction we should walk in," he said. "Do you know the way through to the other side of the forest?"

"No." Janna's face fell. "I lost the path at that clearing by the pool." She looked around her. "I have no idea where we are now."

"We're at the place I've made into my home." He jerked a thumb behind him. Looking past him, Janna noticed a small shelter fashioned from branches and stuffed with mud and leaves. Longer branches were laid on top of the primitive walls to form a rough roof; they were covered with a layer of reeds for extra protection. She had to look hard to see the shelter, for it was almost indistinguishable from the surrounding forest. It would give Edwin some cover from rain, but was too small for anyone to live in any comfort. Nearby was a small circle of blackened flints, with three branches meeting at a point above the space in the middle—Edwin's fireplace.

"What do you do for food? Do you have any?" she asked, suddenly ravenous.

Edwin looked shifty. "I trap small creatures with this," he admitted, pulling a snare of plaited fibres from the front of his tunic. "I cook them and eat them."

Janna felt juices seep into her mouth. "I'm so hungry," she said. "Do you have anything we can eat now?"

"No." He smiled slightly. "I could offer you some water, but I saw you drink your fill in the pool."

"You have water? And something to cook in?" Janna's gaze flicked across the forest floor, settling on several plants of interest to her. Edwin nodded. "Then light the fire," she instructed. "Before we go anywhere, I'll make us a pottage of herbs to fill our bellies for the journey."

"We can't, not in daylight! The smoke will betray us." Edwin cast a nervous glance about him.

Janna hesitated. Her stomach growled with hunger. She was famished. "Let's risk it," she said. "The forester is probably miles away, and even if he does see the smoke we'll be gone long before he can track its source." Not giving Edwin a chance to protest, she drew out her knife and hurried to a clump of nettles. She plucked the nettles by the stem and carefully harvested the young leaves. She held up the front of her smock like an apron, and dropped them in. All the while, she kept an eye on Edwin's movements. Although her treasures were safe in her purse, she still didn't trust the young outlaw. While it was true they might help each other, she remained wary. His boast had not been an idle one, she thought, as she recalled how powerless she'd been in his grip. In a fair fight between them, he would be the winner. He was taller, and he had a wiry strength that became evident as he wrestled with a dead branch to break it up for kindling.

A patch of chickweed drew her on, and she plucked a handful of green shoots before gathering dandelions and a snippet of wild garlic to add flavor. She glanced back, and noticed that Edwin had now lit a fire and was pouring water from a small, crudely made jug into an iron pot. As she watched, he hooked the pot over the flames to heat. Reassured that they had a common purpose, Janna ventured further, hoping for some mushrooms to add bulk to the brew. Pale gray plates fanned out from a rotting tree stump, and she gathered those. She inspected them carefully for insects before adding them to her collection. She glanced up into the branches above her, hoping to spot a bird's nest. Some eggs, or even some berries, would make a welcome addition to this most basic of broths.

She found a nest, but it was empty, and while the berries she spotted were still unripe, she espied something even better. She smiled with anticipated pleasure as she hurried toward the big white splats of lacy elderflowers peeping through the green cover. She cut several and added them to what she'd already gathered, before circling back to the fireplace.

The pot hung over the fire, steam rising in the cold air, but there was no sign of Edwin. With a sinking feeling, she called softly, remembering to keep her voice pitched low, "Edwin? Where are you?"

There was no response. "All the more for me, then," Janna muttered. Carefully laying aside the elderflowers, she threw the mushrooms and plants into the pot and, shivering, stepped closer to the fire to warm herself and dry her clothes. All sympathy for the outlaw had vanished along with him. Beaten by his lord indeed, she thought, as she recalled the scar on his chin. Got that in a fight more like, probably while he was trying to steal from someone else!

A slight rustle set her fumbling for her knife. She whirled around, frantically trying to recall the moves Edwin had taught her. The eyes. The nose. The neck! She was about to lunge forward and strike when she saw who it was. Wearing a proud grin, Edwin dangled a limp, furry form in front of her nose.

"Erk! What's that?" Janna jumped back.

"A leveret." He set down the hare and pulled out his knife.

"But it's only a baby!"

"God's breeches, Janna, it's food!" Edwin looked proudly at his prize. "It must be ailing or I wouldn't have caught it." He began to strip the fur from the small body before cutting it in half. Janna shuddered, but she didn't stop him when he threw the pieces into the broth. He peered at the boiling mixture, and sniffed suspiciously. "That's poisonous." He pointed at the mushrooms.

"No, it's not."

"I don't eat fungus. It can kill you."

"I know. You have to be careful. But these are oyster mushrooms. They're quite safe."

Edwin looked at Janna. "How do I know you're not trying to poison me?"

"You don't," Janna said cheerfully, "but you don't have to eat them if you don't want to. I'm hungry enough to finish them all." She offered him an elderflower. "Have one." She stuffed the sweet lacy flower into her mouth and chewed it with relish. Edwin took a cautious bite, looking dubious. Then he licked his lips in appreciation, and quickly scoffed up the rest of it. It seemed he'd decided to trust her after all. Janna smiled to herself as she picked up another flower.

They ate the pottage with their fingers, taking pleasure and comfort from the hot food. It went some way to settling the ache of hunger in their stomachs. Even the hare was shared between them, although Janna tried to close her mind against what she was eating as she picked the flesh from the small bones.

"A feast fit for King Stephen himself," Edwin commented, licking his fingers.

Janna pulled a face at him. If Edwin really believed that, he must be truly deluded. But his ready grin showed her that, even if he'd never attended a royal banquet, his imagination was every bit as vivid as her own.

"Are you ready to leave now?" he asked, when every last morsel was finally eaten. He stood up.

"You should first break up your shelter," Janna suggested, "just in case the forester comes this way."

"I doubt he will. I've never seen him anywhere near here." But Edwin began to dismantle the branches that had made up his home. Eager to be gone, Janna lent a helping hand by throwing away the flints that marked the fireplace, and scuffing the scorched earth inside the circle to disguise it.

She picked up a last lump of flint and clay, but it flaked and began to crumble in her hand. It slipped from her grasp so Janna gave it a kick instead. The clod fell apart under the impact of her boot. She was about to walk away when she realized that there was something twisted and misshapen at its center. With quickening interest, she crouched down to examine the remains more carefully.

It was a small figurine, fashioned from pale clay and baked hard as iron. Janna jumped up and fetched the jug that Edwin had put by. There was still some water in the bottom, and she poured it carefully over the figurine, wiping away the last clods of earth that disfigured it. A mother holding a child came to life in her hands. Janna caught her breath as their features washed clearer. Was this Jesus with the Virgin Mary? Or was this something much, much older? She looked at the little statue, tracing the lines of the mother's face, the tenderness of her expression as she looked down at her child. A lump came into Janna's throat as she thought of her own mother. She stole a quick glance at Edwin. He was still busy pulling his shelter apart and hadn't noticed. Janna opened her purse and placed the figurine carefully inside. It was ancient and precious but, even more important to Janna, holding it had brought some comfort, some ease to her own aching, lonely heart.

"Now are you ready?" Edwin demanded as he walked over to her and picked up the sword. He handed Janna the staff she had carried, but kept a firm grip on her weapon.

"That's my sword. I found it," she said indignantly.

"But do you know how to use it?"

"Do you?" she challenged, and snatched it from him.

31

"Some of us villeins used to practice our fighting skills against each other. We'd talk of cracking our lord over the head to pay him back for all the beatings he gave us. But we had no swords to practice with, only stout sticks."

"Then here's a stout stick for you." Janna handed over her staff, stepped aside and waited for him to pick up the pot and jug. "Where did you get those?" He looked away and didn't reply, instead setting off toward the clearing. Janna didn't need to be told that he'd probably stolen them. But who was she to judge, when they probably made all the difference to his survival? She walked after him, consciously imitating the easy swing of his stride.

"We need to make up some story to tell once we come to a village or town." She addressed her remark to his back. "If we're going to be Welsh, perhaps we should call ourselves something other than Edwin and John."

"It's too hard. Complicated. What if we forget and don't answer when people talk to us?" Edwin threw the question over his shoulder without checking his stride.

Janna thought for a moment. "Could our mother have been Saxon, wed to a Welshman?"

"Good idea. It would also explain why we don't speak as the Welsh do." Edwin turned, flashing his easy smile at her. Janna found herself smiling back at him. She began to relax, rolling her shoulders to ease tight muscles. The past few days had taken their toll.

"And where are we bound on this quest of yours?" he asked.

Janna shook her head. "I don't know," she confessed. "I can't read my father's letter, so I don't know where to start looking for him." She looked at him with sudden hope. "Can you read it for me?"

He shook his head. After a moment's silence he said, "What about Winchestre?"

"Why there? What about London?"

"Winchestre is closer to us than London. And it's where the King's Treasury is kept. If the king isn't in Winchestre, people there will know where he's gone." He looked back to make sure she understood him. Seeing her look of incomprehension, he continued impatiently, "You said your father was wealthy and important. If you don't know where your father's manor is, maybe your best hope is to find him through the king?"

Excitement blazed across Janna's face. "I didn't think of that!" She touched her purse, feeling the shape of the folded parchment through the rough woven fabric. Winchestre! It was certainly worth a try. She took comfort from the fact that Edwin seemed to be trying to help her, but reminded herself to safeguard her own interests. Edwin had been living wild in the forest, doing whatever it took to stay alive. Therefore she must take care never to come between him and his safety and freedom when they came to a village or town, for she might end up paying with her life.

Chapter 3

"Do you know the road to royal Winchestre?" Janna asked, as they came once more to the forest clearing where she'd spent the night.

"No. Do you?"

Janna shook her head. "Once we reach a village we'll look for someone who knows the way."

"First we have to get through to the other side of the forest. I've never been as far as that, so which direction do you think we should go?" Edwin asked.

Janna shook her head once more. "I was hoping you knew how to find the path. I don't even know which direction I've come from."

Edwin laughed. "You came from over there," he said, and pointed.

"Then we should keep walking this way." She pointed in the opposite direction.

Edwin nodded. "I have been some way along there."

As they skirted the shallow dew pond, a smile twitched Janna's mouth. Reaching out, she gave Edwin a hard push. "Hey!" he yelled as he slid down into the icy water.

"You saw me having a wash, so now it's my turn!" Janna

retorted, and began to laugh as she noticed Edwin's horrified expression. "Go on," she encouraged. "If you clean up the scratches on your cheek, I'll find some herbs to help them heal."

"But I don't want to be clean!" Edwin protested. "I put the mud on my face and clothes so I can blend into the shadows when the forester comes along."

"Oh." That made sense to Janna. "But we're walking out of the forest now, so you won't need to hide for too much longer," she pointed out. "If you're really dirty, people will notice you, and they'll talk about us. You'd better clean yourself up, Edwin." She flashed a wicked grin. "I can wash your back, if you like?"

"You'll turn around, and not look again until I say so," he contradicted firmly.

Smiling, Janna complied.

"So what will you do when we get to Winchestre?" Edwin asked. Soft splashings told Janna that he was profitably occupied.

"I'll ask around, see if anyone can help me." Ready to fulfil her promise to Edwin, Janna began to wander, keeping a lookout for pink flowering betony, mallow, strong-smelling yarrow, or the creamy flowers of wood sanicle.

"You need to find someone who can read."

The thought of a stranger reading her father's letter made Janna uneasy. Her mother had gone to such lengths to protect the secret of her birth. She risked setting her father against her for all time if private, maybe even dangerous, information about his liaison with Janna's mother became known to others.

"I just thought of something else," Edwin continued. "Does your father support the king or his cousin Matilda in their battle over the crown?"

"I know not," Janna admitted. She spied the bright yellow flowers of ragwort and stopped to pluck some sprigs, wrinkling her nose at the strong smell from the bruised leaves. But they would make a good cleanser and healer, as would the hairy Herb Robert growing nearby.

"If he is of fighting age, your father may not be in Winchestre at all," Edwin warned. "Not only does King Stephen wage war against his cousin and her half-brother, Robert of Gloucester, but he's also having to fight his barons to keep them under control. It seems they're using this time of unrest to grab more land, they're becoming too powerful. Maybe your father is one of them, Jan—John?"

Janna straightened slowly, feeling discouraged as the difficulties of her search became apparent to her. "I have to start looking somewhere. Winchestre seems as good a place as any." She stayed silent for a few moments, lost in thought. "How do you know all this if you've been hiding here in Gravelinges?"

"I follow the travelers sometimes. I listen to them talking."

"Just like you tracked me?"

Edwin stopped splashing. "Yes," he admitted after a pause. "I was planning to surprise you, to fell you with a blow and rob you of whatever you carried. But when I heard you cry out, I suspected you might not be a boy at all and so I stayed hidden to watch you. I was curious, you see. It's not often a young woman travels alone through a forest like this one."

"What about last night?"

"I slept close by. I knew I'd hear you once you woke up." The splashing started again.

Janna gave a snort of disbelief. She raised her voice so as to be heard over the noise. "You were hoping I'd fall out of that tree and break my neck, so you could rob me without any blame to yourself!"

"No!" he protested. "Suspecting you were a young woman, I was worried about you. I planned to protect you from harm should any come our way."

He sounded sincere, but still Janna wondered how far she could trust him. "Hurry up," she said gruffly. "I certainly don't want to spend another night out here." *With you.* The words remained unsaid, but she didn't care if Edwin understood her true meaning.

Yet in spite of everything, her lips curved into a smile as he said cheerfully, "You've only had one night in the forest. I've had days, weeks, *months* out here! I was even beginning to talk to the trees and the birds and the animals. Imagine!"

Janna could. After all, she used to talk to the hens and goats she and her mother kept on their small plot of land. Even the bees in their hives used to get a daily report on what was happening. She could quite understand how a lonely youth might find comfort in pouring out his troubles to something that would neither judge him nor give him a harsh reply. In fact, she fancied Edwin might have had little in the way of warmth and companionship even before he fled into the forest.

"You've heard all about me, but you haven't told me much about yourself," Janna commented, as he emerged from the pool. His skin was clean now, and the marks from her nails showed clearly. She pulled a regretful face over the damage she'd done.

"Phwoar!" Edwin's nose wrinkled in disgust as he smelled the ragwort. But he stood quietly until Janna had finished spreading the astringent juice over the scratches on his cheek. He was shivering in his wet clothes.

"Why don't you take off your tunic and squeeze out the water?" she suggested. He nodded, and did as he was bid. Janna drew breath in a shocked gasp. His back was marked and criss-crossed with scars from old beatings. Some were still not healed and looked red and painful. "Come here," she said. She made Edwin bend over so she could examine the wounds more closely. With a gentle touch, she used the remains of the ragwort to cleanse the worst of them. "I'm not surprised you ran away," she said, as he pulled on his tunic once more.

"Like I said, he was a vicious old devil." Edwin stepped around the clearing, examining it carefully for signs of the path they should follow.

"So where does this vicious old devil live? Where have you come from?" Janna prompted.

"He has a manor near Tantone in Somer Shire. I walked for many miles, for it was in my mind to seek work in Winchestre, or even in London. Then I became lost in this forest. I decided to hide here until my time was up, for by then I'd realized that my lord had sent his servants in pursuit of me."

"Why did he do that? Why did he bother?" Janna didn't mean to disparage Edwin, but she was genuinely curious to know the answer. Certain it was that a lord would pursue a missing serf, but the chase would not last long, especially if the serf was as poor and as lowly as Edwin.

"He is miserly as well as vicious. He guards what is his and holds on to it far beyond reason. Everyone on his manor has cause to hate and fear him, for everyone has been called to account for some act of carelessness, some slight or misdeed, some imagined oversight. We have all been punished, even when we were not guilty. Walter of Crice will not listen to any explanation or any excuse but takes the whip to all, even to his own wife and children, so it is said. In truth, I think he goes out of his way to find reason for punishment, for he seems happy only when he's causing misery for someone else."

Janna was silenced by the bleak picture he painted. Yet her imagination couldn't leave it alone; she was sure he hadn't told her the full story. "Were you accused of something? Is that what made you run away?"

Edwin looked up abruptly, abandoning his search for the path. A tide of red washed over his face. "My lord's favorite steed went missing, and I was held to blame for it." His voice was bitter with hatred. Was it guilt or indignation that stained his countenance?

"And did you steal his horse?" Although Janna kept her voice carefully neutral, both of them knew that Edwin was guilty of at least one theft.

"Of course I did not! Do you see it here? I would have kept it if I'd stolen it! And I would have ridden to the far end of the kingdom to escape that devil." His face set in sullen lines as he began to search once more for any faint signs of a way out of the forest.

Janna berated herself for asking such a stupid question. Yet the thought still troubled her: what if the horse had gone lame? Edwin might well have had to abandon it somewhere.

"If you didn't take it, then who did?"

Edwin shrugged. "I don't know. It was a fine beast; any man might covet it. All I know is that my lord will not rest until he reclaims it—which means he will not rest until he finds me. There it is!"

Bewildered by his unexpected outburst, Janna looked for signs of the horse, then realized that Edwin was pointing at a faint mark in the grass.

"Well done!" Ready to forgive him, and forgive herself for her lack of trust, Janna gave him a congratulatory whack across the back, instantly regretting the action as she recalled the deep cuts she'd just treated.

"Ow!" he protested loudly.

"Isn't that the sort of thing men do to each other?"

"Who goes there in the king's royal forest?" A loud shout startled them both into silence. They stared at each other, momentarily numb with fear. Then, putting a warning finger to his mouth to caution silence, Edwin grabbed Janna's hand and began to run, pulling her with him along the trail he'd found. Janna sprinted beside him, hoping she could trust him to find the way. Despite her fear of being overtaken by the forester, she reveled in the freedom of movement the breeches gave her as her legs pumped up and down, pounding downhill through the trees.

"Stop! In the name of the king, I bid you stand and give me your names and your reason for trespass in the king's royal forest." The voice was uneven, somewhat breathless—the forester was chasing them.

Edwin tugged harder on Janna's hand, and she kept running. Both of them knew that there'd be no mercy shown if they were to stop and meekly surrender. They stumbled into hollows and tripped over rough flints hidden among the tangled, weedy undergrowth. They let go of each other, needing their hands to protect themselves from the brambles that snagged their clothes, whipped their faces and tore at their skin. A long strand of sticky goosegrass wrapped around Janna's ankle; she yanked her foot free and, panicking now, put on a burst of speed to catch up with Edwin. The sounds of pursuit were louder but she was tiring. A pain cut into her side, sharp as the sword she carried. *Aelfshot.* The Saxons believed this sudden stab was caused by darts shot by elves, but Janna knew she felt it only when she'd run too far and for too long without rest.

"You go on," she panted hoarsely as Edwin turned to check her progress. "I'll climb a tree and hide till he's gone."

"No!" He stopped and grabbed her. "My safety lies with you, just as yours lies with me. We're in this together. Quick!" Instead of heading deeper into the trees he hauled her to an opening in the forest. Janna had no choice but to follow him, and saw the sense of his action when he dived headfirst into a patch of tall weeds. At once he was hidden from sight, and Janna wasted no time going in after him, although she felt exposed and vulnerable away from the shelter of the trees. Bracken and tall herbs formed part of their shield, but so too did stinging nettles and prickling thistles. Janna had to clench her teeth tight to stop herself crying out. She lay still, listening to the pounding of her heart and the heavy rasp of her own panting breaths. She pressed her lips together to stifle the sound, while the thudding footsteps of their pursuer came nearer.

"Stop!" he shouted as he passed close beside them. "I know you can hear me. Come back here at once!"

They stayed silent, even when a blackbird alighted nearby to forage for a juicy worm. It took one startled glance at them and squawked loudly before taking off to find a less menacing hunting ground. The forester's calls ceased, but Janna could sense him waiting, and watching. She prayed that they were invisible, and that Edwin would keep still until all danger had passed. For herself, she was too frightened even to blink. Any movement, the slightest sound, might give the forester the clue he needed to pounce on them.

Time passed. Janna felt as if she'd been lying hidden for an eternity. She desperately wanted to poke her head up, to see if the forester was lying in wait for them. Instead, she lay silent beside Edwin, and waited for the danger to pass. Her heartbeats had quietened and her breathing had returned to normal by the time the forester eventually gave up watching for them. He began to call once more, his voice growing ever more distant as he demanded that they heed him and obey.

More time passed. The pressure of Edwin's hand on her arm confirmed the need for stillness and silence, lest the forester be waiting down the track to ambush them as soon as they showed themselves. Edwin trembled beside her and she thought at first that he was fearful, until the shudders grew stronger and she realized he was shivering with cold in his wet clothes.

"We must leave here before you freeze to death," she breathed softly into his ear. He nodded and cautiously raised his head above the cover of the weeds. Once he'd made sure the forester was really gone, he stood up and began to run on the spot, rubbing his arms to get the blood flowing through his body. Janna nodded in approval but, seeing the warning finger come to his mouth once more, she didn't say anything. Instead, she extricated her sword from the weedy growth. She jabbed a thumb toward where she thought they'd left the path, and raised an enquiring eyebrow. On receiving his nod, she set off, stepping quietly across grassy patches so that no crackling leaves or twigs would betray her, but ready at an instant to melt into concealing undergrowth if it was necessary.

She couldn't hear Edwin. Had he run off and left her? Alarmed, she spun around, and was reassured to see him pacing silently behind her. He grinned. She flashed a smile in reply, ashamed that she'd doubted him. The trail was wider now, and more distinct. It was becoming well trodden, just like the beginning of the trail on the other side of Gravelinges. It, too, must be used by farmers in autumn, some of whom, for a fee, were allowed to bring their pigs into the forest to eat the beechmast. With a sudden lift of her spirits, Janna realized they must be coming close to Wicheford, and safety.

"Stay where you are!" A triumphant cry punctured her confidence and set her heart leaping with fright. Her first thought was to hide, but even as she searched for cover, the forester sprang out onto the path to confront them. She stepped back, cannoning into Edwin. He shouldered her aside and, with one almighty shove, sent the forester staggering to the ground.

"Run!" he shouted.

At least we've had a chance to rest, Janna thought, as she sprinted beside him. She felt proud that she could keep pace with Edwin even though she was a girl, but she knew she would also tire more quickly. Still she ran valiantly, following the trail down through the trees, through gloomy shadows under leafy canopies where every bush and thicket seemed to conceal a threat to their safety, and through open weedy clearings where she felt even more vulnerable to the hunt.

"Stop!" The cry sounded behind them. The forester was in pursuit once more. Janna forced her aching limbs to work harder, and sucked breath deep into her burning lungs. To be caught by the forester was bad enough. To be caught after striking him to the ground and running away would invite a punishment too dreadful to contemplate. Flight was the only answer, their only hope of salvation. Fear added a burst of speed to Janna's feet.

They ran on. Janna felt now as though she'd passed into a new dimension, a place where her body no longer seemed part of her consciousness. Her chest rose and fell with her breaths; her feet flashed briefly in front of her, left, right, left, right as they sped onward, but she felt nothing past the desperate need to escape. She sensed Edwin check slightly and matched her stride to his, looking past him to see for herself what had given him pause. Only a narrow fringe of forest separated them now from water meadows and a river lying ahead. Behind them, the forester kept shouting, but in front of them danger also lay, in the form of a mounted man. By the stillness of his stance, and the direction of his gaze, Janna understood that he'd already spied them and that trying to hide from him was futile. Nor could they turn back. And so they kept on running, while he spurred his horse to meet them. They came together at the edge of the forest.

"What frightens you? What do you run from?" In spite of his handsome mount and the elegance of his tunic, the man spoke in the Saxon language. Janna found the courage to answer truthfully.

"We're running from the king's forester." She kept the sword hidden behind her back, knowing that the man would suspect the worst if he saw it. His expression hardened. Janna wondered if she'd misjudged him. The king's forest laws were popular with no-one save those of his favorites who'd been granted hunting rights in the royal forests. The Saxons especially had reason to hate and resent the edict set in place by William the Bastard, who had conquered their country and killed their king. Forced off their own lands, forced to work for their hated enemies, thegns and villeins alike were also prevented by forest law from cutting wood to build their homes, or trapping wild creatures to fill their empty bellies. Was this man on their side, or was he only speaking their language?

"Take shelter in there. Hurry!" The man pointed at a long, timbered shed nearby. It was so close to the forest edge that Janna hadn't noticed it before.

"Our thanks," she breathed, even as Edwin pushed her toward it. The door had hardly closed behind them when they heard a cheerful shout.

"Master Roger! What brings you through the forest in such a hurry?" This time, the man spoke the language of the Normans, but Janna had been taught to speak it by her mother and she understood his words. Edwin, however, tensed.

"He's trapped us here like rats, and now he's going to hand us over to the forester," he hissed into Janna's ear.

"No, he's not. Shh. Let me listen." Janna bent and put her ear close to a space in the wooden palings. She heard the jingle of the bridle as their rescuer dismounted to talk to the forester.

"Where are they, Serlo? Two youths? You must have seen them." The forester also spoke in Norman French now. His voice was rough with fatigue; he struggled to catch his breath. The chase had taken its toll.

"I've seen no youths. Are you certain they came this way?"

A short silence confirmed that the man's shrewd question had hit home. Just as Janna eased a sigh of relief, the forester said petulantly, "They were following the trail through the forest. They must have run past you."

"Do you doubt my word?" Their rescuer sounded resentful.

"No, not at all. I'm merely surprised you haven't seen them."

"If they realized you were after them, mayhap they're still hiding in the forest. Did you have them in your sights all the while?"

"I did not." The forester's voice was sharp, accusing. "One of the ruffians struck me such a blow that I fell to the ground. By the time I got after them, they had disappeared from my view. I was sure they were coming this way and so I made haste to follow them even though I can scarce move from the pain of the attack."

Janna stiffened, sure that the forester's lie would make their rescuer think twice about his chivalrous action. While Serlo might be prepared to save villeins fleeing from a harsh and unjust law, he wouldn't harbor anyone who'd resort to violence to escape from a king's man. She peered through the crack in time to see the forester rubbing his head, an aggrieved expression on his face. Hardly daring to breathe, she waited through a long silence as their rescuer weighed the pros and cons of confessing his lie or continuing to shelter a pair of dangerous villains.

"What are they saying? Do you understand any of it?" Edwin whispered nervously.

"Yes. Shh." Janna clamped a hand over his mouth and leaned closer to the gap between the wooden stakes, straining to hear what else might be said.

"...but if I see them, I'll be sure to keep hold of them and send word to you."

Janna felt slightly cheered as she understood what Serlo was saying. He had hold of them already, but hadn't spoken of them to the forester. That must mean he was prepared to let them go free, once the danger had passed. She released Edwin, and put her eye to the crack, trying to see what the forester would do next. Fear slammed into her with the force of a body blow as she found herself staring directly into his eyes. Had he seen her? Did he know someone was hiding inside the shed? She dare not blink lest she betray their presence.

"What are you...?" Edwin subsided into silence as Janna gave him a hard jab in the ribs. Her eyes stayed fixed on the forester, who continued to stare at her. Moments passed. Hours. Months. Years.

And then the forester turned to Serlo and asked, "What's in the shed over there?"

"Nothing now, Master Roger." Their rescuer gave a shrug. "It's a winter shelter for my sheep, to keep them out of snow and flood, but it's not time for that now. See how well my flock is doing." There was pride in Serlo's voice as with one hand he grasped the forester and deftly turned him around, while with his other hand he indicated a distant flock of white-faced sheep grazing peacefully under the watchful eye of their shepherd. The generous sweep of his hand also encompassed the fields beyond the river: plowed earth lying fallow, golden barley and ripening wheat. "We shall have a goodly stock of wool to sell at the fair this year, and a bountiful harvest too if the weather stays kind."

Janna felt a great warmth toward him as she understood how successfully he'd managed to deflect the forester's attention from the sheepfold and their suspected whereabouts. Serlo kept a grip on the forester's arm and, still talking, led him away, following the green wall of trees at the edge of the forest.

Once she judged they were safely out of earshot, Janna whispered an explanation of what had transpired to Edwin, including the forester's version of how he was attacked.

"I gave him a shove and he fell over," Edwin protested. "I didn't mean to hurt him, I just wanted to buy us some time."

"I'm sure you didn't hurt him. There was no sign of any mark on him, but that didn't stop him trying to make a greater cause against us. Lucky for us, his ruse didn't work."

"So what do we do now?"

"Nothing, for the moment. I don't know where Serlo's taken the forester. They may still be close enough to see us if we leave. Besides, where would we go? We can't cross the river in daylight, and we certainly can't go back into the forest while the forester is still about. I think we should stay here until nightfall. We can make our escape as soon as it's dark."

Edwin grunted uneasily. "Serlo? Is that his name? He thinks I hit the forester. He thinks we're dangerous. He may want to hand us over to the shire reeve instead, and claim a reward for his trouble." He shook his head. "I think we should go now."

"It's not safe. At least, not yet. Let's wait a while," Janna insisted.

Edwin huffed a sigh. "It's all very well for you to say wait. You're not the one on the run. You didn't thump the forester. You're not suspected of stealing a horse either."

"You can go if you want to, but I'm staying here." Janna sat down. To underscore her intention, she shifted around so that her back rested against the timbered frame of the shed. She stretched out her legs in front of her, and closed her eyes. For safety, she casually folded her hands over her purse. If Edwin decided to make a move, it would not be with any of her belongings—at least, not without a fight.

"You still don't trust me, do you?" His voice was amused.

Janna was embarrassed that he'd read her mind so easily. Or was it shame for doubting him? Uncertain now, she recalled how he'd taken her hand, matching his speed to hers as he pulled her along. He hadn't run away to save himself. Instead, he'd helped her hide from the forester.

"No, I don't trust you," she said truthfully, pushing aside her uneasy conscience.

"I've already apologized for stealing your purse. It's safer for both of us if we stay together, but we have to trust and even pretend to like each other if we want people to believe that we're brothers."

"Stay together? I thought you were leaving right now?" Janna opened her eyes to study him.

"No. Not yet. You're right. It's not safe. We'll go as soon as it gets dark." He stretched out beside her.

"Go where? We still don't know the way to Winchestre."

"Shh. I hear voices. I think they're coming back."

The voices grew louder. Janna tensed, waiting for betrayal, but the voices passed, becoming softer until there was silence once more. Just as she started to relax, the door of the shed was flung open with a sudden crash. A tall figure blocked the light, and blocked all chance of their escape. It was the horseman, Serlo. They scrambled to their feet to face him.

Serlo was in his mid-years; his freckled face was burnished red by the sun and topped with a shock of red hair. From his commanding air and confident speech, Janna guessed he must be the lord of this manor. A quick inspection confirmed her guess: his tunic was made of good linen and decorated with a border of embroidery. His boots, although mud spattered, were made of fine leather.

"Now," he said, "you'd better tell me what really happened in the forest." He planted his hands on his hips and puffed out his chest. "Tell me the truth, for you can be sure I'll beat it out of you if I suspect either one of you is lying."

Janna was thankful then that she'd understood his conversation with the forester, and that she'd repeated it to Edwin. They might otherwise have tried to bluff their way out of trouble, and would have earned themselves a beating for it. But how much of the truth should they tell? She stole a quick glance at Edwin, then looked away. One of them had to say something. It had better be her, for Edwin had far too much to lose. She would speak for both of them—and in as low a voice as possible.

"We thank you kindly, sire, for hiding us from the forester," she began, thinking it wise to flatter their rescuer as well as show themselves humble and well-mannered, so that he might think twice before believing all that the forester had said of them. As an added precaution, she addressed him in the Saxon tongue, not wanting him to know that she'd heard, and understood, his conversation with the forester.

Serlo grunted acknowledgment, all the while looking them over as if to assess their worth. He frowned as he took in Edwin's damp and tattered appearance, his half-starved, wild air. His attention moved then to Janna. She quickly looked away, not wanting to show her full face to him lest she betray her real identity. Instead, she studied the earthen floor intently as she launched into explanation. "We are two brothers from beyond the Welsh Marches, sire, come to seek employment wherever we may find it."

Their rescuer eyed them suspiciously. "Has your lord given you permission to leave his manor?"

"We—we are not tied to anyone, sire." Janna's thoughts raced as she tried to come up with something to satisfy the man's curiosity. "Our father was Welsh, a craftsman, but he died when we were just babes. Our mother found a living…" Janna flushed as the man's eyes glinted in anticipation, "…working in an alehouse." If the man believed her mother was a whore, he might well think the daughter one too! Except she wasn't a daughter, she reminded herself. "My name is John," she said hastily, "and my brother is called Edwin."

"You do not speak like a Welshman, John."

Janna felt a flash of triumph that he'd not seen through her disguise. "Our mother was of Saxon stock, sire, and often

49

told us stories of her home near Winchestre, and of the kin she'd left behind. Now that she has died we come hoping to find some of them still living thereabouts, but we must find work along the way to support us while we search."

She was rewarded by the brief flash of sympathy in his eyes. But he was not yet done with them. "One of you struck the forester. Which of you was it?"

Janna glanced at Edwin. As she opened her mouth to defend him, he said, "It was me, my lord. I gave the forester a hard push, to give us time to get away from him. He fell to his knees, but I swear to you that I did not hurt him. I did not strike him either."

"I should hand you over to the shire reeve for such an act." Yet a faint smile curled Serlo's lips.

Emboldened, Janna asked, "Will you allow us to leave now, sire? If the forester is gone and it is safe?"

"No." The smile grew broader as the man shook his head.

"No?" Janna's voice skidded dangerously high. Sweat dampened her palms. Did he mean, after all, to give them over to the shire reeve for punishment?

"There is much to be done on the manor, and I am short of labor, especially as half the villeins are struck down with some poxy disease. You may stay a while, and repay your debt to me by doing their work for them." Serlo was no longer smiling. Janna knew that even though his words were couched as an offer, he expected to be obeyed. She glanced at Edwin, uncertain what to say or do. To her surprise, he nodded acceptance.

"Good," the man said briskly. "My name is Serlo. I am the reeve of this manor." Janna felt a moment's surprise that she'd so misjudged his position here. But Serlo was still speaking. "You will follow my commands and work in return for your bread and lodging until I no longer have need of you. Do not cross me for I will raise the hue and cry should you try to leave."

Janna's heart sank. She fingered the shape of the small figurine in her purse, the mother hunched so protectively over her child. It gave her the courage to ask a question. "How long will you keep us here, Master Serlo?"

"What does it matter? You said you were in search of work. I am offering it."

Janna wondered how to convey to him the urgency of her quest to find her father, without giving too much away. As she struggled to find the words, Edwin forestalled her.

"We are grateful for your kindness, Master Serlo. Be sure that we will repay our debt to you in full."

"Come with me." Mounting his horse, Serlo beckoned them to follow. Janna cast a glance at the sword she'd salvaged from the pond, now lying half hidden behind a rough wooden feed trough. Edwin caught her glance and shook his head. He started off after Serlo. Janna quickly stowed the sword out of sight, along with Edwin's jug and pot, and scurried after the pair. Serlo had said that the shed stood empty through the summer. The sword should be safe enough for the moment, but she would come back for it once they were given permission to leave.

It was a long walk over the marshy ground of the water meadows. Mud and dung stuck to Janna's boots and she wished she had a pair of wooden pattens to protect them from the muck. Serlo led them across the ford and up to the manor house. He bade them wait while he entered the yard and dismounted to fetch some implements. To Janna he handed a heavy wooden mallet; to Edwin, two pairs of long-handled sticks, each pair comprising one stick with a Y-fork, and with a small sickle blade on the other. Once more he mounted, and walked them on and up into the fields beyond. Some of the plowed fallow land was studded with fat horned sheep and their long-tailed lambs. They nibbled at new shoots of weeds and grass, and dropped the dung that would be spread out to make the soil more fertile for the next cycle of planting. The earth was dark, marked with patches of white chalk and studded with flints that glinted in the watery sunlight. Scarlet poppies turned their faces to the sky, bright splashes of color among the green wheat growing nearby. Looking more closely, Janna could also see an abundance of prickly purple thistles, red deadnettles, charlock, dock and hairy pink corn-cockle. The flowers made a pretty picture, but Janna knew they would spread and choke the wheat if left unchecked.

Weeding fields and spreading dung was back-breaking work. It was normally done by the villeins of the manor in return for a small plot of land and shelter for their families, yet these fields seemed almost deserted. She wondered how Serlo could be so careless with his lord's property, and why his lord let him get away with it. Then she remembered the disease Serlo had mentioned, and understood why the reeve was forcing their service to his cause. She became aware that he was talking to them, throwing words carelessly over his shoulder as he rode along. She hurried to catch up with him and Edwin. To her dismay, the reeve's words confirmed her fears.

"I'm behind with everything here because of this cursed pox. The sheep are still to be washed and shorn and the hay to be cut, just as soon as we get some sunshine. There are new ditches to dig, and hedges to repair around the growing crops. But you can begin by weeding the wheat, breaking up clods, and picking large flints from the fallow fields, clearing them of anything that might get in the way of the plow. You will also spread them with the sheep's dung to make next season's crops grow better. I shall arrange for you to sleep with the servants in the hall, and break your fast with them. Mistress Tova, the cook, will give you food and ale to take out into the fields for your dinner and supper. I don't want to see you back at the manor until it's dark. Understand that I'll be keeping an eye on you and how hard you are working, for I am out every day keeping watch over everything in my lord's absence."

Janna groaned inwardly. With the sun rising early, and the summer light fading ever later from the sky, it made for a long day's labor. But at least they'd be meeting new people, any of whom might know the way to Winchestre. Besides, their service here could not last forever; sooner or later they would be given permission to leave. The thought cheered her somewhat.

Edwin gave her a hard nudge. "What?" she asked, startled out of her reverie. He began to walk with exaggerated strides, swinging his arms manfully by his side. Puzzled, Janna stared at him, then became aware that Serlo was watching them both and frowning. Suddenly catching on, she squared her shoulders and lengthened her stride. "He's only young," Edwin called, as he drew nearer to Serlo, "but he's strong." He jerked a thumb toward Janna. "He's a good worker, you'll see."

Another grunt met this observation, but Serlo finally turned and set his horse for home. Edwin flashed a grin at Janna and she pulled a rueful face at him. It was so easy to forget her new disguise. So easy, and so dangerous.

Chapter 4

After a few days out in the fields, Janna ached all over. Her fingers were torn and bruised from picking up sharp flints and uprooting thistles, while her back felt bent out of shape from bending over to beat out hard clods of earth with the heavy mallet. The stink of sheep dung permeated everything. Although she'd washed her hands and feet in the river before coming in for the night, she could still smell it. She stretched out on her straw pallet, trying to find ease for her tired body and her unquiet mind. To stop herself from recalling her past life with her mother in their small cot at the edge of Gravelinges forest, which always brought with it a slow burn of anger coupled with tears, she thought instead about Urk and what had happened that day while she was out culling weeds.

Urk was by far the oldest of the group of children who had been sent into the fields to scare away the crows, rooks and other scavengers that swooped down to eat the ripening wheat. The youngest of them, aged three or four, banged drums and shouted. Older children carried slingshots, and it was a matter of competition and pride between them who could fell the most birds. Behind the children came Urk's mother, cutting weeds and keeping an eye on the youngsters to remind them of their purpose should their natural high spirits lead them astray.

Urk was tall and heavyset, and slow by nature. He reminded Janna of a scruffy hen she'd owned, called Laet because it was always last to get to the feed. The hen would not have thrived without her special care. She suspected that Urk's mother might also need to give her oldest son special attention. Yet he was a merry lad, with a sweet smile and a willing nature. He was also the most accurate of them all when it came to using the slingshot. This day he'd had the misfortune to bring down a dove in front of Serlo, and had his ears severely boxed as a result. Janna cringed as she remembered how Mistress Wulfrun had pleaded on her son's behalf.

"Please don't punish him, Master Serlo. He really doesn't understand what he's done wrong."

"It was eating the wheat, Master Serlo," Urk chimed in. "You told us to kill all the birds who eat the grain."

Serlo glowered at the unfortunate boy, then gave him another clip across the ear. "Doves are for my lord's sport, not yours," he shouted, as if the boy was deaf rather than slow. "Don't you dare kill another dove. Don't ever touch them again, or I'll take your slingshot from you and you'll never get it back!"

Urk's lip quivered; he looked on the verge of tears.

"And no more playing with fire either!" Serlo turned on his heel and marched off.

Mistress Wulfrun placed her arm around her son and gave him a hug. "Don't take it to heart," she comforted him. "Master Serlo doesn't mean it."

Feeling sorry for the boy, Janna had bent once more to her task. Mistress Wulfrun moved to work beside her, with Urk a pace behind. "Master Serlo is usually more patient with him," the woman confided, as she stooped to cut weeds. She glanced at Urk. "And you don't play with fire, do you, son?"

"No." Urk stood still, watching them. Janna wondered if he was too afraid now to use his slingshot.

"He sometimes wakes up and goes outside," Mistress Wulfrun explained further. "We stop him if we can, but on this occasion no-one heard him leave. He said he wanted to look around the manor in the moonlight, while everyone was asleep. He was quite young at the time, but still he had the good sense to take a rush light so he could see his way. But when he tried to explore the byre, a cow mooed and frightened him. He dropped the light into a pile of hay, and the byre caught on fire. He didn't do it on purpose—and there was no harm to the animals," she added quickly, forestalling Janna's question. "But my son got such a fright he started screaming. Everyone came running. The animals were led to safety, but the byre burned to the ground." She looked at Urk, concern scoring deep lines across her pleasant, homely face. "Of course, he shouldn't have gone near the manor, but my lord was very good about it, very understanding. Only Serlo was angry, I suppose because he feels responsible for whatever happens here. He is usually fair in his dealings with us, but it seems he has neither forgotten the fire nor forgiven my boy." She looked up at Janna. "I can't be with him all the time. Will you also keep watch over him out in the fields, John, when I'm not here?"

"Of course I will, mistress." Janna didn't know what else to say to comfort the woman or her son, but she wished now that she'd thought of something, anything, to ease the situation, to make Urk feel better about himself, and his mother less worried about him.

She yawned, and shifted on the straw pallet, trying to compose herself for sleep, but her bed was prickly and her whole body ached. Contributing to her unease was the crowded hall she shared with all the servants of the manor, most of them men and boys. Edwin had set their pallets in a corner, away from the crowd around the fireplace. He'd put Janna next to the wall, keeping himself between her and the others. She was grateful for his protection, but even so she lay awake, unaccustomed to the night noises, the sighs and murmurs, the cries of nightmares, and the odors of farts and sweaty clothes and dirty feet.

When at last she fell asleep, her dreams were full of endless fields waiting for her attention. She stooped over them, with the smell of animal excrement in her nose and the knowledge that her tasks would never be done. And so it seemed still when she woke to yet another gray dawn and a new day before her, and one after that, and then another and another. She groaned softly. Hot tears stung her eyes.

Edwin stirred beside her. "What's wrong?"

"Nothing." Janna was conscious of the servants nearby, any one of whom might be wide enough awake to carry the tale to Serlo if she confessed to Edwin how sad and desperate she felt. She wiped her eyes on the back of her sleeve, and tried not to sniffle.

Edwin seemed to understand. "My body is one big ache, and my arms feel like they're on fire," he muttered, as he stood up and squared his shoulders to face the day.

"At least our bellies will soon be full!" Janna felt a little more cheerful as she stored her straw pallet in an alcove off the hall. She looked around, but there was no sign of the bread and ale with which they normally broke their fast. The table stood bare, and Janna's stomach rumbled with hunger. Beckoning Edwin to follow her, she hurried down the stairs to a stone building nearby. There might be other pickings waiting for them in the kitchen, a scrap of bacon perhaps, or even a pasty. Saliva flooded Janna's mouth at the thought, and her steps quickened.

She loved going into the kitchen every morning to fetch the dinner they would eat later, out in the fields. It was a source of wonder to her that anywhere could hold such an abundance of food. She took a deep sniff, anticipating the delicious smells of meat roasting on a spit over the fire, newly baked bread, the rich aromas of a bubbling pottage, the spicy fragrance of herbs. Instead, she smelt a sharp and acrid stink. A young maid stood at the large table in the center of the room, chopping onions and weeping over her task.

Janna sniffed again and realized that it wasn't onions she could smell, but smoke and burnt offerings. Bewildered, she looked around for the cook, but there was no sign of Mistress Tova, only Serlo and the kitchen servants. Hands on hips and face red with anger, Serlo was berating one of the skivvies. Feeling sorry for the boy, yet reluctant to attract the reeve's attention, Janna stopped abruptly.

Edwin crashed into her. "What are you...?" His words died on his lips as he took in the situation. But it was too late. Serlo had seen them.

"The cook has gone and got the pox now. She's all over spots," he said, by way of explanation. "And no-one seems to know anything about baking bread." He flung out a hand toward some flat, blackened rounds that must once have been small loaves.

"I can bake griddle cakes, Master Serlo," Janna said quickly, hoping to keep the young boy out of trouble, and themselves too. She noticed the flare of surprise in his eyes as he turned to her, and realized, with a sinking heart, that she'd have done better to hold her tongue. "My—our mother taught me how," she added, sneaking an anxious glance at Edwin as she did so.

"Hmph," Serlo grunted. He cast a glance around the kitchen, at the silent kitchen hands and lowly skivvies huddled near the door, waiting only a chance to disappear from his sight.

His glance settled on a young woman, and he reddened slightly. "Hasn't your mother taught you how to cook, Gytha?" he demanded, in a softer tone than he'd used with the boy.

"No, Master Serlo, she has not." The girl tossed her long dark ringlets. Janna waited for an explanation or an excuse for her lack of skill, but none came.

Curious, and rather impressed by Gytha's impertinence, for Janna judged the girl even younger than herself, she leaned slightly to one side for a better view. Gytha was beautiful, she decided with a pang of envy and of pain, as she recalled her own lost locks and her rough disguise. Evidently Gytha was the cook's daughter, yet Janna hadn't seen her in the kitchen before. Now she faced Serlo with pride, secure in her own beauty and a position that seemed equal to his own.

He's smitten with her, and she knows it! Janna hid a smile. But Serlo was well in command of his emotions when he turned his hard gaze back on Janna.

"Make some griddle cakes then, John, quick as you can. There's much work to be done today." With a last suspicious glance at her, he hurried out.

"I'll help you." The beauty moved toward Janna with a friendly smile. "I wouldn't admit it to him," she jerked her head in the direction of the disappearing reeve, "but my father taught my mother the arts of the kitchen while he was alive, so she was able to keep his position here after he died. In turn, she has taught me all she knows. I can cook, and cook well, but I will not be a skivvy to the likes of Serlo. I have set my sights much higher than the reeve." A dreamy smile tugged at the corners of her mouth.

"You plan to cook for the lord of the manor when he returns?"

"No, indeed. I shall do more, much more, for my lord than cook for him."

What did Gytha mean? Janna's insatiable curiosity prompted her to probe further. "Are you the lord's mistress then?"

"Certainly not!"

"I beg your pardon," Janna apologized hastily. "I meant to ask if you were betrothed to him?"

"Not yet." A calculating expression briefly marred the young woman's beauty. "But it's only a matter of time before he sees that our destiny lies together." Head tilted to one side, she studied Janna. "You're new here, aren't you, John?"

"Yes, mistress." Janna answered without thinking. "Yes," she said again on a deeper note.

"My name's Gytha." She took Janna's hand. "Come on, I'll show you where everything is kept. It'll be a blessing if you can look after the kitchen while my mother is ill. Not for anything will I have Serlo tramping around after me, breathing down my neck and telling me what to do."

Yet you have no hesitation in shifting the burden onto my shoulders, Janna thought. With a wry smile, she acknowledged that she would far rather slave in the kitchen all day than break her back out in the fields. She rinsed her hands, and began to rub fat into the flour, noticing how fine and white it was compared to the gritty brown flour that was all she and her mother had been able to afford. She poured some goat's milk into the mixture. Edwin sidled over, edging closer to Gytha, looking hopeful. Gytha fluttered her eyelashes and gave him a demure smile.

"This is my older brother, Edwin," Janna said, amused. Gytha might have designs on the lord of the manor, but it seemed she also enjoyed flirting with any other marriageable prospects. "What ails your mother and the villeins, mistress?" she asked, thinking it was possible she might know of a preparation that could help them to heal.

"They burn with fever and they're covered in itchy spots. They are too sick to leave their beds." Gytha looked genuinely concerned now, and Janna could understand why. She'd seen the ravages of this disease before, how it could scar skin and destroy hearing and sight, and even kill. No wonder Gytha looked frightened. Her ambitions for her future were dependent on her youthful beauty.

"You must stay away from your mother if you can. I hope it's not too late," Janna advised. "Once one gets the disease, it's likely everyone else around will get it too." She hung a flat tray over the kitchen fire and waited for it to heat.

Gytha whisked into a larder and came out with several eggs cupped in her hands. "Put some eggs with that."

Trying not to look too impressed by such riches, Janna cracked them open and spilled the contents into the bowl. Once the eggs were beaten into the milk and flour, she ladled the mixture in small dollops onto the hot tray.

"My mother looks so ill. She burns with fever, while the spots plague her and she can't stop scratching them. Now they ooze yellow matter and look even worse," Gytha confided. She seemed genuinely concerned. "I bathe her with cool water, but it doesn't seem to help."

Janna thought of the potions she had made up for her mother when a similar disease had struck down a number of villeins in a hamlet near their own. "If you wish, I can brew a decoction for the fever and make up a lotion to soothe and heal the spots," she promised. "But you must help me first," she added quickly. "These cakes are almost ready. Could you please fetch the ale and take it up to the hall?"

"And what would a youth like you know about fevers and lotions?" Serlo's voice made Janna jump. She hadn't heard him return.

"Our mother was a—a *wortwyf*, a healer," she stammered, thinking it safest to keep as close as possible to the truth. "But she also worked in an alehouse," she added hurriedly, as she recalled what she'd first told Serlo.

"She was renowned as a healer, Master Serlo," Edwin cut in swiftly. "People came from all over to see her when they had a pain or a disease." Edwin spoke the truth—even if he couldn't possibly have known it, Janna thought sadly.

"Then let your brother do the cooking, and you can see about making my villeins well again," Serlo told him. "The sooner they are able to go about their tasks, the sooner you can both leave the manor farm."

"I... have not my brother's talent for healing," Edwin stuttered. "I can't cook neither." He brightened as he thought how best to embroider the tale. "In fact, our mother always said that young John here was by far the more skilled when it came to indoor work such as this. I am more use out in the fields." He raised an arm and flexed the muscles to make his point.

"Then you can work alone in the fields today. Your brother will stay here and brew his concoctions—and also make sure that my people are fed." Serlo gave them a curt nod, and stepped back to watch their final preparations. Even though most of his attention was reserved for Gytha, Janna could understand how the proud beauty sought to avoid him. Such close proximity to Serlo was making her nervous, and that in turn made her clumsy. She stifled a cry as her wet, greasy fingers slid off a bowl and it crashed into pieces on the floor. Scarlet with shame, she kept her head bent as Serlo berated her for her carelessness. Her gratitude toward the reeve was waning; she was beginning to wonder if they might even have been wiser to take their chances and keep running from the forester.

Once they'd all broken their fast, the men left to go about their work while Gytha returned to the kitchen to supervise the servants over preparations for their dinner at midday. Janna made her excuses, and escaped out to the kitchen garden to seek the herbs she needed to bring relief to the cook and the manor's villeins. She was pleased to recognize several familiar plants from her own garden. She plucked feverfew, intending to add it to a syrup with mint and valerian; it would help to dull pain and cool the fever. She continued to browse among the herbs, searching for marigold, septfoil, elecampane or mallow. All or any of them could be useful in a lotion to soothe the itchy spots and help them to heal.

Harvesting the herbs, smelling their fragrance, reminded Janna of the last time she'd collected herbs for healing, when a child's life had been at stake. She sighed with regret. The child had been ailing from the start, and had died. But if her mother had allowed her to administer to the sick as well as preparing and making up potions, she might have known enough to help the child thrive, just as she would have known more about the disease that afflicted those she was expected to treat now.

Clutching her handful of herbs, she hurried back into the kitchen. A quick glance told her that Serlo had left off interfering, and that Gytha was now supervising the plucking of fowls, the gutting of herring and the dicing of vegetables in preparation for dinner. Janna resolved that if any of it came her way, she'd keep half for Edwin, who would not be nearly so well fed out in the fields. She'd seen his hunger as he ate the griddle cakes she'd prepared; how every last crumb had been wolfed down. In spite of his strength he was too thin, but regular meals would soon restore him to full health and vigor. Perhaps, then, he might have a chance with the lovely Gytha?

Ignoring the activity going on around her, Janna carefully washed her hands and the herbs she had collected, just as her mother had always done. Then, with Eadgyth's instructions whispering through her mind, she set about preparing what was needed. She had only Gytha's and Serlo's description of the disease to go on, but even so she was almost certain that she had seen its like before. She knew how to make up the preparations that would bring relief, even if she wasn't sure she could cure the pox. Of course, prayers and holy relics might also help—for certes the priests would think so—but Janna had little knowledge of such things so the patients would have to look for that sort of cure themselves.

She hung a pot of water to boil over the fire, moving a dish of savory pottage to one side to make room for it. "This won't take long," she told Gytha when the young woman protested. She added leaves and roots to the steaming water. Leaving the decoction to simmer, she began a survey of the kitchen, bemused at the array of spices, and the abundance of grain, fruits and vegetables stored in huge barrels and baskets in the larder. A hock of ham hung beside the fireplace to be cured in the smoke from the fire. She took a deep breath, inhaling the potent mix. Bread and vegetable pottage had been their staple diet, but she and her mother had often known great hunger at this time of the year, after what little grain that remained had grown moldy and the new wheat was still too green to harvest.

She prowled around the kitchen while she waited, testing and sniffing the spices. Some she remembered from her encounter with the spice merchant at the market at Wiltune. She wished now that she'd asked their purpose. At the time they had seemed so far out of her reach she'd been reluctant to bother him with too many questions. Now she tasted and sampled them, enjoying the unexpected heat of some, the elusive fragrance and piquancy of others. She could see how they would add flavor to meat, vegetables and puddings. She longed to try them out.

"Pray, take me to visit your mother, Mistress Gytha," she said, once her medicaments were ready. The cook and her daughter did not share the common sleeping quarters upstairs in the hall; they had a separate cot of their own, set close behind the kitchen. Janna had come across the cook in the mornings when she and Edwin broke their fast and waited to collect their dinner. She was a disapproving, thin-faced woman whose tongue had been sharpened on the misfortunes of others. But she was a sorry sight now, Janna thought, as Gytha pushed open the door and led the way into their cottage.

Mistress Tova lay on a straw pallet. She was flushed and sweating. Her hair lay in lank strands on her forehead, and her restless fingers scratched first at her face and then at her arms.

"Don't scratch!" Janna said quickly. "Some of those sores have already begun to fester; they will take longer to heal and you will be left with scars."

The cook's gaze moved from her daughter to Janna, who walked closer so that she might see her patient more clearly. With a conscious effort, she made her voice deeper. "I beg your pardon for scolding you, mistress." She was about to curtsy but remembered in time to catch herself and bobbed awkwardly instead.

"Is that you, John? What are you doing here?"

"I've brought you an infusion to drink. It will dull the pain and cool your fever." She held up a phial and a jar of lotion to show the cook. "There's also a lotion to bathe your skin. It will soothe those itches and help the spots to heal. Please try not to scratch them; you will only make them worse."

The woman nodded, and even managed a faint smile. "I would be glad of some comfort, John, for in truth I think my head is about to burst. And my skin feels as if it's been branded by the devil's own fire."

Janna was somewhat relieved to hear the cook's words. Her mother's patients had described their symptoms in similar fashion. As she set about ministering to Mistress Tova, the woman gave her daughter a sharp glance.

"Get back to the kitchen, Gytha, and make sure you prepare a goodly feast just in case my lord returns today. John can minister to my needs."

Gytha ducked her head in obedience and vanished outside, leaving Janna alone with the cook. She kept her head bent, for Mistress Tova's sharp eyes seemed to miss nothing.

"You are very young," she said now. "You have not even a hint of a beard."

Janna cleared her throat. "I may be young, but I am strong, mistress," she said, fending off any implied criticism.

"And skilled too, it seems." The cook sniffed the draught that Janna handed to her. "What is in this? I'd like to know, for it is usually my task to minister to any who might fall ill here on my lord's demesne."

As Janna detailed what she had used and her method of preparation, the cook nodded approvingly. Her eyes were alight with interest. After a first suspicious sip, she drank the mixture down. "And how did you prepare this?" she asked, when Janna unstoppered the cooling salve she had made.

"Septfoil?" she queried, interrupting Janna's recitation.

"It goes also by the name of tormentil." Using a small piece of cloth to keep her fingers out of contact with the sores, Janna began to dab the lotion onto the cook's skin.

The cook was silent for a few moments. "You have a wide knowledge," she commented.

"My mother was very skilled at healing. She wanted me to learn her craft and so she taught me what she knew."

"And your brother? Does he have the knowledge too?"

"He has no aptitude for healing. He...he prefers to work outdoors in the fields, tilling the earth, or caring for the animals." Janna hoped this was true.

The cook grunted. "Master Serlo will keep him up to the mark. He is a hard taskmaster, but a fair one, you'll find. Do as he tells you and he's kindly enough. Go against him, and you'll live to regret it. He tends the manor farm as if it were his own and he expects the same from all of us. Indeed this is his life, for he has no family to distract him. My lord relies on him completely."

"Master Serlo has indeed been kind to us," Janna said. She continued to dab the cooling lotion onto the cook's face and arms. The cook gave a quiet moan as the liquid touched several raw spots. "Am I hurting you, mistress?"

"No, indeed. I am grateful for your aid and comfort."

"If you will remove your kirtle…" Janna remembered her new identity just in time. "You could also use this lotion on your stomach and your back. I will leave it here with you."

"Thank you." The cook nodded gratefully.

"And I will mix up some more medicaments, and visit you again tomorrow." Janna moved to the door.

"You should ask Master Serlo if he would like you to attend other villeins who are too sick to work, John. There is so much to be done, and too few hands now to do it. I know the reeve is anxious, for my lord is expected home at any time. He will want to give a good accounting of his stewardship during my lord's absence."

"I will do what I can," Janna promised. Curiosity prompted her to probe further. "You have a very beautiful daughter, mistress. I pray that she will not contract the disease."

"As do I," the cook said promptly. "My daughter is of an age to wed, and I have great hopes of a good match for her. In fact, Master Serlo has already spoken to me. He would be a good catch for Gytha. I have urged her to consider his offer, but…" She hesitated. Pride overcame prudence. "I believe my lord is also attracted to Gytha and I know she cares for him. If he was to suggest that they wed…" The cook smiled at the thought.

"Then I hope they will find happiness together," Janna murmured. "God keep you, mistress. I'll call in tomorrow."

Smiling to herself over the high hopes of the cook and her daughter even while wondering if they were deluding themselves, she opened the door and let herself out of the cottage.

Chapter 5

The next few weeks were busy for Janna. She physicked her patients and thus learned her way around the manor farm and the hamlet outside the manor gate where dwelt those villeins who gave service and goods to their lord in exchange for a few strips of land and somewhere to live. Urk and his mother she'd already met, but Janna now came to know everyone else in that small community, husbands and wives, brothers and sisters, sons and daughters. At first they were watchful, suspicious of the boy who claimed to possess the power to heal their hurts and lessen their misery. They asked instead for Mistress Tova, and Janna had to explain over and over again that the cook herself was struck with the pox and confined to her bed. But at Serlo's urging, and as they themselves began to feel the benefit of Janna's healing salves and lotions, they came to accept her, and welcomed her into their homes.

For Janna, this was something new. She had no experience of living in a close community; she found that she enjoyed the villeins' friendship as well as their appreciation. Tending the sick also gave her new confidence, and the hope that her years of watching her mother treating her patients in the confines of their own home might count for something after all. With practice, she might yet come to possess her mother's skills. It was a source of pride that Mistress Tova made a good recovery, with only a few scars to show where the spots had been. Gytha escaped unscathed. Others were not so lucky and bore the scars of their misfortune, but it was a consolation that no-one died.

As soon as they were well enough, the villeins returned to work in their own fields, although their time was restricted by Serlo, who insisted they also catch up on tasks on the lord's lands. Rainy days postponed haymaking so, instead, Edwin and Janna continued to cut weeds, dig ditches and repair the hedges that protected the crops from hungry animals. Whenever she could, Janna fled to the kitchen garden to tend the plants and herbs that grew there, for the villagers continued to come to her with their complaints.

The days were long and the work was always hard and despite the fact the villeins were now well enough to work in the fields, Serlo continued to find chores for Janna and Edwin. He seemed determined they would repay their full dues for his silence. He traversed the manor and surrounding fields tirelessly, keeping an eye on everyone and everything, making sure that whatever was needed would be done. Janna had come to admire and respect the reeve, even while she grumbled over the toll paid by her body. Yet she knew she was also growing stronger, and she gloried in the fresh air, exercise and freedom that her new life afforded her.

Of the lord of the manor there was still no sign, although Gytha was forever preening herself in case he returned unexpectedly. "He's much older than me, but not so old as Serlo," she confided on one occasion, when Janna found her staring at her reflection in the still waters of a small duck pond. "He has at least twenty-five years." She puckered her lips to blow a kiss to herself.

"And has he spoken to you of marriage?"

"He wishes first to make his way in the world." Gytha tossed her head. Janna could see that she was out of sympathy with her lord's ambition.

"Is this not enough for him?" Janna spread out her hands to encompass the fields stretching before them. "Surely this fine demesne brings in a good income?"

"It is not his to inherit." Gytha sounded resentful. "And it's not fair, when my lord works so hard. It is his aim to make this the finest manor farm in the shire, but he will be left with nothing once the young lord comes of age!"

Janna nodded. She knew it was generally the custom for the first born to inherit everything, but life was hard for those sons who came after, or for any noblemen lacking property or wealth of their own. They had few options other than to enter the king's service and hope to earn bounty in battle, or else go into the church. A third option was to marry a woman with a dowry and lands of her own—if they could find someone willing to be wooed. Watching Gytha admiring her reflection, Janna felt sorry for the young beauty. She might have her hopes pinned on the lord of the manor, but unless he was either blind in love or very stupid, he would be looking to wed someone far more suited to his ambition than the cook's daughter.

"When you grow up you should try to be just like him, young John. He's very brave, and so handsome," Gytha gushed. Janna wondered how many noblemen Gytha knew that she could make the comparison with such confidence.

"When will he return?" she asked, thinking that perhaps even now he might be off scouting marriageable prospects.

"We expected him home long before this." Gytha scowled. "He went to visit his family, but the country is in such unrest mayhap he's been summoned by the king to Sarisberie. It's not so very far from here. Or he might have gone on to Winchestre."

Janna's ears pricked up. "Which is the road to Winchestre?" she asked quickly.

"I don't know." Gytha pouted, her mind fixed on her own problems rather than Janna's question. "Really, there is no reason for him to be anywhere but here. While there's fighting between the king and his barons, who keep changing their allegiance in the hope that it might profit them, none of the trouble comes anywhere near here. Besides, my lord mentioned that the king's brother, Bishop Henry, arranged a council of peace between Stephen's queen and the Empress Matilda's half-brother, the Earl of Gloucester, only a month or two ago. The bishop hopes to bring about a reconciliation between the king and his cousin so that she will give up her claim to the throne."

This was welcome news to Janna. "Pray God he succeeds, for all our sakes," she said.

Gytha nodded absentmindedly. "Perhaps my lord is still with his family," she said, coming back to the topic that most interested her. "Perhaps even now he is arguing his right to keep this demesne for his own. Oh!" She clasped Janna's hand in sudden hope. "I pray that they will listen to his plea, John, so that our future together may be assured."

Janna wondered whether to sound a note of caution, but decided it was none of her business. "I hope your wish may come true, mistress," she said, and gently removed her hand from Gytha's grasp. She did not intend to become involved in the young woman's schemes.

It was not so easy, however, to keep herself detached from the villeins and the servants of the household for, having come to know them all as she ministered to their needs, she was popular and much sought after as a result of her skill. She stood in the kitchen early one morning, waiting for the cook to pack up their dinner while half-listening to Mistress Tova's gossip. She had taken special care to stay on friendly terms with the cook, for it meant that she and Edwin sometimes gained extra meat, or a stale pastry or some fruit along with their bread and ale for the day. Their hard work out in the fields meant that they were always hungry, so Janna was happy to put in extra time and care in return for extra food.

"Of course, that girl would look at anyone who wore breeches." The cook's lips tucked down with disapproval as she continued her petulant whine. "Only yesterday, I saw her walk past him. She pretended to stumble, and kicked aside her kirtle so that she could show off her legs. One of these days, you mark my words, that girl will—"

Was the cook speaking of her own daughter? Janna hid a smile, and bent her head closer to hear more.

"You must warn your brother against her." Mistress Tova clicked her tongue vigorously. "He's handsome enough, I grant you, but he shouldn't encourage her. No good will come of it, you'll see. She'll break his heart before she's done, for she's a flighty girl, that Bertha. Besides, she has her sights set much higher than Edwin." There was an extra note of sourness in the cook's voice "Not that she'll get anywhere with my lord. He might have a keen eye for a pretty girl, but he's not for the likes of Bertha."

Janna nodded in agreement, even while wondering how the cook could show so little common sense when it came to her own daughter. Yet she had some sympathy for Gytha, and also for Bertha, as she remembered her own dealings with the handsome Hugh of Babestoche. Truly, she'd been dazzled by his kindness. But Hugh also had his way to make in the world. Janna knew that he was not for her, although his easy kiss had shaken her heart and soul, shaken everything she'd thought and believed. How easy it would have been to lose her heart to him, even knowing that he would have broken it. She shook his image out of her mind. Hugh belonged to the past and besides, she was a youth now and so would not attract the eye of any man, be he as highborn as Hugh, or even as lowly as Godric, who had protected her so bravely, and who would have done even more if she had been willing.

She turned her face away so that the cook wouldn't notice her sadness. The whine continued, as relentless as a midge in summer. "Young as you are, John, you should also guard yourself against Bertha's wiles. That Bertha will set her cap at anyone. Young or old, it matters not."

Janna wondered if the cook realized she was contradicting herself, but was too weary to defend the young woman in question. Instead, she pondered what the luckless Bertha had done to attract so much spite and ire. Bertha was the carpenter's daughter. Although she was not as comely as Gytha, she had a pleasant countenance that matched her friendly disposition. Perhaps it was her popularity that soured the old biddy? It was a popularity that the cook's daughter lacked because of her airs and graces, and her aloofness. Perhaps it was also because others resented the favoritism shown to Gytha by Serlo, for servants and villeins alike worked every hour of daylight while Gytha seemed to please herself. She was seldom found in the kitchen, but spent a lot of time sitting beside the well in the yard, or under a sheltering tree, where all might admire her dainty stitching and her efforts at embroidery.

"…but you'll see him soon enough."

"Who?" Janna realized her mistake as soon as she spoke.

The cook pursed her lips. "If you are not bothered to listen to me, you'll have to stay ignorant, John," she said. "Besides, I haven't all day to stand here gossiping."

"I beg your pardon for delaying you, mistress." Janna quickly made her escape before the woman relented enough to regale her with another half-hour of malice. Yet she would have liked an answer to her question. The cook's words had piqued her curiosity.

"Is someone expected at the manor today? Have you heard anything?" she asked Edwin, once she joined him in the fields.

Edwin stopped weeding, and leaned on his sticks to ponder the question. "Mayhap the lord? He was supposed to be here in time for the haymaking. It's late, but they'll start scything as soon as this rain stops." Edwin looked worried. "I hope he won't ask too many questions about us."

"Who is the lord?" Janna was surprised to realize that after all this time, she didn't even know whose manor they were on. Serlo held such firm control over everything, she'd almost forgotten that the manor belonged to someone else.

Edwin shrugged. "Don't know his name. Don't care, so long as he don't find out who we really are."

"I believe he's quite young and very handsome, although to hear Gytha tell it you'd think he was as ancient as God."

Edwin laughed. "He might be as handsome as the devil himself, but it can't matter to you. You're a youth, remember?"

"Oh, he'd be far too busy to look at me, even if I were a young woman," Janna said cheerfully. "I'm told he has his eye on Gytha, and that Bertha has her eye on him."

"What?" Edwin swung around to confront Janna. He took a savage cut into a deadnettle as he waited for her answer.

"It was just idle gossip. You know what Mistress Tova is like." Janna remembered how Edwin had sidled up to Gytha when he first saw her, and wished she'd kept her mouth shut.

"She's a wicked old crone," Edwin muttered. Turning his back on Janna, he began to hack into a patch of weeds as if his life depended on eliminating every single one.

With a sigh, Janna looked about her. No matter how many thistles they uprooted or cut, there were always more to find; she was beginning to think the harvest would be more bountiful if they reaped thistles rather than wheat! Although they used long-handled sticks to cull the tall, prickly weeds, Janna's hands were scratched and sore. She could feel the sting of their spikes through her smock and breeches whenever she came too close. She hated them! She turned her back on them and, instead, began to cut into a clump of hairy pink corncockle. In the freedom her smock and breeches provided, she'd almost forgotten how it felt to be constrained in a long kirtle. Her past life was beginning to seem more and more like a dream, and yet her quest nagged at her conscience. She needed to find her father. She wanted justice for her mother's death. Finally, she gave voice to her thoughts.

"If Master Serlo won't give us permission to leave the manor, we must ask the lord if we may go."

"Master Serlo needs our help with haymaking. He told me so only yesterday."

"You work too hard, that's the trouble." Janna paused a moment to survey Edwin's efforts as he slashed through a spiky thistle. "If we were both of us as useless as Gytha, he'd get rid of us tomorrow. Today, even." She stopped abruptly as she remembered the distress she'd already caused Edwin.

"Gytha has other uses so far as Master Serlo is concerned," Edwin said dryly.

"True enough." Janna felt slightly reassured that Edwin had come to realize he was wasting his time on Gytha. She decided to jolly him along. "And what is this I hear about Mistress Bertha showing off her legs to you?"

"Who told you that?"

"Do you need to ask?" Janna continued before Edwin had a chance to respond. "I'm meant to warn you that she's a flirty, flighty girl, and that she'll break your heart."

"Mistress Bertha cares nothing for me, whatever Mistress Tova might think!" Edwin's voice was gruff with embarrassment.

Janna looked at him. Edwin's wild, half-starved appearance was gone; he was filling out, becoming a man. He still had a beard, but she realized that at some stage he must have cut his hair, for it was shorter than when she'd first met him.

He was also much cleaner and tidier. No wonder young women looked at him when he passed by, although he never stopped long to talk with them, to tease them or flirt with them as they obviously wished he would.

"You might not stand a chance with Gytha, but I reckon you could have your pick of anyone else if you weren't so shy," she observed.

Edwin flushed. "Look at me!" he countered angrily. "I'm a fugitive from my lord's demesne. How can I woo a maid when I have nothing to offer her, nothing at all?"

"That'll change when you've waited out your year and a day."

"It may, but I need to get to Winchestre so I can find work and start earning a wage."

"Then we might as well get started," Janna said cheerfully. "We'll ask the lord's permission to leave as soon as the opportunity arises."

"I'd rather stay until we're told to go," Edwin said. "Serlo is a good reeve, far better than my own lord, and we have food and shelter here. Trust me, it's much more comfortable living here than living wild in field and forest, having to scavenge and steal to stay alive. Besides, Serlo saved us from the forester. We owe him for that."

"We've already worked hard enough to repay him a hundredfold," Janna grumbled.

"More important, it's much safer for me to stay here, tucked out of sight." Edwin thought a moment. "It's not as though you have any real plan to find your father. A few weeks more can't make any difference either way."

Janna gave a grudging nod.

"Besides, I hear there's to be a great feast after haymaking is done, with much ale and merrymaking," he continued. "You wouldn't want to miss that, would you, even if it means you'll have to ask a maiden to dance with you?"

Janna threw back her head and laughed at the thought. Then her gaze sharpened and she straightened abruptly. feeling light-headed with shock. A sleek, black destrier! She could swear she'd seen the horse before, had even ridden on its back. She closed her eyes, remembering how she'd leaned against Hugh on the long ride back to her cottage; how his arms had folded around her to keep her close and safe. Heat suffused her body as she recalled his kiss at the end of the journey.

She squinted her eyes against the light, trying to see the rider more clearly. He was cleanshaven, with brown, shoulder-length hair. A green cloak almost covered his long tunic. She looked into his dark eyes. Yes, it was, it truly was! Her legs folded under her and she collapsed, faint and giddy with fear. She bent her head to her knees, knowing that the rush of blood would make her feel better. More than anything, though, she needed to hide her identity. Hugh thought she was dead, burned in the fire along with her cottage, and buried by Godric. It was safest for Janna if everyone thought so.

"What is it? What's the matter?" She heard Edwin's anxious voice through the heavy pounding of her heart.

"Hide me, Edwin! Stand in front of me." Janna didn't raise her head. "The lord Hugh is coming our way. What's he doing here?"

"Keep working, or you'll be noticed." Edwin hauled Janna upright and spun her around so that her back was turned to the approaching horseman. He, too, bent to his task while keeping a sharp eye on the figure coming toward them. "I've seen him before, in the forest," he commented. "He rides alone, so he must know the way. There'd be a guide with him else."

"I suspect he knows the way very well. I suspect he's done the journey many times." Janna remembered how Gytha had talked about her lord, and how he would have to give up the manor once the heir came of age. Hugh himself had told her that he was visiting his aunt to report on his custodianship of her property, while his cousin, Hamo, had boasted that in time he would inherit everything. If she'd asked Gytha more questions about the lord, she would have made the connection in time to flee before Hugh's arrival. Janna berated herself for her stupidity.

"The lord Hugh has been away visiting his aunt at Babestoche, which is on the other side of this forest," she said slowly. "Dame Alice must own this manor farm, for Hugh is her nephew and Gytha has told me he's in charge here until the heir comes of age. Oh, Edwin!" Her voice shook as she looked up at him. "This is the worst possible place we could have chosen to come for shelter!"

"Have courage," he murmured, as he bent and began to slice into a patch of nettles. "You are a youth now, remember, and the lord comes very near to us. Keep on cutting weeds or he'll certainly stop and give you a piece of his mind."

Janna quickly moved toward a patch of yellow-flowering charlock. All her senses were alert as she listened to the clopping of the horse's hooves and the jingle of its bridle. In spite of herself, a slow blush mounted her cheeks.

Hugh's cheery voice rang out. "God be with you this day."

"God be with you too, sire," Janna mumbled in reply. She didn't turn around, but heard Edwin's voice echo her greeting. To her horror, the sounds had stopped, which meant that the horse had too. She risked a quick glance behind her, unable to resist seeing Hugh once more, but also wondering if he would consider it rude if she ignored him and kept on working.

"You are strangers to my manor, are you not?"

Janna waited, her heart thudding, for Edwin to reply.

"We are, my lord. Your reeve, Master Serlo, gave us shelter in return for our labor. He has asked us to stay and help with the haymaking."

"Which is very late." Hugh cast his eyes skyward, assessing the chance of sunshine.

"There has been much illness as well as bad weather, sire," Edwin explained.

Watching from under lowered lids, Janna saw Hugh nod silently. "Who are you? What are your names?" he asked.

"I am Edwin, and this is my brother, John." Janna turned to Hugh. She ducked her head in obeisance and kept it bent to avoid his gaze.

"And where are you from? Do you have permission from your liege lord to leave his manor?"

As Edwin launched into an explanation, Janna captured a bristly stem of charlock between her weeding sticks, and felled it.

"Your young brother seems determined to earn his keep," Hugh interrupted, sounding amused. Janna did not dare to look at him.

"He's young, sire, and shy. But he's a good worker. Our mother always said that young John here was never at rest until all that was needed was done and done proper."

Janna stifled a giggle. Edwin sounded so convincing!

"I can see your mother was right. I'll have a word with Serlo when I find him. It may be you can stay on to help with the harvest too. There is always a need for good and willing workers." The jingle of the bridle told Janna that Hugh was on the move once more. Only when the sounds had faded into the distance did she dare to raise her head and look after him.

"There, you heard him! He wants us to stay." Edwin sounded wistful. "I'd like that, John, I really would. Especially if we can also work our way through the bitter months of winter."

"Don't even think about it!" Janna said furiously. "Didn't you listen when I told you how the villagers set fire to my cottage, with me in it? And how they all now think I'm dead? It's too dangerous for me to stay here!"

"You didn't tell me he had anything to do with it." Edwin jerked his head in the direction of the dwindling figure of Hugh.

"No, but—but—" If Hugh found out that she was alive and living on his manor, it would only be a matter of time before Dame Alice and Lord Robert found out too. Janna had managed to escape with her life once; she didn't intend to take any further chances.

"But what?" Edwin raised an enquiring eyebrow.

"He was part of it. Hugh, I mean," Janna muttered. "It's not safe for me to stay here." Even as she said the words, she knew that really she wanted to stay, just to be near him. Coming so close to him again had utterly unnerved her. In spite of her short hair and men's garb, she longed to see him again.

Gytha was also longing to see Hugh. The thought quenched Janna's ardor as efficiently as a bucket of cold water thrown over a fire. It seemed that the lord had a weakness for pretty serving girls, along with the glib tongue to convince them that they were special in his eyes.

"We have to leave here. We must," she insisted.

"We can't. Not without Serlo's permission."

"He can't stop us if he doesn't see us go." Janna wondered why Edwin was being so obstinate.

"He can raise the hue and cry after us with the forester and with the shire reeve. I've done enough running away, Ja—John. I would rather stay here for as long as we can."

Janna was silent, torn between wanting to help Edwin and the need to protect herself.

"We probably won't see him again," Edwin said. "He'll be far too busy and important to bother with the likes of us, and we can also make sure we stay out of his way. Our dealings are with Serlo, not him. Besides, he doesn't suspect a thing. In fact, he thinks well of you for being such a hard worker!"

Janna gave a grudging nod. "Then you must speak for me, and protect me from him," she conceded, adding fiercely, "but only until our time is up! Then I am going to Winchestre, whether you come with me or not." She bent to cut into the hated weeds once more.

Chapter 6

After her unexpected encounter with Hugh, Janna spent as little time in the hall as possible in case he came in and found her there. She'd break her fast with speed and, while Edwin waited to hear Hugh or Serlo give those villeins on week work their orders for the day, she would hurry to the kitchen and wait for Mistress Tova to pack up dinner and supper in a sack for those who were unable to provide for themselves. Listening to the cook's tattle meant that Janna was always abreast of what was happening around the manor, along with Mistress Tova's thoughts about it all.

Not everything was going smoothly and Mistress Tova had plenty to say. A fox had got into the henhouse one night. The rumpus had woken the servants sleeping in the hall, and they'd rushed down to investigate, but several hens had already been savaged and killed. The maid in charge of feeding them and collecting their eggs had been harshly scolded, although she tearfully repeated over and over again that she was sure, positive, absolutely certain that she'd shut the coop tight for the night.

Next, a young lamb had been found dead. They'd been put back in their fold for the night, but the lamb's body was discovered some distance away, although the shepherd said he'd counted them and had stayed close in his little hut all night. The lamb's carcass was cut and bloody. It was certain that no natural illness or weakness had killed it, while the shepherd swore no wolf could have carried it off without his hearing it. He, too, had felt the sharp edge of Serlo's tongue.

On another occasion, cows managed to escape from their byre and had plunged through a hedge into a field of ripening wheat. Before the hayward could sound the alarm, their hooves and their appetites had destroyed a large portion of new grain, which meant there would be less for the harvest and therefore less to tide everyone over through winter and the hungry months before the next harvest.

What intrigued Janna most was her suspicion that the incidents had been planned, and for a purpose. Walking past the henhouse on the day after the hens had been savaged, she'd noticed a small posy of rue beside the gate of their run. It had seemed odd at the time, so odd that she'd paid close attention when she found another bunch of rue near the sheepfold after the slaughter of the lamb. It seemed unlikely that the herb had been dropped by accident. Did it mean, therefore, that the perpetrator regretted his acts of violence afterward? Was this his way of saying he was sorry?

No-one seemed to think anything of it, but Janna didn't believe in happenstance. Perhaps to the others rue was just a useful herb, but she understood its special significance. "*Rue is for repentance,*" Eadgyth had told her. "*Rue stands for regret.*" The bunches of rue must surely mean that there was some reason why these things had happened. But what could it be?

The question had niggled her so that, after the cows went wandering, Janna searched for rue near the byre. It had taken some finding, for by then the ground around was pooled and muddy and the herb had been trampled underfoot, but Janna found enough scraps to know that rue had been picked and placed there.

No accident then, but for a purpose. Who was responsible, and why? Janna had a growing suspicion that she knew the answer to the first question, and possibly even the second. She resolved to keep watch, and wait until she had some grounds for accusation. Meanwhile, she hoped with all her heart that her suspicions were wrong.

Mistress Tova was still talking. "... and these accidents have all occurred since the lord's return. This sort of carelessness isn't tolerated when Master Serlo is in charge." Mistress Tova gave Janna a long and meaningful glance, before adding, "Of course, Gytha is delighted to have the lord home at the manor again, but even so..."

Janna stopped herself from defending Hugh, not wanting to betray any special interest in him to the gossiping cook. But she couldn't help worrying about it, for although Serlo had questioned everyone after the incident with the cows, no-one seemed to have any knowledge of how they might have escaped the byre, nor any intention of revealing the secret if they had. The cowherd seemed blameless; his family could vouch for his presence in their midst at the time the animals must have gone astray. Someone else was therefore responsible, and Serlo was making every effort to find the culprit. Janna was quite sure that the reeve suspected her and Edwin, being the newest arrivals on the manor farm. He'd certainly questioned them for a long time.

Janna's thoughts went back to that interview, and how uncomfortable she'd felt under Serlo's accusing gaze as he'd made them recount where they'd been and what they'd been doing. He had a nasty rash on his hand, Janna remembered, and she'd sought to divert his attention by offering a healing salve. But he'd brushed her concern aside, clearly determined not to be deflected from his purpose. Someone was going to be held responsible for the destruction; someone was going to get the blame. Yet at the end he'd made no accusations, instead ordering every villein out into the field to plant peas, beans and vetches, so that there might be something to eat in place of what had been destroyed.

"Of course, you and your brother are newly come to the manor." Mistress Tova's voice broke into Janna's thoughts. She didn't have to say anything else for Janna to know what she was thinking.

"Edwin and I aren't responsible for any of these accidents. We know nothing about them!" Janna hoped that her denial would be believed, and also passed on with the rest of the gossip that Mistress Tova shared so freely.

The cook looked thoughtful. "No-one wants to think the worst of you, John, not when you were so good about curing us of the pox. No." She went quiet for a moment, as if wondering how far she could trust Janna with her suspicions. "No," she continued, "we must just be having a run of bad luck." She tied up the sack of food and thrust it at Janna. "I've put in a small meat pie for your dinner," she said generously, and Janna beamed her thanks.

*

The sun had finally come out, the long days had settled into sunshine, and haymaking had started at last. Hugh was present for the ceremony that marked its beginning, when at dawn the hayward tied a bunch of flowering grasses to his scythe and crossed himself in prayer before making the first cut. Janna had stayed as far away from Hugh as she could, mingling with the villeins as they followed the hayward in a line through the water meadows, scything the long grass that would keep the animals from starvation during the lean winter months when the meadows were flooded. When she next looked around for Hugh, he had gone. She smiled with relief, her smile returned by the women and children who followed behind. Their task was to spread the grass out to dry, and turn it so that it bleached to a pale gold in the hot summer sun. The sweetness of cut grass, and the fragrant herbs that were felled with it, scented the air.

All able-bodied villeins, plus their wives and children, were expected to take part in this boon work for their lord, just as they were pressed into service at other busy times on the farming calendar. Their reward, at the end of each day of haymaking, was to take home as much hay as they could carry on their scythes. Only when all the grass was cut, dried, bundled and stored would they be released from their extra days of labor. While this caused some grumbles, they mostly worked with a will so that they could finish the task and get back to tending their own fields.

After the fuss about the straying cows, there'd been no further incidents. Janna had begun to convince herself that the culprit was truly repentant, and that they could all rest easy now. So she was happy and quite unsuspecting as, sack of food under her arm, she walked past the stables on her way down to the water meadows for the day's haymaking. The sound of Hugh's voice stopped her. After a quick look around the yard to check that no-one was watching, she sidled over to the door and peered around it. Hugh was in a stall with his destrier, swearing loudly as he inspected its hoof. Janna knew an instant of alarm, but then calmed her fears with the thought that horses often went lame, and that a sharp flint must be to blame. As she watched, Hugh removed a loose shoe and carefully extracted an iron nail from the horse's hoof, swearing profusely all the while.

Hoping to allay her suspicions, Janna inspected the ground in front of the stable door for any telltale sign, but there was nothing to see. Then she noticed the silvery green leaves and small yellow flowers of rue peeping out from under her boot. She stepped aside and snatched them up. This was proof, if proof was needed, that this was no coincidence. All these so-called accidents had been planned deliberately. As she hurried through the water meadows, she cast the sprigs of rue into the long grass to hide them. If her suspicions were correct, then she needed to say something. But first she had to be sure. If she was mistaken, if she made a false accusation, she would never forgive herself. And pray God that she was mistaken.

Once more, Janna ran through the names of everyone she knew. From everything she'd heard and witnessed, Hugh was a good overlord, kind and fair, while Serlo was respected and trusted by everyone. Any one of those employed at the manor might have had the opportunity to carry out these acts, but there was only one person that Janna could think of who had a personal reason to want to cause this sort of damage. Urk.

Everything pointed to him. He was free to come and go as he liked, particularly at night. No-one paid much attention to him, or took him seriously. Although slow, he was quite capable of carrying out all that had happened, for all that was needed was a cloak of invisibility. Plus he, alone of anyone she knew, had a reason to cause trouble and then repent of his actions. Although she'd tried to keep her promise to Mistress Wulfrun, it was impossible to watch the boy all the time. Janna was sure that he brooded over his punishment at the hands of Serlo. He might well want to hit back at the reeve, while the posies of rue seemed to confirm his regret for the harm he had done. She should warn Urk's mother to keep a more watchful eye on her son, although she was reluctant to cause the woman even more grief and worry. Perhaps she should wait a while longer and, instead, keep close to Urk herself? She could warn him that she knew what he was doing, and counsel him over the consequences. If she could make him realize that if he was caught, retribution would be horrible, both for himself and for his family, perhaps he would stop this childish mischief-making?

Pleased to have formulated a plan of action, Janna skipped a few steps. After checking that no-one was about, she next tried a couple of cartwheels, copying the actions of some children she'd seen larking about. She'd been dying to have a go and, to her satisfaction, she almost succeeded. She had another try and then another. A bit wobbly, she decided, but she was sure she'd improve with practice. She strode on, feeling happy, healthy and almost content. She was used to the labor now, and reveled in the growing strength in her muscles, and in her freedom to run, to shout, even to turn cartwheels and do anything else a boy might do. She smiled to herself, and hurried on to join Edwin and the others, who were busy forking up the dry grass and stacking it into bundles.

Urk was among the group. He was almost as tall as Janna, and far stronger and quicker in his movements. He smiled when he noticed her. It was the perfect opportunity, and Janna took it. "Are you very angry with Master Serlo, Urk?" she asked, moving closer to him so that they could talk without being heard.

"Angry? No. I'm scared of him."

It was true. Janna had seen him cower away and try to hide whenever Serlo came near. "I wonder, did you hurt that baby lamb we found the other day? The one that was all bloody and lying out in the field?"

"No! I like baby lambs." Urk's lips set in a straight line, and he forked the hay with renewed vigor.

"Do you know who hurt it?"

"No." Urk shook his head without slackening his pace. "It's not right to kill baby lambs."

"No, it isn't," Janna agreed, feeling rather at a loss. "What about the cows that got into the field? Did you let them out of the byre?"

The boy shook his head, not bothering to answer.

"And the hens? How did the fox get into their coop?"

"I don't know!" Urk kept on forking up hay.

"What about my lord's horse? Was it you who hammered the nail into its hoof?" Janna pressed.

"No!" Urk stopped and turned to her then. "I'm scared of horses. They're too big. It wasn't me, John. None of it was me!"

"None of what's happened here was an accident," Janna said. "Someone did these things on purpose. Someone who wants to cause trouble to Master Serlo and to the lord Hugh. Do you know who that could be, Urk?"

He lowered his head and began to kick at the green stubble left from the newly cut grass.

"It's all right to tell me if you know anything about it," Janna urged. "I won't tell anyone else what you did, I promise, just so long as you stop causing trouble."

"But I didn't do anything!"

"If Gabriel says he didn't do it, then he didn't do it." Mistress Wulfrun stepped in front of Janna and pulled her son behind her, out of harm's way. "I know what you're thinking, John, but he's a truthful boy. I've never known him tell a lie, even when he's got in trouble for it."

"Gabriel?" Janna asked, confused.

"His name is Gabriel," Mistress Wulfrun explained. "He may not be the brightest star in the sky, but he's kind and loving, and he has such a sweet smile we believe he's been touched by God's own hand."

Urk peeked out from behind his mother and smiled at Janna, as if in proof of his mother's faith in him. "I didn't do none of those things," he said, softly but firmly.

Janna wondered whether she could believe him and his fond mother. "I hope that's true," she said, "because you can be sure that when Master Serlo finds out who is responsible, that person will get such a beating he may be half-killed." She read the fear on Urk's face and was briefly repentant, yet she'd spoken only the truth. If Urk's conscience was clear, then Serlo couldn't touch him or his family. Meantime she had delivered her warning. It was all she could do. And if Urk was telling the truth, then she would have to think again.

Could Edwin be responsible? It hardly seemed likely when he was so keen to stay on at the manor, and was so grateful to Serlo for giving them food and shelter. Yet Janna had formed the impression lately that Edwin was keeping something hidden from her. She hadn't thought much about it, for although the two of them had become firm friends, she thought of him only as a friend and no more than that—she certainly didn't expect him to confess every little thing to her. But where once he'd been always at her side, now he was often absent, gone off on some errand of his own. On occasion she had questioned his absence, but had received no satisfactory answer. Had he gone off to kill a lamb? To lame a horse?

No! Janna shook her head, unable to imagine Edwin doing any of those things—and yet, by his own admission, he'd stolen from travelers in the past without it troubling his con-science—or so it seemed. Yet he seemed happy here, and wanting to stay. He certainly didn't seem to be harboring the sort of resentment that must lie behind acts of this sort.

What most worried Janna was the thought of what might happen next. If someone was causing problems for a reason, he'd be unlikely to stop until his purpose was achieved. What could that purpose be? If she could find that out, perhaps she might be able to put a stop to these so-called "accidents" and so ensure her and Edwin's safety.

*

Questions continued to bedevil her as the villeins prepared to enjoy medale, the drinking festivity to celebrate the end of haymaking. The grass had been cut and dried, and either collected into stacks with thatched covers to protect it through the winter rains, or carted off to be stored in the barn. For the moment, their task was done, although Serlo had already warned them that sheep-shearing would be next, followed by the harvest, and that he expected them to stay on and help with those too. She took comfort from the notion that he must not suspect them of causing the problems.

It was with a sense of anticipation that she followed Edwin up to the manor hall on the night of the celebration. Mistress Tova, Gytha and the rest of the kitchen servants had been busy. Trestle tables were set up in long lines and were laden ready for the feast. Wooden platters were piled high with food, with brimming pitchers of honey mead and ale set beside them.

"This'll do me," Edwin said cheerfully, as he surveyed the spread. "You can have the leftovers." He patted his stomach and gave Janna a wolfish grin. Janna laughed, but her mirth vanished as she looked beyond Edwin and saw Hugh standing beside Serlo at a table raised up on a platform. He was surveying the crowd below.

"I have to go," she muttered, and swung around.

"You can't miss out on medale!" Edwin caught her arm and dragged her back, looking horrified at the thought.

"But he's here! The lord Hugh is here!"

"So what? Why are you so afraid of him? What makes you think he'll even remember you?"

It was a fair question and one Janna couldn't answer unless she told Edwin how kind Hugh had been to her after her mother died; how they'd played ball with his cousin, Hamo, and how he'd taken her home on the back of his destrier afterward. And kissed her! She blushed at the memory.

"Stay," Edwin urged now. "He thinks you're my brother. He doesn't know who you really are. Don't let him spoil this feast for you."

Janna risked another glance in Hugh's direction, her heart jolting painfully as she noticed who else was standing beside him. Gytha. She wore a new kirtle for the occasion, homespun but dyed a greenish tinge that became her dark locks and creamy complexion, and added a bewitching green tint to her hazel eyes. Hugh sat down at the high table, accompanied by Serlo and several others. After he'd said grace, Gytha began to serve him, bending over so that she could smile into his eyes while giving him time to glimpse the slight swell of her breasts above the lacing of her kirtle.

Janna stood still, swept by a tide of pure envy. She wanted to flee, to hide from the sight, yet a painful curiosity bid her stay to watch the interplay between them so she would know for sure whether the girl's trust in Hugh's intentions was well founded. She would feel sorry for Gytha if the girl's high hopes came to naught, but she knew she'd feel even worse for herself if Hugh defied common sense and became betrothed to the young woman.

Edwin nudged Janna, unwittingly adding to her distress as he said, "See? You don't need to worry that he'll notice you. He has eyes only for Gytha."

"As she has for him," Janna said, wondering how Edwin could sound so cheerful. "Don't you mind?"

"About Gytha? No, why should I?"

So Edwin was over his infatuation with the cook's daughter. Good. She must work on him anew to persuade him to leave the manor with her. Flight was her only choice, both for her peace of mind and to pursue her quest.

She sat down beside Edwin, but she found now that she'd lost all appetite and could only look without interest at the mound of food he'd piled on the trenchers of bread in front of them.

"Do you mind if I sit with you two?" Without waiting for a reply, Bertha took a seat on Edwin's other side, flashing a cheerful smile at Janna as she did so. The two of them set about wolfing down huge portions of fish, fowl and mutton, but Janna was too sick with envy to eat. Instead, she picked up her cup of ale and drained it, then sneaked another glance at Hugh and Gytha. It was clear that the young woman was doing all in her power to woo him. Janna wondered if it was only wishful thinking that made her question whether Hugh was quite so enamored with the serving wench as she was with him? She knew Hugh to be kind and courteous, and so he was now, bending his head to listen to something Gytha was saying. Yet his gaze roved the room until it alighted on Janna. She blinked and looked quickly away, while her face flamed scarlet. His glance had been questioning; he was frowning slightly. Had she done something wrong? Worse, did he suspect that she or Edwin might be behind the laming of his horse and the other disasters that had befallen the manor?

Janna wanted to leap up, to go to him and protest her innocence, but she stayed seated and tried to look as if she was enjoying herself. She sneaked another look, and found Hugh still watching her. Her heart thudded painfully; her chest felt too tight to breathe. She cast about for a chance to escape, but knew there was none. It would be unforgivably rude to leave the hall until after the lord had arisen from the table and retired to his solar. In case Hugh was still watching, she poured herself another mug of ale and quaffed it down, trying to look as unconcerned and as boyish as possible.

"You should eat something, John," Bertha urged, and held out a portion of fat hen in her fingers. "You'll never grow as tall and strong as your brother, else." She smiled at Janna. Distracted from her dark thoughts, Janna felt a flash of amusement as she took the food from Bertha's fingers.

"Thank you," she said, wondering if the cook's sour gossip had some truth in it. Was Bertha indeed flirting with her as well as with Edwin—and everyone else who wore breeches, if Mistress Tova was to be believed? Janna ate the fowl, her appetite reviving somewhat as she savored the delicacy, so that she continued then to help herself from the trencher. "Are your family here tonight, mistress?" she asked, seeking to distract herself from the scene being played out at the high table.

"Yes, indeed." Bertha waved an arm toward the tables opposite. "That's my father and mother over there, and my two sisters sit next to them. Not for anything would any of us miss this feast." With an expression of bliss, she began to tear the flesh off a bone with her teeth.

Janna had met one of Bertha's sisters when she'd taken medicaments to cure her of the pox. Now she looked with interest at the rest of Bertha's family.

"Bertha's little sister wants to meet you, John," Edwin told her, with a sly smile. "She thinks you're very handsome. Perhaps you might like to dance with her later?"

Janna choked on a piece of fish, and began to cough. Edwin thumped her on the back. Scarlet in the face, she took some ale. "Fish bone," she spluttered, by way of explanation.

Bertha smiled in ready sympathy. "I had an uncle who choked to death on a fish bone," she said, and embarked on a long story, giving Janna a chance to recover her equilibrium.

Only when every last morsel was eaten were the tables cleared and stacked, and benches placed along the sides of the hall. Now I can leave, Janna thought, but Hugh still stayed seated at the high table, gazing serenely at the scene in front of him. Gytha leaned over him to pour wine into his goblet, her arm against his, her breast almost brushing his cheek. Janna clenched her hands and turned away, knowing she was trapped for the while. Several villeins stood together at one side. Janna recognized the shepherd with his pipe, then noticed that the others also carried musical instruments. Occasionally she'd heard someone playing a tune in the marketplace; sometimes people sang words to the music, or even danced around. Janna hadn't paid them much mind. Music had never been part of her life, so she could hardly contain a gasp of surprised pleasure now as, with one accord, the musicians turned to the eager crowd gathering around them and began to play a carol. The shepherd held his pipe to his mouth and blew through the holes in it, dancing his fingers up and down to produce the sounds. Another villein struck a small drum, setting up a rhythm for the dancers who were now swirling around in pairs, stamping in time to the beat and shrieking with delight. The third member of the party held a wooden bowl with a long neck along which several strings were tied. His fingers plucked and stroked the strings so that his sounds and the sounds from the pipe spoke to each other, sometimes blending together and sometimes taking turns to create different sounds altogether. Janna listened, enchanted, while her feet tapped in time to the rhythm.

"John? I would have a word with you."

Hugh's voice dragged Janna from her reverie. She gave a start of surprise, and looked anxiously for Edwin and Bertha to save her, but they had joined the throng of dancers and she sat alone. She leaped to her feet and bobbed her head.

"Sire," she murmured, remembering to keep her voice deep. She did not dare look at Hugh. Instead, she moved closer to a shadowy recess where the light from the candles scarcely reached.

"I believe I have you to thank for ministering to my workers when they were ill with the pox. I am grateful to you. Serlo tells me we would have been even further delayed but for your cures." He was addressing her in the Saxon language. Although Janna was sorely tempted to prove that she was something better than a lowly serf, she knew it would be folly to answer him in the Norman French in which they had conversed before. She hoped that speaking Saxon to him now might further disguise her true identity. Hugh seized her hand. Something round and cold was pressed into it. Janna looked to see what he had given her. A dull glint told her what it was: a silver penny.

She thrust it into her purse. "I thank you, sire," she stammered, glancing quickly at him before looking away again.

"I have a horse gone lame—a nail awry in a loose shoe. Will you see if you can do aught to help my steed? Arrow is in pain, and I fear he may become crippled if the wound festers."

"Yes, my lord. Of course I'll do all I can." Janna's heart lurched at the thought of ministering to Hugh's destrier under his watchful gaze. She kept her head bent.

"Come to the stables tomorrow, after you have broken your fast. I'll wait for you there."

Janna nodded. "My lord," she whispered, wishing that he would go and leave her alone yet wanting him to stay, wanting to prolong this moment alone with him.

"You have no need to fear me, John." Hugh's voice was kindly. But his next action filled her with alarm. He reached out and tilted up her chin so that she had no choice but to look full at him. "I thought so," he murmured, peering more closely at her in the shadowy darkness. "You remind me of a young healer I once knew. Her name was Johanna. Do you know of her, John? Was she perhaps a sister, or a cousin to you?"

"No! No, sire. My brother and I come from Wales." Janna's voice shook as she told the lie. She longed to confess to Hugh, and also to ask if he had kept his promise to her, but she dared not. "We have no living kin here in England that we know of for certain," she said, in case he still harbored any suspicions.

"You look so like her," Hugh mused, adding as if to himself, "but Johanna is dead."

And are you sorry? Janna pressed her lips firmly together so that she could not ask the question, although she burned to know the answer. It was some comfort that Hugh remembered her; she took additional comfort from the regret in his voice when he said, "Johanna had a great gift for healing, and so did her mother. They are greatly missed at the manor of Babestoche, as well as in the neighboring hamlets, for there is no-one now to physick the sick and help the dying."

"Surely there is a midwife in the village with some healing knowledge, my lord?" Janna knew he was mistaken about the villagers' regret, but she was curious to learn what had become of Mistress Aldith, one of the few of her mother's acquaintances who had shown her any kindness.

Hugh shrugged. "Her business is to birth babies, but my aunt has little faith in her ability, that I know." His eyes narrowed as he inspected Janna. "Where did you learn your healing ways?"

"From...from my mother, sire." Janna knew she must stick to her story. Others had heard it, and could repeat it to Hugh if he asked. It would increase his suspicion if she told him something different now. "She was Saxon born, but when she wed my father she went to live with him in Wales. He died when we were still quite young, but my father had a cot and enough land to keep us so my mother stayed on, for she believed her own family were either dead or had moved and she knew not where to find them."

"I thought Serlo told me your mother worked in an alehouse?"

"So she did, sire, for she had us to help her about our home and in the fields," Janna improvised rapidly. "As soon as he was old enough, my brother tended the fields, planted crops, and looked after our sheep and goats. I helped by growing vegetables for the pot, and herbs for my mother's medicaments.

My mother was settled in Wales. It was her home. And ours, until she died." Janna knew she was gabbling, but hoped that the wealth of detail might serve to convince Hugh. She hated lying to him, hated it, but their safety depended on her lies.

"Why, then, did you leave Wales?"

Janna gulped. "I...er...my oldest brother has wed. He has taken the land and the cot for his own, so Edwin and I decided to seek a living in Winchestre and, perhaps, find out if any of our kin are still alive. We are free born, sire," she added for good measure.

"This isn't Winchestre," Hugh commented dryly.

"No. No, my lord, it isn't. But we have no money of our own so we are forced to find food and shelter along our way, which we repay with our labor."

"Then I wish you both good fortune." Hugh paused a moment. "I've watched you and your brother. You are both hard workers, while your skill as a healer is also welcome here. You may stay here as long as you desire."

"Th-thank you, sire." Janna stepped away from Hugh and bowed her head, desperate for him to leave. To be so close and not tell him the truth was torture to her. When she looked up again, he had returned to his place at the table but he watched her still, his face screwed up into a thoughtful frown. Knowing she must act, and quickly, Janna turned to a young girl standing nearby. She was Bertha's young sister and she was looking at Janna with a hopeful expression on her face. Without giving herself time to think, Janna grabbed the girl's hand and led her into the throng of laughing, dancing villeins.

Just as she had no notion of music, so Janna didn't know how to dance either. It didn't seem to matter among all the noise and confusion, but still she tried to imitate the actions of those around her, clapping her hands and stamping her feet in time to the beat. When the villeins linked arms or whirled their partners around by the waist, so did Janna, and when they formed into a long line and danced around the high table, Janna joined them along with Bertha's sister. She hoped Hugh was still watching and that he was satisfied she was who she claimed to be. But in truth, she thought, as she stole a quick glance at him, it was Gytha who had his attention now, for she held a plate of sweetmeats before him, tempting him both with the delicacies and with her eyes.

Janna looked quickly away and concentrated on following the pattern of the dancers. She was just beginning to enjoy herself when a loud cry sounded above the music.

"Fire!"

At once there was pandemonium. Some began to scream, some froze to the spot with terror, while others pushed past and over them in a desperate effort to get through the door and down the stairs to safety. It took some time for the hall to clear and everyone to see that the danger lay not in the manor house but outside in the fields.

One of the haystacks was alight. They could see the glow above the palisade of sharpened stakes that fenced the manor house and yard. Cold dread gripped Janna as she listened to new cries of alarm. If the fire moved on and destroyed the other haystacks, the winter fodder would be burned and the animals would starve. Yet everyone milled around, waiting to be told what to do until Hugh shouted out above the hubbub: "Follow me to the stream!" He raced ahead through the gate, and all fell into line behind him.

Janna saw that he had already left instructions with Serlo for he, with a group of his own, ran to the shed where all the farming implements were housed. Undecided how best to help, Janna followed the crowd through the gate and up into the field, then stopped to watch. In the light from the flames, she saw that Hugh was now dividing the villeins into two groups, sending some to the small stream that ran down into the river, and beckoning others to follow him to the flaming haystack. As Serlo and his helpers raced to the stream with leather buckets from the shed, the villeins formed into a long line, making a chain that led from stream to haystack. At once they began to fill the buckets and pass them from hand to hand up the line. Serlo stayed by the stream to keep the buckets moving, while Hugh took up station beside the haystack to direct the flow of water to where the flames were fiercest.

Once the contents were thrown, the buckets were thrust at a knot of children waiting nearby. They took turns to race back with the empty buckets to the stream to be refilled. Janna noticed Urk among them, carrying two buckets at a time and racing faster than anyone. Had he been in the hall with everyone else before the haystack caught alight? She couldn't be sure. All her attention had been on Hugh, and then on her dancing partner as she tried to convince Hugh that she was a youth. It was certain that Urk was on the spot now, and doing all he could to help put out the fire—but had he set it in the first place? It seemed unlikely when he was making such an effort to help now. Or was this part of his repentance for his act?

Janna looked about. Was anyone missing? Who else might have fired the haystack? She had little doubt that this was no accident, but she feared that Urk would be blamed for it. After all, he'd set fire to hay once before. Serlo would certainly believe he was capable of doing it again.

She stepped closer to scrutinize the chain more carefully. Hugh was beside the burning haystack, his face illuminated in the blaze as he directed the villeins to throw the water where it would be most effective. Serlo was still down beside the stream, keeping a watchful eye on the buckets moving up the chain, and also on the children to make sure they ran back to the haystack once they'd handed over the empty buckets to be filled. There was order amid the panic, for everyone knew how vital it was to keep the fire from spreading. Janna's glance narrowed as she tallied off the line of peasants laboring to pass along the heavy buckets without spilling their precious contents. There was no sign of Edwin. Where was he? She was filled with dread as she moved along the line to search for him.

"You! John! Get down to the stream and help fill those buckets!" Serlo had seen her. Janna knew that to disobey him would invite his wrath as well as his suspicion. She hastened to do as she was told. There was barely enough light from the flickering flames to make out the identity of her companions. But Edwin was not among them, she was sure of it.

She bent to her task, grabbing buckets from the children, sweeping them through the water to fill them, then heaving them up and into a pair of waiting arms. It was back-breaking work, but Janna had been toughened by her weeks in the fields and she knew she felt the strain less than the women who worked beside her. But they carried on without complaint, desperate to save the fodder that would keep their animals alive through winter, with meat on the table for themselves and their families.

"Give me a bucket." She heard Edwin's voice beside her, and turned to him with a mixture of relief and fury.

"Where have you been?" she hissed. He hung his head. She thought he looked guilty, and feared the worst. "What's going on?" She grabbed his shoulder and shook him hard. "Did you set fire to the haystack?"

"Of course not." He pulled away from her and leaned over to fill a bucket. "I came to help as soon as I realized what was happening."

"I just hope no-one else noticed your absence! Don't you see, Edwin, we are the last to come here so we must be the first they will blame when they understand that these are not accidents but deliberate attempts to harm the manor and those who live here."

"Don't be silly! This was an accident, surely." Edwin handed over a brimming bucket and grabbed another from a waiting child.

"How could it be an accident? Why would a haystack suddenly catch fire in the middle of the night?"

"Sometimes they overheat, especially if the grass is still green. It happens."

It was true. Janna hadn't thought of that, but in her heart she was sure it hadn't happened that way. "What about the dead lamb?" she asked. "That wasn't an accident."

"A fox? A wolf?"

Janna shook her head. "A wild animal would have eaten the lamb, not killed it and left it for someone to find. Besides, its wounds were made by a knife, not teeth."

"Yes, 'tis true." Edwin's forehead knitted into a frown.

"And the cows that got out and the fox that got in? And the lord's lame horse? Do you really think all those things were accidents?"

"What happened to the horse?" Conscious that Serlo was keeping an eye on the water chain, Edwin hastily dipped his bucket into the stream. His frown deepened as Janna told him what she'd seen and found at the stable.

"These things have all happened since the lord returned to the manor," he interrupted her recital. "It seems he's not as good at managing the farm as his reeve."

So Mistress Tova was still spreading her poison. This time Janna was determined to defend Hugh. "That's not true. You can't blame my lord for any of this."

"I'm only saying what everyone else says."

Janna shook her head. "These are not accidents, they're deliberate actions by someone wanting to cause harm."

"How can you be so sure?"

"Because of the posies of rue left behind at the scene."

"Rue?"

"For regret. And for repentance. That's what the old ones say, anyway. I wondered at first if the rogue felt regret for his actions after he'd done the deeds, but now I'm not so sure." Without meaning to, Janna looked for and found Urk. He was coming their way, an empty bucket dangling from each fist. In spite of the gravity of the situation, his face creased into its customary cheerful smile as he thrust the buckets at Janna and Edwin.

"He looks happy enough. Maybe it's him," Edwin commented.

"No, it isn't." But Janna wasn't as sure as she sounded. She decided it was time to voice her concerns. "Actually, I wondered if it might be you."

"Me?" Edwin looked astonished. "Why in God's true name would I do something like this?" He gestured toward the haystack. "What have I got to gain by it? Truly, John, I think your wits have been addled by the ale you've drunk tonight!"

"Where were you when the fire started, can you tell me that?"

Edwin shook his head, and did not answer. He bent to fill another bucket and passed it along the line.

"Tell me!" Janna insisted.

"I swear by a snake's tits this is nothing to do with me," he said, and grabbed another empty bucket.

Wishing she knew who or what to believe, Janna turned away. She glanced up at the haystack, aware that the flames were dying at last. Smoke and the stink of wet, burnt hay tainted the air, but it seemed the remaining haystacks had escaped the fire. Janna stood up and stretched, easing her cramped, sore muscles. "If you won't tell me your secrets, then I shall just have to go on suspecting the worst," she said.

Chapter 7

Worry kept Janna wakeful and restless through the night. Her eyes felt puffy and pricked with tiredness when she finally rolled off her pallet and prepared herself to face Hugh. She longed for a wash, for her monthly courses had begun. She'd managed to scavenge some rags to use, but maintaining her disguise was proving difficult. Although she could wash out the rags, there was no privacy to wash herself and preserve her modesty along with her true identity unless she left the manor farm—and that she couldn't do, not without Serlo's permission. Nor could she sneak out at night and plunge into the river, for if anyone saw her undressed they would find out the truth. So she sighed, and wet her fingers and tried to smooth the singed stubble that covered her head, which was all she could do to make herself presentable. With a catch of alarm, she realized that her hair was growing long again. She patted the knife in its sheath. She must ask Edwin to cut her hair this very night.

With bread and ale consumed, she left Edwin to wait for the cook to assemble their dinner, and to chat to the serving maids, for he had become a great favorite in the kitchen. She was trembling with fear and excitement as she gathered soapwort, mallow leaves and woundwort from the kitchen garden, before walking to the stables.

There was no sign of Hugh anywhere, nor anyone else other than a youth who was leading a small herd of nanny goats and their young through the yard toward the gate. As Janna watched, the boy raised his arm and aimed a pebble at one of the kids. It struck the goat on the rump and it jumped, bleating pitifully as it did so.

"Stop that!" Janna shouted. The boy hardly glanced at her before picking up another, larger stone. This time he aimed for the goat's head. The animal dropped, stunned, and lay in the dirt, kicking feebly. Without thought, Janna raced toward the boy. Before he could run away, she had caught him, and she boxed his ears hard, packing all her new-found strength into the punch.

"Ow!" he shouted, wriggling and squirming in Janna's grasp. "Let me go!"

"How dare you!" she panted. "How dare you harm that baby goat!"

"It's for our dinner." The boy had turned sullen now. "First finders of a dead animal gets to keep it, so Master Serlo says."

"But I'll wager Master Serlo doesn't say you may first go out and kill it!" Janna gave the lad a hard shake.

"There's no-one here to see me, 'cept you. Why should you care? Anyway, I'm not the only one what does it. There's plenty others too."

Janna doubted it, but she wasn't prepared to debate the point with the lad.

"Then I'll tell Master Serlo what you've done. If everyone else is doing it, he won't mind, will he?"

She felt the goat boy cower against her. He began to tremble with fright. Janna understood why when Hugh's cool voice interrupted them.

"What's happening here, boy? Why are you throwing stones at my goats?"

Janna let the boy go. She stayed silent, leaving him to talk his way out of the situation as best he could. All bravado gone, he began to cry.

"Take the goats out and look after them properly, Eadwig," Hugh said sternly. "Be sure I shall count them when you bring them in tonight. And when you get home, tell your father he's to come to the manor house and bring you with him."

The lad fled, leaving Janna alone with Hugh. She knelt to pick up the herbs she'd dropped when she'd grabbed hold of the goat's tormentor, and smiled in relief as she watched the kid rise to its feet and stagger off to find its mother.

"I saw everything that happened," Hugh said into the ensuing silence. "I was waiting just inside the stable. I heard you shouting at Eadwig. I saw it all, Johanna."

Janna froze.

"I'm right, aren't I?" Hugh continued softly. "Your appearance might have changed, but your voice—and your manner—not at all!"

Janna stayed on her knees, clutching the herbs. She did not dare move or say anything. Hugh put his hand underneath her elbow, and yanked her upright. "I think you owe me an explanation," he said coldly, and began to propel her toward the stable. "You can minister to Arrow while you tell me why you burnt your home to the ground and left us all to think that you were dead."

"I did not set fire to my home, sire!" Janna was outraged that he could think such a thing.

He cocked his head to one side, studying her. "The abbess is wroth, for the cottage was her property and now it is destroyed. And Godric, the villein, told us that you died in the fire and that he has buried you in the forest. Why so many lies, Johanna, and to what purpose?" His voice lost some of its hard edge as he continued more softly, "Was the fire an accident? You know, because I told you, that Dame Alice agreed to pay heriot to the abbess and mortuary to the priest after the death of your mother, so there is no money owing. And if the fire was an accident, I doubt the abbess would hold you to blame, while the villagers would surely have helped you to rebuild your cottage and given you shelter until it was done. There was no need to flee, or to tell lies."

How little you know of the villagers, Janna thought, as bitter memories filled her mind. She did not know what to say to Hugh, and so she stayed silent.

"In truth, I am disappointed," he said, as he snicked open the latch and led her into the stable. "I thought you were honorable, and that you had more courage. I didn't take you for a coward, Johanna."

Janna could stay silent no longer. "I am not a coward, sire!"

"And yet you have run from the village, and even disguised yourself as a boy to escape detection." Hugh stalked past a line of horses and stopped at Arrow's stall. The destrier blew a gentle greeting as Janna caught up with him. She wondered if the animal remembered her. She stood awkwardly, uncertain how to make it lift its hoof so that she could inspect it. Hugh solved the problem by doing it for her. Janna clicked her tongue, distressed by the ugly wound that already was beginning to fester from the dung and dirt that had worked its way into the cut.

"I need boiling water and something to wrap the hoof," she said. "I'll have to cleanse it first. Then I'll bind these healing herbs against the wound. You must not ride him, sire, or even take him out from the stall." She glanced down at the dirty straw on which the horse stood. "It would be best if the horse stood on clean rushes for the while."

Hugh grunted. But he released the horse's hoof, and shouted for a stable lad to fetch what Janna needed. While they waited, he fixed his dark gaze on her once more. "Who is Edwin? What is he to you?"

"He's..." Janna was going to claim him as her brother but knew that Hugh would not believe her. She decided to stick as close to the truth as she could. "I came across him in the forest, sire, in Gravelinges. I was alone, and frightened, and I asked if I might journey with him. It is true that he comes from Wales and that he has to seek his fortune after his eldest brother inherited both cot and land when his mother died." Janna kept her fingers crossed behind her back against yet another lie. She hoped Hugh would not doubt her word as she added, "Please believe me, sire. I did not set fire to my cottage. That was the work of the villagers, and that is why Godric seeks to protect me now by saying that I died in the fire, and that he buried me."

"The villagers burned your home?" Hugh sounded horrified. "Why would they do such a dreadful thing?"

"Because..." But even Janna's quick wits could not come up with a convincing enough story other than telling Hugh the truth. But that she could not do for she was sure he would not believe her.

"I am sorry you did not bring your troubles to me, or to my aunt," Hugh said, when it became clear that Janna would say no more. "We would have helped you. Dame Alice had great respect for your mother's skill, and yours too."

"I am sorry too, sire," Janna said softly. "I was alone and frightened. With no home and no family to call on, it seemed best to flee and so I did."

"You are safe now." Hugh gave her a troubled glance. "There is no need to disguise yourself any longer, Johanna. You may stay here and help Mistress Tova in the kitchen. I know she would be glad of an extra hand. And heaven knows we often have need of a healer for burns, and broken bones, and especially the pox if it comes again. You could be very useful to me, if you wish to stay."

"I thank you for your offer, sire. Of course I am happy to help anyone in need of a healer, but I would rather stay as I am—or as others think I am," Janna said stiffly. She wanted to tell Hugh he was wrong; that she was no longer safe now that he knew her true identity. She would have to talk to Edwin, persuade him that they must leave and swiftly.

"You have nothing to fear from showing yourself as you truly are." Hugh looked more puzzled than ever. "In truth, your disguise does not become you."

Janna felt a painful blush stain her face as she recalled how he'd once looked at her with admiration in his eyes. No more, nor ever again. The thought stung. "I beg you, sire." She forced herself to look into his eyes so he could see that she was in earnest. "Do not allow anyone to punish the villein, Godric, for his lies. He told them for my protection, just as I would ask you now, sire, to keep the truth about me to yourself. I–I cannot explain to you why my life is in jeopardy, but I beg you to believe it, and keep my secret if…if you care about my safety."

Hugh stayed silent, still looking troubled.

"Please, sire!" In her desperation to secure his silence, Janna realized she'd grabbed hold of Hugh's arm. Quickly, she released it. "Please, sire," she said more quietly. "I matter to no-one other than those who wish me harm. Please protect me with your silence."

"Very well." The promise was given grudgingly. Clearly Hugh was unhappy about the course Janna had urged on him. "I know that the priest stirred up trouble against your mother, and that he might have influenced some of the villagers because of his refusal to bury her in consecrated ground," he conceded. "I spoke to Dame Alice about the priest but she will not take action against him." He stopped, and gnawed on his bottom lip. He seemed to be wondering how far he could take Janna into his confidence. "You must understand that this is a difficult situation for her," he said at last. "My aunt married unwisely. Robert was her father's steward, and after her father died he wooed Alice. Being her father's only heir, and with all that property at her disposal, Alice was supposed to petition the king for permission to marry, but she was desperate to have Robert and no other. With a baby on the way, it became urgent to find someone who was prepared to wed them. This priest obliged and, when the living at the new church at Berford became available, he asked my aunt to put in a word to the abbess—"

He broke off as the stable lad came clattering in, bearing a bucket of hot water and the linen Janna had requested. But Hugh had said enough for Janna to understand the situation. Anger flared anew as she reflected how worthless Robert had proved to be. First, and to secure his future, he had seduced Dame Alice. Next, and for his own pleasure, he had seduced Cecily, the dame's tiring woman. Janna wondered how many others Robert had seduced—and abandoned—during his marriage.

"You should know that I petitioned the Abbess of Wiltune for a requiem mass to be said for your mother's soul, and for your own," Hugh said, once they were alone again. "I must confess she was reluctant at first. It seems she knows something of your mother's past, but I managed to convince her that both of you were worthy, and so it was done." Hugh surveyed Janna, his face grave as he added: "Obviously a mass for the dead was not necessary on your account. I can only hope that you walk in the grace of God's blessing, and that you will continue to do so."

"Oh yes, sire, and thank you. With all my heart I thank you for your kindness." So he had kept his promise to her! Janna felt almost giddy with relief.

"Hmph." Hugh looked as if he needed convincing that he'd done the right thing. "And what plans do you have for the future?"

To go in search of my father, Janna thought. But she wasn't prepared to take Hugh so fully into her confidence. "To go to Winchestre, sire, to seek employment there." It was part of the truth.

"With Edwin?"

"With Edwin."

"And still dressed like a youth?"

Janna nodded confirmation.

"Why don't the two of you stay on here? I've already told you of your worth to me, and Edwin is a good worker."

"Thank you, sire. You are very kind." Janna had no intention of accepting his invitation, but she wasn't about to tell Hugh that she was proposing to run away immediately, now her secret was uncovered. Instead, she set to work, crushing the waxy green leaves of soapwort into hot water and bathing the wound. The stable lad had returned with another bucket of clean, hot water, and this time he stayed to help Hugh keep tight hold of the destrier so that it would not move, or kick out at Janna while she worked. She was grateful for the lad's presence, for it made further conversation difficult. Hugh had already given her much to think about, but she needed time alone to mull over what he had told her. For the moment, she concentrated on her task, feeling the great horse flinch as she set about binding its hoof, wrapping the linen tight to keep the healing herbs in place, and to prevent any dirt from entering the wound.

"Clean out this stall," Hugh ordered, once Janna was finished and the horse was standing firmly on its feet once more. "Then go and cut some clean rushes to lay on the ground." As Janna made to do what she was bid, Hugh grasped her arm. "Not you," he said, angling his head toward the lad. "Him."

"I am capable of doing the work just as well, my lord, and it will go quicker with two of us."Janna felt an uneasy thrill in defying Hugh.

A smile hovered at the edge of his mouth. "I can see you haven't changed anything other than your clothes. You are still as independent as you were when you lived with your mother. Very well, then. Do as you wish."

"Thank you, sire." Janna kept a smirk of triumph off her face with difficulty, as she seized a rake and began to gather the dung and dirty straw into a pile. When she looked up, Hugh's silhouette blocked the light from the door; the next moment he had disappeared from view.

Rebuffing Janna's attempts at conversation, the stable lad worked in sullen silence as they cleared Arrow's stall. She wondered how much of her conversation with Hugh he had overheard. Enough to let him know that Hugh regarded her so highly he'd arranged a mass to be said for her soul? Had Hugh said her name in the boy's hearing? Janna cast her mind back over their conversation, hoping her secret was still safe.

The lad went over to a row of implements then, and selected two scythes. He gave one to Janna. "To cut the rushes," he said shortly, and led the way to the river.

Looking up at the fields, Janna noticed the blackened remains of the burnt haystack. With a feeling of dread, she realized what she needed to do. "Let's cut the rushes further upstream," she said, pointing in the direction of the haystack. The stable boy frowned at her, seeming resentful that she was taking charge. "It means we can carry the load downhill instead of up," Janna pointed out.

He gave a grudging nod and changed direction. Janna followed him, veering off to the haystack as they walked past. She bent to examine the ashy remains. The scene and the smell reminded her of the time she'd searched the burnt ruins of her own home, and how her search had uncovered her mother's secret cache with its clues to her father's identity, the clues she could not read and didn't know how to interpret.

Hugh's words came back to her. He'd said that the abbess knew something of her mother's past. She wondered now if, instead of fleeing in a blind panic, she should first have sought an audience with the abbess. Was it still possible? It would certainly be worth the risk of being seen by the villagers if the abbess could tell her where to begin her search for the truth about her mother—and her father.

Janna pushed the thought aside for consideration later, and began her search. She knew exactly what she was looking for and she examined everything very carefully, first the ruined remnants of the haystack, then widening her search to encompass other haystacks nearby. It didn't take her long to spy it, the leaves a silvery green, the flowers a bright splotch of yellow tucked into the pale straw of a nearby haystack. Janna snatched out the posy of rue, and ground it to shreds under her boot. Too late, she wondered if she should have kept it to show Hugh or even brought him out with her to search the haystacks. Now that he knew the truth about her, would he have believed her suspicions, or had she already stretched his trust too far?

She looked to the stream, where the stable lad was already hard at work cutting rushes for Arrow's stall. She hurried to join him. There was no sign of Edwin, or her dinner either. With haymaking over, the sheep had been washed and shearing had begun. The hurdles had been taken down after haymaking, so the animals were free to graze in the water meadows, but she couldn't see them or their keeper. She wondered where shearing would be taking place and where she needed to search for Edwin if she wanted her dinner.

She was sweating, hot and filthy by the time she and the stable lad had finished cleaning out Arrow's stall and spreading armfuls of clean rushes over the bare earth floor.

It seemed to her that the horse stood easier now. She knew Hugh's pride in his sleek black destrier and, having an affinity for all living creatures and this one in particular, she hoped that the cure was already working, and that the wound would heal without leaving any lasting harm.

With her task over, Janna hurried to the well, keen to slake her thirst. She sank the bucket down, and wound it up again. After splashing cool water over her hands to cleanse them, she cupped them and drank her fill. She was glad to get away from the sullen stable lad, glad to have a few quiet moments alone to ponder her conversation with Hugh. She was mortified that he had recognized her and had found out all her lies, but she also felt an easing of mind that she no longer had to pretend, that he knew the truth—or most of it. She hated lies, hated deceit, and her anger flared anew at the memory of those who had made this subterfuge necessary.

Her thoughts turned then to the abbess, who knew something about her mother. Hugh had indicated that the abbess thought badly of Eadgyth. She would also think badly of Janna once she discovered that Janna was still alive, for she would believe that Janna had fled to escape the consequences of the destruction of her cot. Was it worth braving the abbess's wrath in the hope she would relent enough to tell Janna what she knew?

With her thirst quenched, Janna sat for a few moments beside the well to rest and ponder the question. She leaned back against the rough stone wall with a weary sigh.

"Hello! My name's Hamo. What's yours?"

A child's voice jerked her from her reverie. She sat upright with a gasp, feeling giddy and disorientated. This had happened once before. Was she dreaming now, or was it happening all over again? She blinked as a little boy's bright face came into focus. She knew him. Just so had he introduced himself to her at the manor house at Babestoche. She looked about her. She was still on Hugh's manor farm. She felt some relief that her mind wasn't playing tricks after all. But what was Hamo doing here?

He held tight to a piece of rope attached to a mangy dog. All skin and bones, with matted fur, it now limped over to sniff around Janna's toes. She scrambled away, her alarm increasing as she took in Hamo's companions with a quick glance. They were just coming through the gate; there was no sign of Hamo's elderly and disapproving nurse. In her place, and still some distance away, came Cecily and...Godric?

Janna blinked and peered more closely. Yes, there was no mistake. It seemed that Hamo had found himself a new nurse, as well as a guide to bring him through the forest. With an effort, she tore her gaze away from Cecily's sturdy escort to meet the boy's questioning gaze.

"I know you," he announced firmly. "You're—"

"My name is John," Janna said gruffly, too alarmed by his unexpected arrival to worry about rudely interrupting the young lord of the manor. Her alarm increased as she noted Cecily's steps quicken to protect her charge. Although Cecily knew Janna hadn't died in the fire, she'd been sworn to secrecy. Would she keep the secret even now? And Godric, how could she face him? He had protected her so loyally, but he didn't know the truth, for she'd stayed hidden when he came looking for her. Her decision had seemed sensible at the time but now she could feel only shame over her behavior toward him.

"My name is John," she said again more firmly, and jumped to her feet, desperate to escape before anyone could challenge her identity. She'd forgotten about the dog. Startled by her sudden movement, it sank its teeth into her boot and hung on, growling.

"Get your dog off me, Hamo," she ordered.

"Bones!" Hamo dropped the rope. He tried to force the dog's teeth apart, but it growled and sank them deeper.

"Be careful! Mind he doesn't bite you," Janna said, automatically protective.

"Godric will help. He brought us through the forest and he found Bones. He'll know what to do." And before Janna had a chance to protest, Hamo turned and shouted the villein's name. There was nothing else for her to do then but wait for the shame of discovery.

"Bones! Let go!" Godric arrived in a burst of speed. He didn't look at Janna. All his attention was on the dog as he bent and firmly prized open its jaw. Janna felt the pressure ease, and wondered if she still had time to make a run for it. But Hamo had grabbed hold of her hand.

"This is John," he said gravely, holding on tight. She had no choice but to stand still and face Godric.

"Thank you for getting the dog off me," she said faintly.

His eyes widened. He said nothing, but he went pale. Janna knew she would never forget the look on his face as he studied her intently. Confusion gave way to elation, which immediately darkened into anger and rejection. He scowled at her, and turned away. Cecily had reached them, and she took in the situation in one quick glance.

"Janna! What are you doing here?"

Godric still said nothing. Janna tried to find the words to explain why she'd acted as she had, and to tell him what was in her heart. She ached for his understanding, but she could think of nothing to say that would make the situation any easier. Stricken mute, she looked down at the ground.

"Janna?" Hamo queried.

"There you are, John! I've brought your dinner." Edwin had come dashing into the yard, and he hailed Janna as soon as he spied her. As he noticed the tableau beside the well, his footsteps slowed.

With a muttered exclamation, Godric pushed past them, moving at speed toward the gate.

"Godric! Wait!" Janna said urgently. "I can explain—"

He ignored her and increased his pace. The dog took off after him, moving as fast as its maimed paws would allow.

"Bones! Come back!" Hamo tried to grab hold of the rope trailing behind his pet, but Cecily grasped him and hauled him back.

"You must stay with me, Hamo," she said firmly, and looked at Edwin. "Who is he?" she asked Janna.

A short silence followed Cecily's question, before Edwin cheerfully gave her his name. "I am John's elder brother, mistress," he added by way of explanation, and sketched a bow. Still no-one said anything, Janna because she was incapable of speech and Cecily because she was utterly confused. Edwin's worried glance moved between them both, and then he looked after Godric's disappearing figure. His frown deepened.

Cecily's glance followed his. "Over here, sire!" She hailed a couple of strangers who were just coming through the gate. Seemingly Godric had guided the men through the forest along with Hamo and Cecily, for one of them put a hand on Godric's arm to restrain him. The other fumbled a coin from his purse but by the time he held it out, Godric had pushed past the pair and was gone.

In answer to Cecily's call they surrendered their mounts, including several heavily laden sumpter horses, to the waiting groom and paused to give instructions. As the groom led the horses away, Janna noticed that one of them had cast a shoe and was walking awkwardly.

"Shearing's started. I have to get back," Edwin said hurriedly. "You'd better come too, John, or you'll feel the sharp edge of Serlo's tongue." He thrust the sack of food at Janna and disappeared around the side of a barn.

"John? Doesn't he know who you really are?" Cecily asked.

Janna sighed. "Yes, of course he does. And so does the lord Hugh." At the mention of Hugh's name, Cecily gave Janna a questioning glance, but she didn't say anything. "I met Edwin while I was lost in Gravelinges," Janna continued. "He..." She was about to tell Cecily the truth of what had happened, but stopped herself in time. This was Edwin's secret, not hers, and his safety depended on her keeping it. "He's from Wales and we're going to seek work in Winchestre," she said instead, wishing there was no need to lie to Cecily, or anyone else. She was sick and tired of telling lies, of having to hide the truth. "We decided to travel together but, by greatest misfortune, we found work and shelter on this farm not knowing that it belongs to the lord Hugh."

"To Dame Alice," Cecily said.

"But he manages the demesne for his aunt."

"Yes, that is why we are here." Cecily nodded thoughtfully. "After the lord left Babestoche, Hamo fretted so much that Dame Alice decided to let him come here for a short visit."

"How is my lady? Is she quite recovered from..." Janna wasn't sure how to phrase the question, but Cecily answered readily enough.

"In truth, my lady still grieves over the death of her infant son. She is low in spirits and in health. She told me it would relieve her mind greatly to think that Hamo is here and happy with his cousin."

Janna surveyed the tiring woman, thinking it also a shrewd move on Dame Alice's part to remove Cecily from her husband's influence. Too much harm had already resulted from Robert's untoward interest in Cecily. Janna wondered how much Dame Alice suspected about their past liaison.

Cecily caught her hand. "I know I said I would stay and watch out for my lady," she whispered, "but I had no choice when she asked me to accompany Hamo. His own nurse is too old to make the journey and besides, Dame Alice believes

Hamo needs someone closer to his own age to take care of him and amuse him now."

"I shouldn't worry about my lady's safety," Janna consoled her. "That is, unless Robert has turned his affection to another young woman in your household?"

"No." Cecily gave Janna a rueful smile. "I think he has learned his lesson—as have I."

"Then Dame Alice is in no danger, for Lord Robert will be trying to convince her that he has always had her best interests in his heart."

"Pray God that you are right." Cecily turned from Janna, and swept a hasty curtsy. "My lords," she said, greeting the two strangers who were now almost upon them. "I trust you are not too weary after your journey? If you will come with me, I will take you to meet the lord Hugh, Dame Alice's nephew." She turned away from Janna.

"I'll see about finding the dog, mistress. And the young lord," Janna said quickly.

"Hamo?" Cecily's hand came to her mouth. "I didn't see him go! Where is he?"

"I'll look for him, mistress." Leaving Cecily to take care of Hugh's visitors, Janna set off to search the manor grounds, bringing with her the sack of food that Edwin had thrust at her. She was hungry and so, she was willing to wager, were the dog and its master. If shouting didn't bring them into view, a sack of food well might.

Chapter 8

"Hamo! Hamo, where are you?" Janna had searched the kitchen garden and orchard, as well as the undercroft and all the barns, workshops and other buildings that made up the manor's demesne. She'd even gone upstairs to peek unobtrusively into the hall, to make sure that he was not among the throng gathered around Hugh. Gytha was there, she noted with a pang of envy, as she watched the beauty circulating among the guests, pouring wine into goblets and offering platters of food.

Hamo was nowhere to be seen, and Janna was growing anxious. The manor was close to the stream and river. Could Hamo swim? She hurried downstairs and peered first into the well. "Hamo?" she shouted, and listened to her voice echoing. There was no reply. Wasting no more time, she rushed out through the gates to check the manor's fishpool, but there was no sign of a child, drowning or otherwise. Janna's anxiety increased as she looked down over the stubbled water meadows to the swiftly flowing river beyond. Although it was quite shallow, the fast current could turn into whirlpools in the deep holes that pockmarked the riverbed. Even more dangerous was the mill race and water mill further downriver.

The great wheel churned in a thunder of foam with the force of the water channeled into it. She looked upstream to the water-logged marsh, which was equally dangerous to a child who couldn't swim. Beyond the river and straight ahead was the solid green wall of the forest of Gravelinges. Might Hamo have crossed the river in safety at the ford, and be on his way home to his mother?

No, she thought, remembering Cecily's words. He'd been lonely at home, pining for his cousin Hugh. So why, then, had he run away?

She remembered the lame and mangy dog. Hamo seemed to have adopted it as a pet, and yet it had run after Godric when he left the manor. Had Hamo slipped away to find it? And if so, where might he have gone? She turned in a circle, trying to spot any signs of the boy and his dog. Behind the manor spread the fields, basking gold and green in the hot afternoon sun. The sounds of frightened baaing and bleating gave direction to the shearers, but there was no sign of Godric, or the dog. Would Godric have gone straight home?

Yes, she thought sadly. He'd made no secret of his disquiet on seeing her. He would not want to encounter her again. Had Hamo followed him into the forest, hoping to find his dog? She shielded her eyes and peered across the water meadows once more, in case she could see anyone walking toward the forest. The thought of Hamo lost and alone made her shudder, but a new horror turned her cold in spite of the heat. She had to force herself to consider the possibility that this might be the next disaster to befall Hugh's manor. If so, whoever was behind what was happening must have had advance warning that the party was arriving today, or else had acted on impulse and with lightning speed to take advantage of Hamo's unexpected appearance. And that denoted a cunning and guile far above Urk's capability. Who, then, was behind this latest calamity?

Fighting anxiety, Janna cast about for any sign of movement. A couple of swans, followed by a line of fluffy gray-brown cygnets, paddled majestically upriver, laboring against the current that dragged them toward the mill. There was no indication of any other living thing either in the water or beside it, but Janna couldn't see very much of the river's path, shrouded as it was by trees. She forced herself to stand quietly, to think things through, for there was no point in alarming herself needlessly, or rushing about looking in all the wrong places. Better by far to think of the most logical explanation for Hamo's absence: that he'd gone in pursuit of the stray dog, and Godric.

It was a hot day. Godric and his party would have had a long walk through the forest, might even have had to stop there to pass the night. Neither Godric nor Hamo had taken water from the well to drink, or any food, so they would be thirsty and probably hungry too. Where might Godric or Hamo have gone for refreshment?

The river, Janna decided. Upstream or downstream? She shrugged. She had no idea, but there was no time to waste, not if she wanted to catch up with the pair.

"Hamo?" she shouted, as she hurried down toward the ford. "Godric!"

If Godric had seen Hamo following him, he would have brought the boy back to the manor. Her pace increased. If Hamo hadn't found Godric, he could be in the most deadly danger. "Hamo!" she shouted. "Where are you?"

A faint cry answered her, and she felt a momentary relief until she realized it was the deeper tone of Godric's voice. She couldn't see him, but his voice had come from the dense thicket of brambles and trees that lined the river's path upstream.

"Godric!" She broke into a run, the quicker to reach him. "Hamo's missing. He's lost," she bellowed. "Please help me look for him!" She pushed her way through trees and bushes, only to find her way barred by the mangy dog, which snarled and bared its teeth. "Get out of my way!" Janna was too worried to be afraid. She aimed a kick in the dog's direction, and it backed off, barking furiously. "Godric!"

"When did you last see Hamo? And where?" He came running, and she realized he'd been up to some illegal fishing, as she spotted a flash of silver on the river bank behind him.

"Hamo left the courtyard while we weren't watching. I thought he might be looking for you and the dog."

"Bones." Godric gave the dog a disgusted glance. "Look at it! I tried to leave it behind, but the stupid thing kept following me."

Even though the dog had given her grief, Janna thought Godric was being a little harsh. That the dog was in pain was evident. A closer inspection revealed that to conform with the harsh forest laws, three claws had been cut off to the knuckle on each forepaw so that the cur could not chase after the king's game. But not enough care had been taken. Its paws were bloody and oozing yellow matter. The dog was also half-starved, reasons enough for its antisocial behavior. But Janna had no time for Bones now. Her anxiety overrode even the awkwardness she felt being face to face with Godric as she quickly explained her fears for Hamo's safety.

"You go on upriver and I'll go down toward the mill," he said at once. "Keep calling. If either one of us finds him, we must go in search of the other." He glanced up at the sun. "If neither of us finds him by the time the sun touches the tree line over there, we should retrace our steps and meet back here so that we can go back to the manor before it gets too dark to see."

Janna nodded in agreement, greatly relieved that he was prepared to help her search and that there were no recriminations—at least, not yet. Godric started off, calling the boy's name, following the river downstream. The dog limped behind him. Janna hastened off toward the marsh, also calling Hamo's name. Along the way, and just to be on the safe side, she quickly kicked Godric's illicit catch back into the river.

She hadn't gone far when she heard a shout.

"He's here!"

She turned and raced downstream in the direction Godric had taken. After some moments, she saw him. Her body went cold with shock as she saw that he carried the limp and dripping body of Hamo.

Pray he isn't dead, she thought, as she rushed up to Godric and fell into step beside him. He was striding in the direction of the manor, bearing his burden at the greatest speed he could muster. The boy was blue around the lips, and he hung lifeless in Godric's arms. Janna fought down her rising panic. She couldn't bear the thought that after all, they had come too late. There was a bloody gash across Hamo's forehead, but Janna noticed one of his eyelids twitch and felt a surge of relief.

She cast her mind back to a time when she and her mother had passed two villeins arguing over the possession of a pig. As the argument escalated over whose pig it was to sell, punches were thrown and one of the villeins pushed the other into the river. Hearing his cry, Eadgyth had turned and run back to aid the culprit rescue his victim, but the man was lifeless by the time they managed to haul him out of the water. Janna remembered what her mother had done next.

"Put him down!" she told Godric.

"We have to get him back to the manor house." Godric's pace didn't check.

"There's no time for that. Put him down! On his stomach." Janna grabbed hold of Godric's arm and dragged on him to make him do as she asked. "We have to push the water out of his chest."

Reluctantly, Godric laid Hamo down on a bed of soft grass. Janna turned his head to one side, then pressed down on the boy's back with all her strength. A gush of water erupted from Hamo's mouth. She lifted his arms to give him a chance to breathe in, then pressed down once more. She kept pushing and lifting until, to her great relief, the boy began to cough and splutter. He took in a great whoop of air, and began to breathe on his own. He was incapable of speech, so Janna turned to Godric.

"Where did you find him? What happened to him?"

"He was face down in the river, drowning."

"Yes, yes," she said impatiently. "I mean, was anyone else there with him, anyone at all?"

"No." Godric looked puzzled. "Only me. If you hadn't sounded the alarm, if we hadn't gone after him, he would have died. He's lucky that we found him in time, and that you knew what to do."

"How did it happen? Can you tell?"

Godric shrugged. "He was probably thirsty, looking for a drink. He must have slipped and fallen into the river."

"But what about that wound on his forehead? Could he have been hit over the head and then pushed?"

"Why should anyone want to do that?" Godric squatted beside Janna, who had her arm around Hamo now and was helping him to sit up. "What's going on? Why are you asking me these questions?"

"I can't tell you." Janna wasn't done yet. She had one final question, but she dreaded hearing the answer. "Did you notice any rue nearby? I mean a posy picked, not rue growing wild?"

"No. But I wasn't looking for anything like that. I didn't have time." Godric lifted a questioning eyebrow. "Why should a posy of rue be lying about?"

"It's for regret. Repentance."

"I wish you'd explain yourself, Janna." Godric lifted the boy into his arms once more. "But I know that you don't care to explain anything to me, anything at all." He strode off in the direction of the manor house, leaving Janna to scurry after him.

A great cry went up as they came inside the gate. It was clear Cecily had confessed to losing Hamo, for everyone came running from all directions to welcome them back. Hugh was at the forefront of the crowd. As Godric tried to pass Hamo over into his cousin's arms, Hamo wriggled free. "I can walk by myself," he announced with great dignity, and looked about for the mangy dog that had followed them in.

"What happened, Hamo?" Hugh asked the question that Janna most feared.

"Nothing." The boy looked up, all injured innocence now.

"Tell me!" Hugh folded his arms and waited, hiding his concern with an appearance of exasperation.

"I-I went looking for Bones." Hamo reached out to pat the dog, but it bared its teeth and whined softly. Hamo backed off.

"I'm afraid the dog followed me when I left the manor, sire," Godric admitted.

Hamo shot him a grateful glance. "I saw Godric walking to the river. He didn't know I was following him," he added, determined that Godric shouldn't get any blame for what had happened. "When I got there I couldn't see him, or Bones, but I guessed he would go downriver so that's where I went. But Godric must have gone the other way."

Janna waited somewhat anxiously for Hugh to ask why Godric had gone up the river at all instead of crossing the ford and heading for home. Fortunately, Hugh was more interested in Hamo than in Godric. "What happened to you? Why are you so wet?"

Hamo shrugged. "I followed the path of the river a little way. I was thirsty, and I wondered if Bones was thirsty too, if he'd gone for a drink and maybe fallen in. I couldn't see through all the reeds so I came closer to the edge to have a look and have a drink, but then I slipped and fell." He touched the gash across his forehead, and winced when he saw the blood on his fingers. "I suppose I must have hit my head."

It was possible Hamo's admission gave his dignity even more of a battering than his head and clothes had taken in the river, Janna thought. She let out a gusty breath as his words sank in. An accident, no more than that.

"Godric saved me." Hamo looked at Janna. "And so did—"

"John," Janna said firmly, before Hamo could say her name in front of everyone.

"And you have my gratitude and thanks." Hugh gave Janna a searching glance before taking Hamo by the hand. "A hot bath for you, young man. Mistress Cecily!" He beckoned her forward, and turned to Godric. "I'd like a word with you too," he said, and hurried off. Godric exchanged an anxious glance with Cecily as they followed Hugh.

"I'll make up an ointment to put on the young lord's cuts and bruises," Janna called after them. Cecily lifted her hand to show that she'd heard, and kept on after Hugh. Ignored and forgotten, the dog trailed them up the stairs and into the hall. The crowd began to disperse, the two visitors among them. Janna watched them leave. She wondered who they were and why they were visiting the manor. One was finely dressed, his tunic richly embroidered and his boots made of good leather, although scratched and stained with mud and muck. The journey through the forest had left its mark. His companion was more plainly dressed, and walked a pace or two behind his master. She looked about for Edwin to ask him who the lordling was. He was always quick to hear tattle from the kitchen staff. There was no sign of him, but Gytha was still lingering. As she caught Janna's glance, she came over to her.

"That boy will be in trouble for running away," she observed, and wrinkled her nose. "I hope he doesn't expect us to find shelter for that smelly, flea-bitten bag of bones he's found."

Janna hid a smile. She was quite sure that Hamo had every intention of keeping his pet. She was also sure that the boy would prove more than a match for Gytha when it came to getting his own way. "We have visitors, I see," she said.

"Master Siward and his manservant. They go to the great fair to buy and to sell for their lord, but one of their horses is lame so they must break their journey here for a spell."

"Have they traveled far?"

"They come from somewhere in the west." Gytha yawned, then brightened as a more interesting subject came into her mind. "Master Siward paid me a great deal of attention when I served the wine and cakes. I do believe my lord Hugh was quite put out by his interest." She gave a self-satisfied giggle.

Janna turned away, telling herself that jealousy was useless. If Hugh wanted a dalliance with Gytha he certainly didn't need her permission.

She remembered her promise to Cecily, and went to the kitchen garden. Pangs of hunger reminded her that she'd dropped the sack containing her dinner while she'd tried to revive Hamo. Should she go after it? She sighted the angle of the sun slanting across the downs. No, it would take too long. She would just have to go hungry. The thought contributed to Janna's misery as she bent to pluck the herbs she needed for the healing ointment. She was on her way to the kitchen when Godric found her.

"I was going to leave without seeing you again," he said curtly, "but I thought you should know, Janna, that your running away has brought ill to my family, to the manor and to the village. I told a lie to Dame Alice and my liege lord, Robert of Babestoche. I told them that you were dead."

Janna cast a quick glance around, making sure that no-one could hear their conversation. "I know, Godric, and I am grateful to you, more grateful than I can say."

"But I have been sore punished for the lie." Godric spoke over her thanks. "The priest has claimed mortuary from me, payment I cannot afford, and—"

"But why? Why claim mortuary from you?"

"Because I said that I had buried you in the forest, and because he claims that we were betrothed. He has taken my best goat in payment, even though the abbess has asked nothing from me. Nor has Dame Alice or anyone else. I told the priest he was mistaken about us, but he will not believe me." There was such a depth of bitterness in Godric's voice that Janna couldn't bear it.

"I'm so sorry." She put her hand on Godric's arm, but he shook it off and pulled away from her.

"That's not the worst of it," he said. "My mother took ill and died. There was no one to physick her as your mother did the last time she had an attack and couldn't breathe properly. By running away, you've left the village without a healer, Janna."

"I—but they drove me out!" Janna spluttered. Surely Godric knew that the villagers wanted her dead, and that she'd had no choice but to flee?

"Everyone mourns your death." He spoke sincerely.

"Everyone?" Janna's voice raised in anger. "The villagers set fire to my cottage, Godric, while I was still inside. They wanted to destroy me as well as my home. That's why I ran away. And that's why I didn't dare show myself even to you!"

He glanced sharply at her. "You should have trusted me."

Janna knew that he was right, but still she tried to justify her actions. "I had to go! It wasn't safe for me to stay. I thought if I—That is, I didn't want—"

"To see me. I know. You've made that clear several times already." Godric's mouth clamped down in a tight, hard line. Without bidding her farewell, he turned and strode toward the gate of the manor.

"I'm sorry about your mother, Godric. I'm so sorry," Janna called after him. But he walked on, not acknowledging that he'd heard her words, or that he'd forgiven her.

*

There was still no sign of Edwin when at last, weary and hungry, Janna went to her bed. She told herself that Edwin was free to come and go about the manor as he pleased, but concern that he might know more about the so-called accidents than he'd admitted kept her troubled and wakeful. She hoped he would return soon, for the events of the day had hardened her determination to flee the manor as soon as possible. So much had happened to add to her unease. She wished she could explain her behavior to Hugh as well as to Godric; she wished they could better understand why she'd acted as she had. "It's not fair!" she whispered rebelliously as she turned and turned again, trying to get comfortable on the scratchy pallet. Restless, and impatient for action, she lay and listened to the night noises, the snarks and snorts and mumbles of the sleepers. She had planned to leave the manor this very night, but in the absence of Edwin she was undecided. Should she go without him?

Yes, she thought, and half rose from her bed. She subsided again as more careful thought advised against it. While she wanted most desperately to run away from Hugh, caution told her that she would do better to wait until Edwin could go with her. Alone, she was vulnerable, even if she was dressed as a boy. Edwin's presence, and their fabricated family history, would protect them both.

Janna passed an uneasy night. The faint light of early dawn found her wakeful and still undecided. She quickly rose, scrubbed at her face with her hands and smoothed back her hair, feeling again its silky growth. She slipped quietly from her bed and pulled her knife from its sheath. She tested its edge against a handful of hair, and frowned. She remembered then the great whetstone outside the blacksmith's shop, left in position for the villeins to sharpen their scythes while haymaking. It was still early; there was time.

She was bent over the whetstone when Bertha walked past, carrying a small sack. Janna greeted her cheerfully. Bertha stopped short, looking startled.

"What are you doing out here so early, John?" she asked, not returning Janna's greeting.

"Sharpening my knife." Janna wondered if she could take advantage of Bertha's good nature. "Are you any good at cutting hair, mistress? Will you cut mine?"

Bertha's attention came full onto Janna then. She hesitated. "Does it have to be done now?"

Janna nodded. "Yes, if you please, mistress." She didn't want to delay, and the alternative was to cut her hair herself. She knew she'd make an awful job of it.

Bertha sighed. She dropped the sack she was carrying and held out her hand for Janna's knife, while Janna sat on the stone block within easy reach of Bertha's hands.

"How does your family, mistress?" she asked, to make conversation while Bertha set about hacking at her hair. She tried not to wince as snippets fell about her feet, curled like small golden snails.

"What?"

"Your family. Are they well?" Janna wondered what preoccupied Bertha, and why she was abroad so early. The sun had not yet arisen. Mist shrouded the cots and turned trees into many-armed ghosts in the pearly light.

"Yes, my family are well, thank you. And you? Are you well?"

"Yes, I thank you." There seemed no more to say on that topic. What else could they talk about to pass the time?

Janna's thoughts turned to the missing Edwin. "I wonder if you've seen my brother at all, mistress? He was not in his bed last night, and I'm wondering what has become of him?"

"Edwin?" The knife slipped in Bertha's hand, nicking Janna's scalp. Janna stifled a cry. She shifted uneasily on her stone seat, wondering at Bertha's clumsiness. "No, I haven't seen him," Bertha snapped. "Why should you think I have?"

"No reason," Janna said hastily. "I'm concerned about him, that's all."

"I expect he'll turn up soon enough. There!" Bertha slapped Janna's shoulders, sending bits of hair scattering in all directions. "You look like a boy again, John."

What did Bertha mean by that last remark, Janna wondered. Had her disguise worn thin, or had Edwin told Bertha the truth about both of them? Was that why she seemed so anxious for Janna to be gone? No. Janna dismissed the notion. Edwin's truth was too dangerous to be told. She was just imagining the worst.

"Thank you, mistress," she said. As she walked past the last of the little cottages toward the manor, she looked back, curious to see where Bertha was bound, but the carpenter's daughter had already vanished.

Hunger drove Janna on to the manor's kitchen, along with the hope that she might find Edwin there, ravenous after his night out and ready to break his fast. She had to jump sideways to avoid the sharp teeth of Bones, who was tethered nearby, before she could enter.

"So there you are," Mistress Tova greeted her. "And where is your brother?"

"I know not, mistress. I thought he might be here, having something to eat."

"I haven't seen him since yesterday afternoon." The cook poked her long nose into the air, and sniffed.

Janna tried to hide her disquiet by stuffing a hunk of bread into her mouth and chewing vigorously, before washing down the mouthful with a gulp of ale. Once her appetite was satisfied, however, she took the chance to question the rest of the kitchen staff. To her alarm, no-one had seen Edwin.

"Run away and left you to face Serlo alone, most like. I always knew he was no good." The cook dusted her floured hands down her apron. "Just wonder what he's taken with him," she said darkly.

"Nothing! He's as honest as I am!" Even as Janna leaped to Edwin's defense she remembered how he'd tried to steal her purse. She also remembered all the lies she and Edwin had told. "Master Serlo has probably found work for him to do elsewhere about the manor that's keeping him busy," she said, conscious of the rising tide of heat that colored her face with shame. Yet she had to defend Edwin, and herself, lest the burning of the haystack was laid upon their shoulders, along with all the other recent disasters.

Mistress Tova sniffed again. "Master Serlo will keep watch over your brother after this. He won't be able to cause any more trouble, not while the reeve has him in sight." Janna knew what she was thinking, what everyone was probably thinking. She was about to tell the cook off for spreading malicious lies, but stopped herself just in time. Her hasty words had caused her trouble in the past; she was learning from bitter experience to put a guard on her tongue, and to think before she spoke.

"Master Serlo is a good reeve," she said instead. "And a good catch for any girl—even if Mistress Gytha doesn't want him for a husband," she added, hoping to divert the cook from her suspicions.

The cook shot her a sharp glance. Janna tried to look demure, but her eyes twinkled with mischief. "'Tis true," Mistress Tova said grudgingly. "My lord certainly knows

Serlo's worth, for he treats him well. Serlo has a good-sized cottage, and he was given the gore acres to cultivate for himself. I've seen the cartloads of goods that Serlo takes to the big fairs, his own bounty as well as my lord's, and good quality, all of it. Fetches a good price too, I'll be bound." The cook tapped a bony finger against her long nose. "There'll be no shortage of pretty girls waiting in line once he decides to take a wife. Of course, he'd marry Gytha tomorrow, if she would only have him. I've told her she could do a lot worse for herself than marry Serlo, for once young Hamo comes of age..." She shrugged thin shoulders, leaving unspoken her wish that her daughter would secure her future with the reeve rather than trying to seduce the reeve's master who, at the end of the day, would be left with nothing.

Janna wondered whether to encourage the cook to urge her daughter to see sense, but decided it was wiser to keep out of their affairs. Instead, she thanked the woman for the sack of food she'd provided, and asked after Hamo.

"Staying in his bed today at Mistress Cecily's insistence, but there's nothing wrong with his appetite."

The cook's words set Janna's mind at rest; Hamo was none the worse for his ducking. She remembered the tethered dog beside the kitchen door. "And Bones?" she asked. "What is to become of the dog?"

The cook scowled. "I'm to feed it and give it water."

Janna saw a bright eye peer hopefully around the doorway at them. "If the young lord is to keep his pet, then I'd like to put some medicament on its paws," she said. "Hopefully, the cur's temper will improve once it is out of pain."

"Get the skivvy to muzzle it," the cook advised. "It'll have a piece of your breeches, otherwise."

Janna laughed. "I know all about that," she said cheerfully, and put down the sack of food while she went to pluck some herbs. Her hands stank from the juice of ragwort as she brewed a lotion with sanicle to put on the dog's paws. Conscious that time was passing, but feeling slightly abashed that she was getting out of the difficult part of the treatment, she gave some of the astringent mixture to the skivvy with instructions to first cleanse the dog's paws and then wrap them tight to protect them from becoming dirty and infected once more.

"Keep Bones tied up and out of trouble," she said, adding, "and ask someone to hold the dog's mouth shut so he won't bite you." Ignoring the skivvy's horrified expression, she gathered up a fresh paste of healing herbs for the big black destrier that awaited her in the stable. She was pleased to find no sign of Hugh inside, while his mount seemed much better. She summoned the surly stable lad to hold up the hoof while she unwound the bandage to check. The wound was healing nicely, and she felt a sense of satisfaction as she washed it with lotion and applied the new paste. Human or animal, it mattered not who or what she treated so long as she could heal them, she thought, as she bound up the horse's hoof once more.

Bright sunshine had burned away the early morning mist. Janna emerged from the dimness of the stables and stood blinking in the sunlight. Shearing was still underway and she knew she should go down to the fold to help, but for a moment she lingered, enjoying a moment's rest in the warmth of the sun.

A flock of geese disturbed her reverie. Honking and hissing, they swarmed around her. Janna drew back, alarmed by the close proximity of the big birds with their sharp, serrated beaks. The harassed goosegirl flapped her arms and shouted at them, doing her best to round them up and drive them on through the manor gate and down into the stubbled water meadows to feast on frogs and grasshoppers. Janna kept quite still until they had moved on, then followed them through the gate.

Her path to the sheepfold took her past the young goatherd. She was surprised he was still in charge of the little flock but then noticed how subdued he looked. Even if Hugh hadn't taken a switch to the boy, his father probably had. In fact, the boy might have had a beating from both of them. Janna felt a little sorry for the lad. It was clear that he'd learned a hard lesson. She gave him a smile as she walked past, and earned a scowl in return.

Dogs yipped and barked as they circled the sheep penned into the fold. All was chaos and confusion. Frightened lambs and sheep baaed in protest as they were caught and thrown to the ground, while the shearers cursed as they fought to hold them still long enough so that they could be shorn. It was important not to nick the animal's skin as they clipped the wool with heavy, one-handed shears, for the skin could be turned into vellum for writing on and was therefore valuable. Excited children laughed and ran about and got in everyone's way, harried by the irate shepherd who was trying to bring some order to the proceedings. Janna looked around, without much hope, for Edwin, but there was no sign of him.

Undecided what she should do, and whether she had the strength to wrestle even one sheep to the ground, she looked to the shepherd for guidance. He surveyed her with a critical expression, obviously sharing her doubts. "'Tis said you have the healing touch, John. Some of my flock have fly sores. They're over there." He jerked a thumb at a small enclosure which had been hastily erected out of hurdles roped together. It was packed with shorn and shivering sheep. "Get one of the children to help you." He beckoned Urk to come forward. The boy smiled happily at Janna, pleased to be singled out for such an important task.

"Take each sheep out of the pen and bathe the sores with that mixture." The shepherd waved a hand toward a large wooden trough propped beside the fold. It was full of a yellow liquid. Janna sniffed the air, picking up what she'd missed before among the stink of animal dung and dust: the distinctive stench of ragwort.

She nodded and let herself into the small fold, followed by Urk. Shorn sheep pressed around her, baaing lustily and pushing at her from all sides. Urk grabbed hold of a ewe and marched it out and over to the trough. He looked at Janna, awaiting instructions.

"Well done, Gabriel." She hastily followed him out of the fold. "I'll bathe its sores if you'll hold it fast for me." The boy nodded. After a moment's thought Janna picked up the handful of wool that stood next to the trough and dipped it in, wrinkling her nose at the smell released by the liquid as it swirled about. There were a few nicks and smears of blood on the animal's skin. Janna bathed them first to get rid of the flies that were already harassing it. Wincing at the sight of the ulcerated flesh on its nether regions, Janna gave the sores a thorough wash. The stinking ragwort would cleanse them and kill any maggots, but she thought she detected also the aromatic tang of tansy, which would repel the flies that had caused the problem in the first place.

After Janna finished her ministrations, getting thoroughly splashed by the struggling sheep in the process, Urk released his charge and went to drag another from the fold. "Thank you, Gabriel. You're being a great help," Janna told him, and he beamed with pride.

One by one, the sheep were washed and released, under the watchful eye of the shepherd who moved about, supervising his flock. Janna was hot, tired and stinking by the time Urk brought the last sheep to her. Taking fright from the stinging liquid on its sores, the animal bucked unexpectedly. Urk's grip slipped. He made a frantic grab but the animal broke free. With the alluring prospect of rich grazing in the water meadows ahead, the ewe bumped past Janna as it set off at speed, followed by Urk in hot pursuit.

Knocked off balance, Janna fell against the edge of the wooden trough. It tipped, splashing its contents over her smock and breeches. Janna surveyed the damage in dismay. Her clothes were soaked through, and she stank worse than ever. She saw that Urk had managed to capture the absconding animal and was bringing it back for her final ministrations. There was a small portion of liquid remaining at the bottom of the trough, and Janna hastily applied it.

Her task was over. She looked longingly toward the cool, flowing river. "By your leave, I'm going to rinse off this stinking mixture," she told the shepherd. Not giving him a chance to argue, she hurried down to the water. She untied her girdle and laid it and her purse on the river bank. She took a quick look around to see if anyone was paying attention then lowered herself into the river. The shock of the icy water on her hot skin took her breath away for several long moments. Recollecting her purpose, she began an opportunistic floundering, determined to make the most of this chance to give herself and her clothes a thorough wash. She also took a long drink of water, relishing its coldness as it slipped down her dry throat. Finally, she regained her footing and emerged from the river. She made her way toward the place she'd dropped her belongings, wringing the water from her smock as she walked. Reveling in her clean skin and clean clothes, Janna picked up her girdle and purse and tied them safely around her waist.

As she returned to the sheepfold, she passed several villeins carrying a pile of washed fleeces back to the manor. She knew that women were already engaged in combing out the tangles, using the dried heads of teasels that were prickly as hedgehogs. The best fleeces would be sold at the annual fair at Wiltune. Janna had been to the fair once, and still remembered the excitement of it all. It was the high mark of the year, both because it was a holy time to commemorate the death of St Edith, but also because merchants and travelers came from miles around to sell their wares.

"Where is your brother, John?"

Janna jumped. She hadn't noticed Serlo's approach. His gaze rested quizzically on her chest. She quickly crossed her arms lest he notice the shape of her breasts moulded beneath the clinging wet fabric.

"He must be working elsewhere about the manor, Master Serlo. Perhaps the lord Hugh has given him a task?"

Serlo frowned. "He should be here, helping with the shearing," he said.

"And so I shall tell him, just as soon as I see him." Janna gave an exaggerated shiver. "I fell into the river and I'm cold. May I have your leave to run in the fields until I am dry?"

With a reluctant nod, Serlo waved her away. Feeling relief, Janna retraced her steps to the sheepfold to retrieve her sack of food, and set off up into the fields. She kept up a fast pace until she was hidden from his sight by a field of growing wheat. She slowed to a walk and looked about for somewhere to eat her dinner, while she considered what to do next.

Edwin had seemed so keen to stay at the manor. What had happened to change his mind? If he'd run away, why hadn't he asked her to go with him? He knew she wanted to leave, and that it was only his wish to stay that was keeping her here. Yet he'd gone without even saying goodbye.

Janna concluded that, if Edwin really had gone, she might as well leave too. There was certainly no future for her here, in spite of Hugh's kind offer. She sat down in the shade of a patch of brambles, and opened up the sack of food. She munched on some bread and sheep's cheese while she considered past events—and whether the "accidents" would continue now that Edwin was gone. His absence seemed to point to his guilt, yet nothing about it made sense, not even his disappearance now. But if not Edwin, then who?

Her years under her mother's tutelage had taught Janna to look carefully, to listen and to learn. As she ate her dinner, she thought through the incidents she'd witnessed. Was there anything to link them together, other than the posies of rue?

No, there was not, she concluded. So perhaps she should approach the problem from another angle. Why rue? What was the reasoning behind it? Janna cast her mind back to everything her mother had told her about the herb. "*It's known as 'herb of grace' to Christians, for they believe rue is a symbol of the true repentance that leads to God's grace,*" Eadgyth had said. But it was clear to Janna that the culprit repented nothing, for the incidents kept on happening. Not repentance, then. What else had she been told?

"*The Romans thought they'd gain a second sight and see visions if they took the herb, but others have used it to curse their enemies.*" Eadgyth's eyes had twinkled as she'd continued. "*You can also wear rue for luck, for protection, or as a cure against disease. In fact, daughter, it seems the ancients couldn't quite make up their minds whether the herb should be used for good or ill. For myself, I believe the herb has many good uses, and these I will show you.*" And so she had, Janna thought, remembering the many medicaments to which rue could be added.

Repentance? Or a curse? Janna sighed. She was no nearer to working out the truth of the matter, but it seemed certain that the culprit wouldn't stop now; something else was going to happen, perhaps something worse than all that had gone before. She felt a shiver of premonition. Something niggled at the back of her mind; something she'd seen, something important that perhaps might tell her who could be responsible. She closed her eyes, the better to recall what she'd seen or heard, but the memory remained elusive.

She was thoughtful as she walked down to the fold, where the last of the sheep were now being sheared. If Edwin had really gone, she should leave too. But not right now; she couldn't risk Serlo seeing her go. Besides, if she left so openly, it would confirm the reeve's belief that she and Edwin were behind the so-called accidents. They would be pursued by Serlo, and also by the forester. Janna had no doubt the reeve would carry out his threat to raise the hue and cry. Nor would he willingly let her go if she asked to leave, not when she was one of his suspects, and not when it was his intention to get more work out of both of them in return for his silence.

Uneasy and afraid, she wondered if she should make a run for it anyway. Whatever her decision, Janna knew she must wait until nightfall. If there was no sign of Edwin by then, mayhap she could sneak out while everyone was snoring? But in which direction should she go? She resolved that her first task must be to find out the way to Winchestre. But as she questioned first the shepherd and then some of the villeins, she found herself more confused than ever by the responses.

"Winchestre lies that way." One shearer stopped clipping to point downstream.

"No, you'll find the road over there," said another, and jabbed a finger in the opposite direction.

"It's behind us," said a villein, who was busy making his mark on his own sheep. He took time to poke his thumb back at the fields.

She would have to go over the fields and see what lay beyond them, Janna decided, as she picked up a bundle of fleeces and carried them down to the river for a wash. Even if the road took her in the wrong direction, it would lead her away from the manor, and also from Dame Alice and Robert of Babestoche. It would lead her to safety. She could always ask about Winchestre along the way, and change direction at a crossroads, if need be.

All these thoughts left Janna's head as, with the day draw-
ing to its weary end, she heard a bell begin to toll. She
recognized the sound. It came from the church at nearby
Wicheford and, on Sundays, it summoned the faithful to
mass, including those villeins from their own manor who felt
obliged to make the journey across the downs. But today was
not Sunday, and the bell rang on and on, clanging its urgent
appeal long past its usual recording of time or occasion.
The villeins hurriedly gathered up the last of the fleeces and
hastened to the manor to find out the cause of the summons,
Janna among them.

"Hamo." She heard the boy's name mentioned several
times as they came closer to the confusion and bustle in
the yard. It was said with annoyance, impatience, and also
with anxiety. Janna's steps quickened. Surely he couldn't have
gone missing again after such a narrow escape last time?
But it seemed that he had. A cry of alarm had gone out
and everyone was being pressed into the search for him. The
yard was full of servants and laborers, all milling around and
discussing what to do. At their center, looking distraught, and
trying to organize the comings and goings, was Hugh. Janna
noticed several unfamiliar faces amid the throng, strangers
from neighboring Wicheford. United in adversity and drawn
by a sense of community, they too had come to join in the
search for the missing boy.

Hugh raised his voice. "Hamo was last seen playing with
his ball here by the undercroft," he shouted above the
hubbub. "I want the women and children to search the
gardens and all the buildings of the manor. The rest of you
will comb the fields and search along the river, up and down.
Pay careful attention to the mill, and also the marsh. I, myself,
will take a small party into the forest. Although the fence
month has passed, the does will still be guarding their young.
Should any of them stray into the fields do not, on any

143

account, do anything to startle or harm them, or the forester will call you to an accounting before the king." With chopping motions of his hands, he began to divide the villeins into groups, ready to send them off in different directions.

Janna hurried up to him. "Where is the dog, my lord?" she cried. "You should also look for Bones."

Hugh glanced down at her. "I haven't seen it, have you?"

Janna shook her head. Hugh raised his voice once more to shout: "Look out also for a stray dog." His face was tight with worry as he continued to issue instructions to the villeins.

"I hope you find him soon, my lord."

Hugh nodded. Janna stood back and waited to be told where to go. A sudden thought came into her mind, and she sidled forward once more. A quick glance confirmed her fears and struck dread through her heart. A small posy of rue lay on the doorstep of the undercroft.

Janna bent down and picked up the posy. Her first thought was to show it to Hugh, and tell him what she thought it meant. Her second thought urged caution. The posy, in itself, proved nothing, for all the other posies were either gone or had been destroyed, some by Janna herself. She had nothing, now, to prove that these were acts of deliberate malice, and that Hamo had not wandered off by chance. This time he must have been taken, and by someone who wished him harm.

Janna felt sick. She longed to spill out her worries to Hugh but a question, and its answer, stopped her even as she opened her mouth. Who stood to gain by Hamo's disappearance—perhaps even his death? The answer had been spelled out to her, only too clearly, on her first meeting with Hamo. "*All my mother's property and wealth will be mine when she dies,*" he had told her. "*I am the first-born son, you see.*"

Hamo, as the first and only surviving child born to Hugh's aunt, Dame Alice, would inherit everything on her death. In the interim, Hugh kept this manor for his aunt, but he would be expected to vacate it once Hamo came of age and married. Unless, of course, the child died before then!

Janna swallowed hard. She cast a glance at Hugh, hating what she was thinking yet understanding that she could not deny the truth of his situation. Only Hamo stood between him and a vast inheritance from Dame Alice. All the evidence pointed to him. These incidents had only started on his return to the manor. He, more than anyone, was free to come and go as he wished; no-one would dare to challenge him. Had he set up a pattern of accidents to convince his aunt that Hamo's disappearance—even his death—while regrettable, was just another accident?

Rue for regret. And repentance. Yes, Hugh might well regret the circumstances that forced him to act in this way. And he might well feel repentance for his actions. But that was still no excuse for murder.

Janna continued to watch Hugh direct proceedings, while berating herself for letting her thoughts run away with her. Hugh murdering Hamo? The thought was laughable, quite out of the question. She herself had seen his fondness for his cousin when they'd played ball together. And Hamo wouldn't have fretted after Hugh left Babestoche if his cousin hadn't shown him genuine kindness. Nor did it seem likely that Hugh would have tampered with his own destrier's shoe in order to lame the horse, for it was his most valuable possession. Besides, his anger then had been apparent, while his concern now seemed real enough.

There must be some other explanation. But if not Hugh, then who? Edwin? Janna shook her head. His absence might indicate guilt to some, but he'd gone missing before Hamo's disappearance. Unless that was to cover his actions and avert suspicion? Janna remembered that this wasn't the first time Edwin had gone missing. He'd been absent on the night of medale, when the haystack had caught fire and the villagers had come together to put it out. Had he gone off to set fire to the haystack, and come back later pretending innocence? Was that what he intended to do now? But why? Try as she would, Janna could come up with no convincing reason for it.

She was assuming that Hamo had vanished for a reason, perhaps forever, but what if she was wrong, what if there was some other purpose behind what was going on? She sighed with exasperation. Her imagination was taking her into dark places where she really didn't want to go.

She wished Edwin would come back and clear his name. Yet he was capable of wrongdoing, she conceded, remembering that he'd been proved a thief—although he hadn't harmed her when he'd had the chance. Her hand went to her purse. She heard the coins clink at her touch, and felt the shape of the small statue she had found, the mother clasping her child. Her fear eased slightly, and she smiled at the notion that the statue had brought comfort.

Mother and child. She felt a sudden pang of deep distress as she recalled Dame Alice. The lady was utterly cast down by the death of her newborn babe. She would surely take leave of her senses altogether if her only surviving child also died.

This won't do, Janna told herself sternly. It's too early for despair. Hamo is missing, not dead. And he hasn't been gone for long. She remembered the mangy dog. Hamo must have gone in search of it once more. He would surely be found soon.

By now, everyone had been summoned by the clamoring bell. Although she'd been ordered to search outside the manor with the men, Janna decided instead to hunt for Bones. Instinct told her that if she could find the dog, she would probably find Hamo too. Regardless of what the rue might mean, it was too great a coincidence that boy and dog should both be missing. So she tried the kitchen first, where she'd last seen Bones. She searched within and without, but there was no sign of dog or boy. She widened her search then, calling as she went, but there was no answering bark or shout for help. It seemed she was right: both of them had vanished. So where had they gone, and with whom?

"You! Boy!" Serlo had his horse on a rein, ready to mount, but now he stopped and beckoned Janna to come to him. His face set in a thunderous frown as he waited for her to draw near. "Where's your brother?"

From the hostility in his tone, Janna understood that she and Edwin were under suspicion for this too. It took all her courage to face the reeve. "I do not know where Edwin is, Master Serlo," she answered politely. She became aware she was still clutching the posy of rue, and hastily secreted it behind her back.

"And the young lord? I don't suppose you know where he is either?"

"No, I do not." Janna hesitated, wondering if she had the nerve. "But I do know he's not with Edwin," she added boldly.

"And how would you know that if you don't know where your brother is?"

"I know Edwin, Master Serlo." Janna hoped that, indeed, she did. "I know he wouldn't take the boy away for any reason, even in fun."

Serlo's frown deepened. "What makes you think there's any reason behind Hamo's disappearance other than that the silly child has wandered away and got lost?"

Janna kept silent. Hamo was anything but silly. He'd run after his dog and got into trouble for it; while he might go in search of the dog once more, it seemed unlikely he'd go so close to the river again, or even stray far from the manor unless enticed away by someone he trusted. But she couldn't blame Serlo for trying to put a good face on things. Besides, it was perfectly possible she'd read the situation wrongly. The fact that there was a posy of rue on the steps of the undercroft might not have anything to do with Hamo's disappearance; it might be a sign of something quite different, something relatively minor. Up until now the incidents had caused harm, but they were not too serious for all that. Kidnapping a child, the heir to this manor, on the other hand, was a very serious crime indeed.

"Get out and look for Hamo," Serlo growled. "I don't want to see you back here before dark. And make sure you bring your brother back with you!" With a scowl he mounted, and rode out through the gate.

Janna grimaced at his departing back. "I'm already looking for Hamo," she muttered. "What do you think I'm doing? Walking about for my health?" Nevertheless, she linked up with a group of women who were busy searching through the manor grounds. Although she joined them in calling out Hamo's name, she also called for Bones. But only silence answered their calls.

The bell began to toll again, a low and mournful sound. A shiver ran through Janna as she came to understand its meaning. The sound was meant to guide the lost child home to safety. It would continue to toll until Hamo was found. And if Hamo didn't come running home, it would mean that he could not; it would mean that he was dead.

Chapter 9

Following Serlo's instructions, partly to avoid Serlo himself, but mostly because she was worried sick, Janna left the manor grounds to search along the length of the river. She stayed out until it grew too dark to see properly. In twos and threes, the villeins began to return, shaking their heads in despair as they asked each other for news. Hugh called for resin torches to be fetched. With flames held high to light their way, some of the men streamed out of the gate to continue their search, a few on foot and some on horseback to ride further afield. Janna was relieved to notice that Serlo was among them. The women and children, meanwhile, went off to their own cots to see about the evening meal and a night's rest.

Not wanting to encounter Mistress Tova's wagging tongue, or questions about Edwin's whereabouts and sly innuendoes about his reliability, Janna wearily climbed the stairs to the hall and settled down onto her pallet, determined to continue her search as soon as it dawned. Unable to sleep, she began to fret over Hamo. She pictured him falling into the river and being crushed by the mill wheel, or blundering through the forest, lost and frightened, not knowing which way to turn.

There were wolves there, and wild boar. Having no weapon, nor anything to defend himself, Hamo would be easy prey.

Janna screwed her eyes tight shut, trying to block out the pictures she'd conjured up. With so many people out looking for him, how could Hamo stay lost—unless someone was determined that he should not be found? She tried to push the thought from her mind but it lay there like a stone, too heavy to shift, too heavy to ignore.

She passed a restless night. Nightmares frightened her awake; she lay, heart thudding, listening to the snores of the sleepers and, at regular intervals, the lonely sound of the clanging bell. In the end, she fell into a deep sleep and didn't wake until one of the villeins gave her a hard shake.

"You'd best get up, John, if you want time to break your fast," he said. "Master Serlo wants us out at first light to look for the young lord."

Janna leaped up from her pallet, but she was still yawning and only half awake as she ate a chunk of bread and tried to come up with a plan. The first thing, she decided, was to give the undercroft a thorough search, just to satisfy herself that the posy of rue was in no way connected with Hamo's disappearance.

"Where's your brother, John? I want a word with him," Serlo said sternly.

Startled, Janna whirled to face the reeve. She hadn't seen him come into the hall but, judging from the thunderous frown on his face, he was in a temper and determined to take it out on someone.

"I-I know not where Edwin is, Master Serlo," she confessed miserably, sure now that she would be punished in place of him.

"I judge him responsible for the young lord's disappearance—and you will be suspect too, if you cannot bring Edwin to account. I'm out of patience with you both, but there's no time to waste on you now. If you don't have Edwin here by nightfall, I'll raise the hue and cry after him. I'll call in the shire reeve. Be sure that I'll also mention your whereabouts to the forester. There'll be no place for you to hide after this, John, not you or your brother. Just think on that."

"I swear we know nothing about the young lord's disappearance, Master Serlo," Janna said hurriedly. "But I will go in search of Edwin. And the young lord, if you'll give me leave?"

Serlo nodded curtly, and turned away to deal with a group of women who awaited further instructions. Gytha was among them, and in spite of her anxiety, Janna felt a twitch of amusement. Serlo couldn't keep his eyes off the girl. All his remarks were addressed to Gytha. She stood before him, hardly responding to his attention, while Serlo watched her as a starving man might watch his last crust disappearing down the mouth of a rival.

Janna turned and walked quickly down the stairs. She had more pressing problems to think about now: was it more important to find Hamo or Edwin? Could they be hiding somewhere together?

Another possible companion for Hamo came into Janna's mind. Urk was older than Hamo, but he was about the same age in his reasoning. Hamo would think nothing of running free on his cousin's property—his own property—while Urk had already shown that he wasn't aware of, or didn't understand, the rules that bound the villeins living on the manor farm. He would be delighted to go searching for Bones, or play a game with Hamo if the young lord still had his ball with him.

Where might the two of them go? After a moment's reflection, Janna thought it most likely that they'd stay right here within the confines of the manor, where the ground was cleared and suitable for play. In which case they would have been found already. Where would they have gone if they'd decided to stray further? Janna decided to try the villeins' cots that spread beyond the manor. Not understanding the differences in their station, perhaps Urk had taken his new friend home with him.

She hurried outside the timber palisade, making straight for Mistress Wulfrun's cottage. There was no sign of Urk, or Hamo, but Janna resolved to check all the cots while she was there. Most everyone already knew that Hamo was missing, but Janna alerted a mother who had just been brought to bed with child, and also an elderly and infirm grandmother, and bade them keep a careful watch out for him. The rest of the cots were empty, the villeins already out on the search.

Remembering her earlier idea, Janna hurried back to the manor house. She could hear the villeins calling Hamo's name as they hunted for him up and down the river, marked by the sonorous tones of the tocsin. If Hamo was anywhere, dead or alive, he must certainly be found.

Several riders flashed past. Janna stared after them. They must be widening the search. She didn't recognize the horses, but she knew at least one of the horsemen—Hugh. He had donned his green cloak for the journey and it sailed out behind him, given wings by the wind. She wished him a silent "God speed," pleased he wasn't riding his own destrier, that he was giving the horse's hoof a chance to heal.

Women and children moved about with a steady purpose, methodically inspecting once again every nook and cranny that might provide shelter for a small boy. The men had fanned out beyond the manor walls, some to continue the search up and down the river, looking especially at the mill and the great marsh, while the rest walked through the tall ripening corn, or searched the meadows on either side of the river, or tramped through the forest beyond.

Janna knew she should join the men, but investigating the undercroft was on her mind now. She would rather discover the real purpose behind Hamo's disappearance, even if only to set her mind at rest. She walked into the undercroft below the hall, and there began a systematic search for anything that might explain the significance of the posy of rue left lying on the doorstep.

She kept her mind and eyes focused on her task. She was looking for something out of place, or something spoiled, perhaps. Even something missing—but how would she know if that was so? She sorted through the few poor possessions stored by the servants who shared her sleeping quarters in the hall, then moved on to the rest of the undercroft where food and grain were kept. Being the hungry month, the time just before harvest, there were few full sacks of grain left. One of the sacks was ripped and precious grain spilled out of it. Janna checked it carefully. Mouse droppings confirmed that it was mice rather than a human hand behind the deed.

There were also barrels, and several chests. She tried the lid of one of them, but found it locked. So were most of the others, she discovered, after trying them all. Only one opened to her touch, but a quick rifle through its contents confirmed that there was only a woolen blanket, worn thin and perforated with moth holes, and some chipped pots and jugs inside. Nothing in the undercroft appeared to have been tampered with; everything seemed in order. Just to be sure, Janna tapped on each chest. "Hamo?" she called softly. She didn't know whether to be glad or sorry when there was no reply.

With her inspection over, Janna walked outside and paused for a moment while she worked out where to try next. She was hot, thirsty and tired. And hungry. There were apples growing on the trees that bordered the kitchen garden. As Janna visualized the juicy fruit, her mouth began to water in anticipation. She hurried to the fruit trees, hoping that the apples were ripe enough to eat, and that no-one was around to watch her steal one.

A long brown snake caught her eye and she stopped, momentarily afraid, until she realized that it was not a snake but a rope. It was tethered to a pole at one end, but the other disappeared behind a large wooden barrel. Curious, she peered over, and found Bones cowering behind.

"Come here!" she ordered. She tugged hard on the rope. The unwilling creature skidded around and came into full view. "Where's Hamo?" Janna demanded. She cast a quick look around, hoping no-one had heard her talking to a dog. But so had she talked to the animals she and her mother had kept at their cottage. "Do you know where he's hiding?"

Her words seemed to soothe the dog, for it stopped cringing and baring its teeth at her and, instead, sat down and looked up at her with pleading eyes. Janna was incensed to see that its paws were still untreated by the kitchen skivvy. She chided herself for passing on the task rather than taking care of it herself.

"Poor old Bones." She dragged the dog inside the empty kitchen and set about finding it some scraps, hoping to bribe it into good behavior so that she could put the medicament on its paws. She wondered if the dog knew anything about Hamo's disappearance. Might it even lead her to Hamo? Her first task must be to take care of its wounds so that at least it could walk with her while she was searching.

Once the dog was busy chomping its way through a piece of raw liver, Janna poured water into a basin and set about cleansing its front paws, clicking her tongue at the damage done, for the wounds were suppurating and filthy. The dog growled as she probed deeper. "Have a bone, Bones," she said, and hurriedly stuffed one of the cook's soup bones into its mouth.

It dropped the bone and began to shiver and whine softly as Janna first cleansed then bound its paws with linen rags smeared with the ointment she'd made up earlier. It seemed to sense that she was friend not foe and even managed a feeble wag of its tail when she was done, while it wasted no time getting back to the feast she'd provided. "You realize I'm going to blame you for stealing this food," Janna told the dog as she scoffed a cold meat pasty while she waited for it to finish eating. She was only half jesting. Mistress Tova would be incensed when she discovered what had gone missing. She hastily drained a mug of ale to slake her thirst.

"Right. Time to go to work," she said, feeling slightly more cheerful after her repast. She pulled on the dog's leash once more. With a last look of longing at the ham that hung enticingly beside the cooking fire, the dog trotted after Janna, still limping.

Holding on to the rope to keep the dog with her, Janna crossed the river. If Hamo wasn't within the manor walls, neither was Edwin, or he, too, would have been found in the search. With Serlo's warning sounding in her ears, she went first to the sheep shed where once they'd taken shelter from the forester. As she'd suspected, it was empty. She peeped behind the rough wooden feeding trough, and felt a great relief when she espied the rusty sword she'd secreted there, along with Edwin's pot and jug. If he had left the manor to go adventuring, he surely would have remembered to take everything with him. Wherever he was, he couldn't be far away. Hunger would drive him home, and soon.

A group of peasants beating through the edge of the forest beyond caught Janna's eye. Urk's mother was among them, and Janna joined them. Edwin could take care of himself; it was Hamo who occupied her thoughts now. A quick glance confirmed that Urk was not part of the group. She made a beeline for Mistress Wulfrun, hoping her suspicions might prove correct.

"Mistress," she greeted her. "I've been looking for Urk—Gabriel. Do you know where he might be?"

Urk's mother nodded. "He went off with the other children to search the barn," she said, looking worried.

"Was he alone?"

"No, I told you. He was with the other children." Mistress Wulfrun shot a suspicious glance at Janna. "Why do you ask?"

"I wondered if he might have gone somewhere to play ball with a special friend, perhaps?"

"Ball?" Mistress Wulfrun couldn't have looked more confused if Janna had asked whether Urk had grown wings and flown to the moon.

Janna nodded thoughtfully. Hamo might have the leisure to play ball games, but it seemed that Urk did not. "And did Gabriel sleep in his bed last night?"

Mistress Wulfrun drew herself up to her full height and glared at Janna. "He was not out setting fire to a haystack, if that's what you're trying to suggest."

"No!" Janna was sorry to have offended Urk's mother. She wasn't sure how to put things right. "It's just that the young lord loves to play with his ball. I wondered if Gabriel had gone off to play a game with him, that's all."

"Gabriel has no time to play games." Mistress Wulfrun strode on, calling out Hamo's name as she went.

Janna clicked her tongue impatiently—she hadn't had an answer to her question. She left the villeins to their search and went back to the manor, dragging Bones on the rope behind her. The clanging tones of the bell followed her passage. Janna scrutinized the knots of people coming and going, wishing more than anything to recognize Hamo among them. Although several small figures brought her to a heart-thumping halt, closer inspection always revealed them to be some other child. She hurried inside the gate and went looking in the barn for Urk and his friends.

Oblivious to the urgency of their task and the real danger to Hamo, the children were playing a game, throwing hay about and shrieking with delight. Urk seemed to be having the most fun. She drew him aside. "Have you seen Hamo, Gabriel?" she asked.

He shook his head. "Hamo's lost," he said helpfully.

"I know. I wondered if you'd seen him. Did you maybe go somewhere to play ball with him?"

"Ball?" Urk looked just as puzzled as his mother.

"Have you seen Hamo today? Do you know where he is?"

"No. Hamo's lost." Urk bent down to pat Bones. "Good dog." Bones' tail twitched in acknowledgment.

Janna sighed, discouraged. "Go on then and look for Hamo," she said, and gave him a gentle push in the direction of the younger children. Urk ambled off, giving her a bewildered glance as he left. Janna walked outside and looked up at the sky. The sun had begun to fall toward the earth; it would be dark within a few hours, and then Serlo would demand an explanation of Edwin's absence. She felt like a watermill in a dry river bed, churning around uselessly and achieving absolutely nothing. She'd been rushing everywhere, but she still had no answers for Serlo, nor any idea where to find them either. What was she to do? With steps dragging, she went back to join the searchers at the forest's edge.

She looked across the water meadows to the manor beyond, with the small cots of the peasants clinging to the lane through the hamlet like pups to a bitch's teats. Behind the manor stretched the cultivated fields, stripes of ripening wheat in one, barley in the other, while the third was left fallow. A small copse of trees occupied part of a triangle left between two of the fields, with a fine stand of wheat filling the remaining space. From the height and distance of her position, Janna could see now that the copse hid a solid, stone-built cottage.

"Who lives there?" she asked, while beside her, Bones began to whine. "Shh." She smacked his muzzle gently to shut him up so that she could hear Mistress Wulfrun's reply.

"Master Serlo. The cottage and those gore acres around it belong to him."

Janna gave a long, low whistle as she quickly revised her opinion of the reeve. Mistress Tova had mentioned Serlo's cottage and fields, but Janna hadn't realized the full extent of his holding. Gytha would do well to encourage him, she thought now, for the young woman's chance of improving her station was far greater with Serlo than it could ever be with Hugh. As Serlo's wife, she would have a certain status; she would also become a woman of property. Yet as she mentally compared the two in her mind, Janna had to admit that in Gytha's position she'd also be hoping for a future with Hugh rather than plighting her troth to the reeve.

She dragged her thoughts back to the more pressing matter of the missing boy. "Has anyone looked around Serlo's cottage for Hamo?" At the sound of the boy's name Bones strained on his leash beside her, still whining.

"Yes, indeed, Master Serlo conducted the search himself." Mistress Wulfrun caught hold of Janna's arm. "Don't think to go anywhere near there, John. Master Serlo does not take kindly to anyone trespassing on his property. Besides, I noticed him return to his cottage at noon for his dinner. So wherever Hamo may be, you can be sure he's not there."

Janna nodded, accepting that the woman was giving her good advice. "You know the manor farm better than I do, mistress," she said. "Where do you think Hamo might be?"

"I wish I knew." The woman scratched her nose, looking thoughtful. "They say the lord has gone to break the bad news to Dame Alice, but in his absence Master Serlo will continue the search until the boy is found. Conscientious as he is, he knows every rock and tree on the manor farm. Wherever Hamo is, alive or dead, Master Serlo will find him."

"Then let us pray that Master Serlo finds Hamo alive!" The alternative was too dreadful to contemplate. As Janna walked on, calling Hamo's name in the silences left between the clanging tones of the bell, she wondered suddenly how Cecily was faring and what she was doing. Newly in charge of Hamo and wanting only the best for Dame Alice, she must be riven with anxiety. And self-blame. How had Hamo managed to escape Cecily yet again? It was something she should have thought to ask right from the start.

Janna turned abruptly and hurried back to the manor, tugging Bones along with her, although the dog continued to bark and pull on his rope to get free. She was crossing the yard when she saw Cecily vanish through the line of pear and apple trees that hedged the kitchen garden. At once she followed, curious to find out what Hamo's new nurse sought there. But it seemed that Cecily had merely escaped to find some privacy, for Janna found her sitting hunched under a pear tree, weeping as if her heart would break. Her head was buried in her lap with her arms wrapped around to muffle the sounds she was making. She didn't hear Janna approach.

"Mistress Cecily." Janna tapped her on the shoulder. At Janna's touch, the tiring woman leaped up in fright and shied away.

"Oh, it's you, Janna," she said, and subsided onto the ground once more. She wiped her eyes on her sleeve, and gave a mournful sniff. "What am I going to do?" she burst out. "The lord Hugh has gone to tell his aunt that Hamo is missing. Dame Alice will never forgive me if harm has come to him. I'll never forgive myself. Oh, Janna, I have caused such trouble to my lady and her kin!" She burst into a storm of weeping once more.

Overcome with pity, Janna put her arm around Cecily, hoping to comfort her. No wonder she was hurting. She had loved Robert once, loved him enough to forget all honor, and all loyalty and gratitude to his wife. That he'd proved so base, so unworthy of her sacrifice, must double both her sadness and her shame. And now there was the added blame of Hamo's disappearance. There was nothing Janna could say to ease Cecily's pain or make things right for her. All she could do, all anyone could do, was keep on looking for Hamo and pray that he'd be found alive.

Janna continued to hold Cecily, patting her as she did so. "Hush," she said at last, offering what little comfort she could. "Everyone's out searching. I'm sure Hamo will be found soon. We mustn't give up hope."

Cecily nodded, and gave a forlorn sniff.

Encouraged, Janna asked, "When did you last see Hamo? How did he come to run away?"

"I know not." Cecily gave her eyes a fierce scrub on her sleeve, and sniffed again. "I needed to speak to the cook about Hamo's meals. I asked him to come with me to the kitchen but he didn't want to, and so I left him playing with his ball."

Janna reflected, with bleak amusement, that Hamo's new nurse didn't yet have his measure. Telling, not asking, would be far more effective if she wanted the child to obey her. She remembered what Hugh had said. "He was playing by the undercroft?"

"Yes. He was throwing his ball at the wall and trying to catch it. Actually, he's very good at it."

Having played ball with Hamo herself, Janna knew just how accurate was his aim, and how skilful his catching. She also knew that Hamo loved to play ball; she could hardly blame Cecily if the boy resisted her efforts to drag him away. "How long were you gone?" she asked.

"Only long enough for the cook to show me what she had in her stores, and for me to give her some directions regarding Hamo's likes and dislikes. She was willing enough to listen and to learn, there was no argument there. But when I came out again and looked for Hamo, he was nowhere to be seen. I swear to you—" Cecily clutched Janna's arm in agitation, "—I was not gone for long. Moments only!" She began to cry once more.

"Was the dog with Hamo while he was playing with his ball?" It was a chance question, but Cecily's answer reinforced Janna's certainty that the two were linked together somehow.

"No," she said. "We'd been looking for the dog everywhere, but we couldn't find it. Hamo was very upset." She looked down at Bones, now sitting placidly beside Janna. "Where did you find it?" She brightened momentarily. "Maybe Hamo...?"

Her voice trailed off as Janna shook her head. "Bones was here, tied up behind a barrel in the kitchen garden," she said. "There was no sign of Hamo."

"But Hamo and I searched all around here just before he disappeared. We would have found Bones; he would have barked when he heard us calling."

"I saw the dog outside the kitchen when I broke my fast yesterday. But I didn't see him after that until I went looking for Hamo earlier today, and found the dog cowering behind those barrels over there. He seemed frightened, I don't know why." It was something to think about later, but for now she was anxious to question Cecily further. If Hugh was somehow implicated in Hamo's disappearance, then Janna vowed to find it out.

"Tell me about the lord Hugh. Does he spend much time with you in the hall and in the solar? Or is he often absent about the manor?"

Cecily frowned at Janna, and remained silent.

"Mistress Gytha is very attractive, is she not?" Janna prompted, hoping to goad Cecily into speaking by throwing in a snippet of kitchen gossip. "I know she cares for my lord and is hoping for a propitious marriage. Does he perhaps spend time dallying with her?"

"Gytha?" Cecily's eyes widened. Too late, Janna remembered that at one time she'd wondered if Cecily herself was enamored with Hugh. She wasn't then, but perhaps that, too, had changed in the time Janna had been away. Janna wished she could unask the question.

"Gytha," Cecily said again. She gave a short laugh. "I think my lord might wish to do better for himself than the cook's daughter."

Although Cecily's words echoed what Janna herself thought, she couldn't help feeling saddened by the reminder that if Gytha was beneath Hugh's attention, she herself must come even lower. She brought herself back to the purpose of her questions. If Hugh was guilty, as she feared, he could have no place in her heart, none at all.

"I doubt that my lord has spent much time with Gytha or any other pretty woman who might take his fancy, for he has been very busy since his return." Cecily said tartly. "He told me he's been going out every day to inspect the fields, and see what's to be done about the manor, to make sure that all is well. I know he's worried that the manor isn't as productive as it should be. I believe there have also been several unfortunate accidents recently. Although my lord Hugh pays tribute to Master Serlo, whom he says is an excellent reeve, I suspect his main aim is to convince his aunt of his own good stewardship, and to stay in her favor so that she will let him keep the manor for himself after young Hamo comes of age—if he still lives." Cecily started to cry once more.

So Hugh could have gone anywhere and everywhere, with no-one to check on his movements. Janna knew she could push Cecily no further. It was clear she had little real knowledge of how Hugh passed his days. But she might know something else of use. "Gytha tells me that the visitors who traveled with you through the forest are on their way to a great fair. Do you know if they are bound for Winchestre?" she asked, sure that Cecily would have shown more interest in them than self-absorbed Gytha would have done. The travelers might be able to tell her the way even if they were not going there themselves. But if they were, she would follow them.

Janna was struck with a sudden thought: Edwin had been present when Master Siward and his servant had arrived—and he'd been missing ever since. Had he already interrogated them about Winchestre? Was that why he'd vanished? Or could it be that he'd disappeared for another reason entirely? She nodded slowly as a different scenario came into her mind. She would think it through later, when she had more time.

"Yes, I believe they are." Cecily's eyes narrowed in suspicion. "You're always asking questions," she observed, "and always to a purpose. What's on your mind, Janna?"

Janna was tempted to share her doubts with Cecily, along with her plans to flee the manor, but she knew she could do nothing or go anywhere until Hamo was found and the truth proved, whatever it might be. "Nothing in particular is on my mind," she lied. "I'm just trying to work out who Hamo could be with, or where he might have gone. I'm trying to help, mistress."

"I doubt Hamo's gone anywhere with Master Siward." Cecily thought for a moment. "In fact, I know he hasn't, for I saw him and his servant earlier. They're taking part in the search." Her voice shook as she fought for control.

"Do you know where they have come from?" Janna asked. It seemed unlikely that these strangers could be responsible for Hamo's disappearance. They would have no reason to wish the boy harm, nor would they have the local knowledge to keep him hidden. Yet their identity was of interest, for in that might lie the answer to at least one of the mysteries that plagued her.

"They come from near Tantone. I think 'tis in the next shire from ours."

Tantone—the demesne of Edwin's cruel lord. Janna nodded as her suspicion was confirmed. "Why have they stopped here?" she asked carefully.

"They needed to break their journey because one of their horses went lame. They plan to reach Winchestre in time for the annual fair of St Giles." Cecily sounded troubled as she added, "But I suspect there might be another reason for their slow progress. I heard them ask my lord Hugh if he'd seen or given shelter to an outlaw over the past months."

"An outlaw?" Janna's voice squeaked in horror at the realization that now Edwin's secret must be known to Hugh. She tried to control her agitation. "What did he tell them?"

"He asked if the outlaw was traveling on his own. When Master Siward said, 'Yes,' my lord replied that he had not come across any man traveling alone. Oh!" Cecily caught her breath. "Is that—did he mean Edwin? Is Edwin an outlaw?"

Janna was furious with herself for questioning Cecily. She was sure the young woman wouldn't have worked it out if she hadn't been prompted into it. But it was too late, now, to take back her words. She nodded.

"Oh, Janna!" Cecily clutched her arm, her own woes forgotten at this new threat. "We might have been murdered in our beds!"

"Nonsense!" Janna could understand why Edwin had gone missing now, but she wished he was here to argue his cause and state his innocence. More than anything, she was grateful to Hugh for keeping both her secret and Edwin's. She felt ashamed of her suspicions about him, yet knew she must not trust him unless and until she could prove him innocent of any knowledge of Hamo's disappearance.

"If the lord has kept Edwin's secret, and mine, I beg you to do the same," she pleaded. "Besides, Edwin left the manor some days ago, so you need have no fears for your safety. I believe those men frightened him away."

"Thank goodness for that." Cecily climbed to her feet, and stretched out her hand to help Janna up. "I must get back," she said. She hesitated, looking suddenly awkward. "Janna, I hate to see you looking as you do. Please let me—"

"It's all right, truly. I don't mind." Janna brushed dust and grass seeds from her breeches. "You go on ahead. You shouldn't be seen with me." Her eyes twinkled, her cares momentarily forgotten. "It might cause talk." Cecily gave her a reluctant smile. "Go on." Janna gave her a gentle push. "I'll follow you."

Chapter 10

A mournful tolling said that Hamo still wasn't found as the villeins returned to the manor, the women and children parting from their menfolk at the gate to make their way home to their own cots. Janna could see the leaping flames of smoking torches. The men had returned only to fetch them so they might continue the search. She could hear Serlo's voice bellowing out above the confusion, and she lingered a little longer, watching as the lighted flares streamed out and disappeared beyond the manor walls. She noticed that the forester had joined the search, and shrank back into the shadows. She must make sure to keep out of his way if he was still around in the morning.

The bell continued to toll, calling out to the lost boy, summoning him home. A wave of desolation swept over Janna. She was sure that if Hamo was lost, or had met with some misadventure, he would have been found by now, either dead or alive. Someone must have taken him, and hidden him away. Could that mean he might still be alive? Janna tried to take comfort from the thought, yet she could not get Hugh out of her mind; he was the only man who had reason to wish Hamo harm. A further thought troubled her: Hugh had gone to fetch Dame Alice. His absence meant there was no-one here to take care of Hamo while he was held captive. So was the boy dead after all?

No! Janna knew she must not give in to despair. She would not. But something else had occurred to her: it might be nothing, but it might mean everything. Cecily had said that Hamo was playing ball against the manor wall while she'd visited the kitchen to talk to the cook about his meals. Why? What had prompted the discussion? And where was Hamo's ball?

Janna went in search of her once more, and found her about to climb the stairs up to the hall. She'd plucked an armful of flowers from the garden, perhaps to cheer herself up. Janna was about to question her, when a sudden roar silenced them both.

"John!" Before Janna could move, could run, Serlo was upon her. He grabbed her smock in one big hand, and began shaking her as a dog would a rat.

"Stop it! Stop that!" Cecily said sharply, and bent to calm Bones, who'd begun to bark hysterically.

Serlo gave her a startled glance. "He is a thief, just as his brother is a thief!" He gave Janna another hard shake. Janna jerked her chin at Cecily, trying to tell her to go away and leave them, but Cecily stayed.

"What evidence do you have for such an accusation, Master Serlo?" she asked calmly.

"A length of fine woolen cloth is missing from a storage chest in the undercroft." Serlo kept tight hold of Janna. "Two silver goblets are also missing." He thrust his face into Janna's, scowling ferociously. "Where are they?"

Janna's first reaction was overwhelming relief. The posy of rue must have been to mark a theft, not the taking of Hamo. In spite of her situation, she felt almost light-hearted.

"I know nothing of those articles," she said steadily, pitching her voice louder to be heard above the noise Bones was making.

The dog had retreated a slight distance from Serlo, keeping a wary eye on the reeve as he snarled and barked.

"I have no possessions for you to search," Janna continued, "but I warrant that no matter where you look, you will find nothing to link either me or Edwin to the missing objects." The storage chests had been locked, she remembered. Whoever had the key must therefore be responsible for the thefts. She opened her mouth to voice her thoughts, and quickly closed it again. It would only increase Serlo's suspicions if she confirmed she'd already investigated the chests.

"What about your thieving brother?" Serlo gave her another shake. "You had until nightfall to find him—and the young lord. Where are they?"

"I don't know where they are, Master Serlo. I wish I did."

"There, Master Serlo," Cecily said. "You have your answer. She knows nothing."

Janna groaned inwardly. Had Serlo noticed Cecily's slip? If so, he gave no sign of it. "You will stay here under lock and key until your brother returns," he said sternly.

And if he doesn't return? Janna dared not ask the question.

"Master Serlo, may I suggest you consult my lord Hugh before locking up this—this youth," Cecily said quickly, trying to make up for her mistake.

The reeve frowned, seemingly puzzled by her intervention. "With respect, my lady, this matter does not concern either my lord Hugh or you," he said coldly.

Cecily looked at him with dislike. "Nevertheless, I will put this matter before my lord as soon as he returns," she said firmly.

Janna's mouth twitched in a smile. It would seem that Cecily had some iron in her spirit in spite of her fragile appearance. Her smile vanished as she heard Serlo's reply.

"And I will keep John safe under lock and key until that time."

Despite Cecily's continued protests, he dragged Janna across the yard and pushed her into the barn. His shove sent her flying into the darkness. She fell against a pile of hay, feeling the hard ground graze her knees through the fabric of her breeches. She heard the snick of the latch as it came down to hold the door fast, and then a frantic howling. Bones was shut outside, and not happy.

"You'll be sorry for this!" Cecily's threat came loud and clear through the wattle-and-daub walls of the barn, and so did her next words: "Come on, Bones, you come with me."

The sounds of whining faded into the distance. Janna kept silent. She didn't know if Serlo was still outside, but she knew that calling out wouldn't change his mind. She would not demean herself further in his eyes.

It was pitch black inside the barn. Janna couldn't see at all. She scrambled to her feet and stretched out her hands, planning to explore her prison. But the barn was crammed full of hay and she quickly found there was nowhere to go. She sat down to consider her situation. While she hoped that Hugh wouldn't believe her capable of theft, it was perfectly possible that he might lay the blame on Edwin. Thanks to the travelers, Hugh now knew Edwin's circumstances, while Janna was the only one who could speak for him and try to clear his name. In all conscience she wondered if she could or should, when Edwin had been so quick to help himself to Janna's own possessions.

A hot wave of shame flooded Janna's cheeks. She was ready to believe the worst about Hugh's intentions toward his young cousin, while expecting him to believe the best about her. But whatever he thought, she knew she couldn't count on him to interfere with Serlo's decision to imprison her, so it was really up to her to help herself.

Meanwhile there was Hamo to consider. As she was not going anywhere soon, she might instead ponder where the child might be held prisoner, if prisoner he was. But try as she would, she could think of no place that hadn't already been searched. Her thoughts took a different tack. Was she making too much of Hugh's relationship to Hamo? Did the theft prove that no-one wished Hamo any harm? She'd already discounted the notion that the child had merely run off in search of his dog and become lost. But could he have become trapped somewhere; or fallen to his death, or drowned in the river and been washed beyond the boundaries of the search? Or was he lying somewhere, bound and gagged—or even worse, already dead?

She shook her head, trying to dismiss her fear. She needed a cool and logical mind for this. Worry over Hamo was taking her nowhere. Once again, she was haunted by the thought that she'd seen or heard something that might shed some light on the child's disappearance. She sat quietly, trying to free her mind of worry so that memory might take its place. The knot of anxiety tightened in her stomach. She was trapped and, if Serlo kept his word, she would face the forester, and mayhap even the shire reeve, in the morning. Face them alone, without Edwin.

Suddenly angry, she punched her fist into the hay. It wasn't fair that he'd run off without a word, leaving her to face this mess on her own. Where could he be? Once he'd recognized Master Siward, would he have hurried off to Winchestre on his own, not knowing that the travelers themselves planned to go there? It seemed unlikely. Edwin knew she wanted to go to Winchestre. He would have told her his plans; he would have taken her with him because his own safe passage lay with her and with their story.

Was he lying low then, waiting for Master Siward and his servant to leave so that he could safely show his face again? But where could he be? Back in the forest, with all this search for Hamo going on? It seemed unlikely. Where else could he have gone, and why had he not got word to her to help him, for he must surely need food and drink after all this time? Who else could he trust if not his traveling companion?

A name came into Janna's mind, and she frowned and sat straighter as she recalled Edwin's earlier disappearances. She hugged her knees to her chest and rested her forehead against them as she began to sift the arguments both for and against the only other person to whom Edwin might turn for help, and trust with his safety. She found that she could think of no arguments against, while everything confirmed her new suspicion.

She jumped up, anxious now for action. She had to get out of the barn and find Edwin. Her eyes had become accustomed to the darkness. A thin sliver of twilight filtered between the overhanging thatched roof and the top of the sturdy wooden walls, helping to faintly illuminate the contents of the barn. She peered at the hay piled behind her and then, with quickening interest, at the solid shapes of farming implements stacked beside the stout door that was now so firmly locked. She hurried to inspect them, hoping to find a sturdy axe to hack her way through, but there were only some curved sickles, which were the wrong shape for an attack on something as solid as the door. She turned next to a wooden plow with its iron cutting parts. She felt the coulter and share carefully, but they were fixed firmly into place and no good for her purpose anyway.

She looked to see what else might be helpful, and saw several flails for threshing wheat once the harvest was in. Janna picked up the long shaft of a jointed flail, and jiggled it experimentally. Yes, it might work. It was certainly worth a try. If Serlo meant to keep her locked up, he should have given more thought to his choice of prison. And he should not have underestimated her need to escape! She tucked the flail under her arm and began to climb the pile of hay, sneezing ferociously as dust swirled and eddied around her.

Her foot slipped; she grabbed a handful of hay to save herself. It came away in her grasp and she fell, landing awkwardly. She whimpered with pain but stood up to try again. Although hampered by the flail, she clambered up, but slipped once more just as she'd almost reached the top of the stack, and her breath jolted from her body as she crashed to the ground. For a third time she tried, and again after that, for she was determined now that Serlo would not find her still trapped here in the morning.

Scratched and panting with effort, she at last managed to reach the thin crack of light that marked the division between the wall and the thatched roof. Janna knew she had to hurry for, once it was dark, the women and children would retire to bed rather than waste a precious rush light, even if their menfolk continued the search. Before that happened, there was someone she needed to see, and much for her to do.

She pulled the flail from under her arm, and thrust the long handle into the thin crack between wall and thatch. Using all her force, she began to push against reeds and straw, levering the stick up and down so that they began to loosen. She sneezed and sneezed again as dust, spiders and earwigs sprinkled down onto her hair and shoulders, but she kept working until she had dislodged enough thatch to form a small hole. A quick slide down the hay to the farming implements, and this time she climbed with a sickle in her hand, hooking it through the hay to give her extra purchase on her way up again.

The small curved blade cut away the loose reeds one by one until there was a hole large enough to wriggle through. Wasting no time, Janna dived halfway through it and peered down. Plunging to the ground head-first would only achieve a broken neck, she realized. She wriggled backward until her feet rested once more on the piled-up hay, and turned around.

This time, taking her weight on her arms and stomach, she thrust her feet first into the hole she'd made. She eased herself through, pushing until she could hold on no longer. She stifled a cry as her ankle twisted painfully beneath the weight of her body when she hit the ground.

At least she was free. Janna stood up carefully, and took a cautious step. She sucked in a breath at the sharp pain in her ankle, and quickly shifted her weight onto her other foot. What she needed was a stout stick to lean on. She peered anxiously into the dusky darkness, half expecting Serlo to pounce on her once more. But everyone who was not out on the search had gone indoors for supper and to bed. Keeping to the shadows, Janna hobbled to the carpenter's cottage as fast as her sore ankle would carry her.

She knocked on the door. It was opened by Bertha herself. Janna watched her closely, looking for any signs she might have missed when she'd questioned her once before. "I give you good night, mistress," she said in a friendly fashion.

"God be with you." Bertha looked out past Janna's shoulder, scanning the track that gave access to the villeins' cots. "What are you doing here?" she asked, bringing her attention back to Janna.

"I'm looking for Edwin."

"Why should you think I know where he is?" A scowl masked Bertha's pleasant features.

Janna wondered if she was going to have the door slammed shut in her face. She quickly leaned against it to prevent the possibility.

"Several reasons," she said cheerfully. "I always thought Edwin was shy with girls. I also know he kept away from them because, with no home and no prospects, he has nothing to offer a wife. He told me so himself. But now I'm not so sure." She peered at Bertha in the pale light of the rising moon. "You're in love with him, aren't you?"

"Why should you think so?" Bertha cast a quick glance over her shoulder, perhaps to check on her family's whereabouts. She stepped outside the cottage, forcing Janna to move away from the door.

"Because you came over and sat with Edwin and me instead of with your own family at medale." Janna noticed Bertha hadn't denied the claim. It gave her the confidence to continue. "Because someone tidied Edwin up, and cut his hair far more neatly than he could have done himself. Because he knew that your sister wanted to dance with me, which meant that he must have met your family at some time. Because he wasn't around when the haystack was fired and the rest of us were trying to put out the blaze. Was he off somewhere dallying with you, mistress?"

Bertha's lips clamped firmly together. Janna waited for her denial, but it still didn't come. "Also," she continued, wondering if she was being rash, building too much into Bertha's parting remark after Janna had asked her to cut her own hair, "you know who—or what—I really am. Edwin would not have told you that unless he trusted you."

Silence greeted Janna's remarks.

"If it's any help, I think Edwin cares for you too, mistress," Janna said, remembering how angry Edwin had been when she'd passed on the cook's gossip concerning Bertha. She'd misread the situation at the time, thinking he was upset about Gytha. But she was quite sure now that she was on the right track. "You were carrying a small sack when I asked you to cut my hair. That was food for Edwin, wasn't it? You're hiding him somewhere."

Still Bertha remained silent. Janna began to lose patience. "You can trust me," she snapped. "Edwin does. We're in this together, you know."

Bertha blinked. She opened her mouth to speak, and closed it again.

Janna decided to help her out. "Do you know that Edwin and I are being blamed for the theft of some woolen cloth and two silver goblets? Have you seen any such things, mistress?"

"No." Bertha licked dry lips. "No, of course not!"

"Then it would be good if Edwin came out of hiding to prove his innocence. As it is, I've been locked up in a barn for the theft and Serlo has threatened to report both of us to the forester and the shire reeve. I managed to escape, but the hunt will be on for me and Edwin in the morning," Janna explained, as she noted Bertha's bewildered expression. "Mistress, if you know where Edwin is, and if you value his good name, I beg you to take me to him now."

Still Bertha hesitated. Janna itched to give her a push, just to get her moving. She restrained herself with difficulty.

"Did Edwin tell you about the visitors to the manor?" she asked instead, wondering just how far he had taken the carpenter's daughter into his confidence. She was fearful that she might be jeopardizing his safety with her question, but she also needed something to convince Bertha to help her.

Finally, Bertha slowly nodded.

Janna decided to put her mind at rest, hoping that it would help her cause. "It is true that the travelers look for Edwin, but that is not their main purpose for being here. They are on their way to trade goods at the fair in Winchestre, and have only delayed their visit while their horse is lame. They are also helping in the search for Hamo." The thought diverted Janna for a moment. "You don't know where Hamo is, do you?"

"No." The answer came bold and clear.

"No? Well, I am sorry for that. But we can both reassure Edwin concerning the travelers, for they have asked the lord Hugh about him, but he has kept our secret."

Now Bertha looked thoroughly alarmed. Janna smiled grimly to herself. "Edwin is safe, but I beg you to tell me where he is, both for my sake and for his."

Reluctantly, Bertha stepped aside and beckoned Janna to enter.

"He's here?"

Bertha nodded. She put a finger to her lips, warning Janna to silence, then led her through the carpenter's workshop and into the room beyond. While Janna greeted Bertha's surprised mother and sisters, Bertha picked up a bucket of slops containing vegetable peelings and assorted greens, and a small sack of grain. Beckoning Janna to follow her, she walked on through to a pen adjoining their cottage. In it were a pig and three small piglets, two goats and several hens. They crowded around Bertha as she walked in, clamoring to be fed, but she pushed past them and on to a small thatched cover at the back of the pen. A pile of wood was set under the thatch out of the weather. Janna's confusion grew.

"Edwin?" Bertha called softly. He peered around the wood pile with a cheerful grin, which quickly turned to a frown of concern when he noticed that Bertha had company.

"Have you been here all the time?" Janna asked, astonished.

"No," Bertha answered for him. "He told me he was leaving the manor, and he showed me where he'd be—up a tree in the forest. You were right, John—Janna. I brought food to him there. But when Hamo went missing, I knew Edwin was in danger of being found and so I fetched him as soon as it grew dark."

"I watched you all go out to search for the boy," Edwin chimed in. "I wanted to help look for him too, but I dared not come out of hiding, for the travelers were part of the search party. You know who they are? You know why I had to run?"

"Yes, I know," Janna reassured him. "I just wish you'd told me your plans."

Edwin gave a regretful shrug. "There was no time. But what about the boy? Hamo? Is he still not found?"

"No." The bell began to ring out its lonely message once more, confirming that the search continued. Edwin's words had reassured Janna that he really knew nothing about Hamo's disappearance, but that still left the problem of the missing length of woolen cloth and the silver goblets.

"Some things have been stolen from the storage chests in the undercroft," she said. "What do you know about them, Edwin? And don't lie to me, either. You stole my purse from me, I haven't forgotten that." A shocked gasp, quickly suppressed, told Janna that Edwin hadn't been entirely truthful with Bertha after all.

"I don't know nothing about stealing goods from the undercroft," Edwin blustered, angry that Janna had shown him in a bad light. "What's missing? And why should you think I had anything to do with it? I haven't been at the manor for days. I've been up a tree instead!"

"Shh, keep your voices down," Bertha warned. "I'll leave you two to argue while I feed the animals."

Watching Bertha empty the bucket of greens and slops, and throw grain to the hens, hearing the clucking, grunting and bleating as the animals fought one another to get to the food first, reminded Janna of her own chores when she'd lived with her mother. She felt a sharp pang of sadness. Their lives had been hard, she'd known discontent, but otherwise she'd been happy enough. But she'd lost her childhood the day her mother died and she'd come face to face with evil. She would never be the same again.

Janna shook off her dark thoughts. While Bertha squatted to milk the goats, Janna began to tell Edwin what had been happening in his absence. Bertha joined in, ranging herself on Edwin's side until Janna was convinced that they knew nothing about either the stolen property or the missing Hamo.

They continued then to confer in low voices, with Janna trying to persuade Edwin to show himself while he and Bertha fiercely resisted all her arguments.

"You've turned me into a fugitive!" Janna said hotly, when she saw he would not be persuaded.

"You were a fugitive when I met you," Edwin reminded her. It was true. But that didn't help Janna now.

"I'm supposed to be locked up in the barn, and I'm certainly not going back there! But I can't leave the manor either, not while Hamo is still missing. What am I to do?"

"You can stay here with me," Edwin offered. Janna investigated the small space between the fence of woven wattle and the woodpile. It was barely large enough to hide Edwin.

"I suppose you could stay here," Bertha said reluctantly. "The animals are my responsibility. No-one else comes out here but me. And my father, when he needs more wood, but Edwin knows to stay hidden unless he hears my voice."

"No, I thank you. I'll find somewhere else to hide." Janna scowled in concentration. Where could she go, and what could she do to help find Hamo? "I wish I knew for certain whether he was lost or taken!" she burst out.

"Taken? Who?" Bertha turned to Janna in confusion.

"Hamo." She was silent a moment, wondering if she could take Bertha into her confidence. Yes, she decided. She'd worried her head until it was sore: maybe three heads would be better than one at working out this puzzle. Besides, Bertha had lived here all her life; she might well know something from the past to help make sense of the present.

"I wish I knew whether Hamo's disappearance was connected in any way with all the other so-called accidents that have happened here," she said carefully, and went on to remind them of each incident and told them how a sprig of rue had been left to mark each scene. Talking about it helped to get the sequence of events clear in her mind, she found.

"I thought Hamo's disappearance was yet another 'accident' when I found the posy of rue beside the door of the undercroft," she continued, "but when Serlo accused me—us—of stealing the woolen cloth and goblets, I thought I must be mistaken, and that the rue was left to mark their loss instead. Now, I'm not so sure."

"Why? What have the accidents and Hamo going missing got to do with each other?" Bertha asked.

"I wish I knew," Janna said again. "It's just that after I found the rue, I decided to search the undercroft myself to see if it meant anything. Serlo claims that the missing articles came from some storage chests, but I know they were all locked when I tried them." She frowned, worried that she already knew the answer to the question she was about to ask. "Whoever took those things must have had a key to open the chests," she said. "So who would have a key?"

"The lord Hugh. Master Serlo. Mistress Tova, and maybe Gytha?" Bertha offered. She laughed, and shook her head. "But that's silly. Why would any one of them wish to cause harm to the manor—or to Hamo? Unless—" She stopped abruptly.

"Unless?" Janna prompted, dreading to have her suspicions confirmed by the carpenter's daughter.

"Gytha's mother wants her to marry the reeve. Serlo has a good position and is held in great respect. He owns his cottage and the gore acres around it and, whatever happens to the lord Hugh once Hamo inherits this property, you can be sure that Master Serlo will keep his position here. But Gytha is determined that she'll wed my lord and no other."

Janna nodded. This she already knew. She waited for Bertha to explain herself further.

"I'm wondering if Gytha knows something about Hamo's disappearance? It's terrible even to think it, but if aught happens to Hamo then the lord Hugh will inherit all Dame Alice's fortune, including this manor. That would please

Gytha greatly. Hamo is the greatest barrier to her becoming the lord's wife and the lady of his manor."

"Gytha?" Janna hadn't considered the young beauty before. She wondered if there could be any truth in Bertha's words.

"Gytha must surely know that if the lord Hugh inherits nothing when Hamo comes of age, he will need to marry someone with a fortune. He certainly won't look at her," Bertha continued. "Has anyone asked Gytha what she knows about Hamo's disappearance? She could even be the cause of it!"

"It's possible, I suppose," Janna said dubiously. Did Gytha have the courage or the guile to carry out such a dreadful mission? It seemed unlikely. It seemed even more unlikely that she was involved in any of the incidents that had gone before. While she would have had the time and the opportunity to carry them out, she had no reason and nothing to gain from it.

"Of course," Bertha continued, "the lord himself has good reason to want young Hamo out of his way. The boy would have followed him willingly; he would not have had to use force."

"Mayhap he and Gytha concocted this plan together?" Edwin sounded doubtful.

"No!" Janna's cry of denial was instinctive. Bertha put a finger to her lips. "I hope you are wrong," Janna said again, more quietly. "But I shall keep a close watch on the lord once he returns, although I shall need to stay in hiding." She turned to Bertha. "Can you watch Gytha? Someone needs to bring food to Hamo, if he still lives. If Gytha knows where he is, sooner or later she'll lead you to him."

Bertha nodded, looking self-important and proud.

"I should go," Janna said, and scrambled to her feet. Bertha stood up to accompany her.

Edwin gave Janna an apologetic smile. "I'm sorry you have to face this alone," he said. "But I'll come out of hiding just as soon as those travelers leave the manor, I promise you."

"And then?" Janna queried. "Will you come on to Winchestre with me?"

Edwin and Bertha exchanged glances. She spoke up for both of them. "It is our wish to be wed, if my lord Hugh permits it," she said. "I have asked my father to take Edwin on as an apprentice and he has already agreed. Edwin's life lies here now, with me."

Janna nodded in understanding. "Good luck to you then," she said, "and I wish you both great happiness." She gave Edwin a farewell salute, and followed Bertha out through the cottage, taking time to give her younger sister an awkward wave as she passed by.

Her first need was to find shelter. Heaving a sigh of resignation, Janna walked to the forest, all the while keeping a lookout for telltale flickers of light from the searchers, and listening anxiously for sounds of the hunt. She'd sworn never to pass another night up a tree again, and so she looked around for somewhere else she might shelter—and thought of the shed where she and Edwin had hidden once before. She hurried to it, sure that she'd be safe there for the night, for it must already have been searched by others as well as by herself. She debated gathering leaves and straw to make a softer bed, but decided against it. Even if she cleaned out the shed in the morning, she was bound to leave signs of occupation behind, signs that could be misinterpreted. Instead, she cleared the sheep's dried dung from a small patch of hard flinty ground, and lay down.

She was exhausted, but her thoughts churned endlessly, keeping her fretful and awake. Hamo. He must be feeling so frightened, and so alone. And Hugh! Her suspicions seemed impossible when she recalled his kindness, his gentle touch as he comforted her after her mother's death. His kiss...Her body ached and burned with memories of Hugh.

At some time during the night she heard the sound of voices and leaped up, trying to judge whether she was safe, whether she had time to run. She opened the door a crack and peered out across the water meadows. The weary villeins were returning home, their torches burned as low as their spirits, judging by the snatches of conversation that came her way through the still night air. Hamo was not found then. The hunt would start again at dawn. She dozed, woke up, and dozed again until a gradual lightening to the east told her that the sun would soon rise, and the searchers with it.

She scrambled to her feet and rolled her shoulders to ease their stiffness, then rubbed her arms to generate a little warmth. She was cold and hungry. She could almost smell the fresh bread baking in the kitchen, the rich scent of pig roasting on a spit, and was tempted to sneak back to the manor and ask Mistress Tova for something to break her fast. Instead, she slipped into the forest to find something to eat. Some mushrooms, hastily collected and eaten raw, helped ease the hollow emptiness in her stomach, while a few early raspberries added a touch of sweetness. The golden aura of the sun peeping above the horizon spoke of a fine day. Her spirits rose with the hope that Hamo was still alive and that he'd soon be found.

Hugh—or Gytha? Janna was certain the answer lay with the one who stood to gain the most from Hamo's death. She resolved to stay hidden until Hugh's return, after which she would become his shadow. If Hamo was still alive, if Hugh was his captor, the lord's first call would be to check on the boy, and when he did so, she would be there to witness it. She took some comfort from the thought that if she was wrong, Bertha would be watching Gytha, ready to pounce if necessary.

Janna walked back into the forest, needing to find shelter from Serlo's watchful eye. She chose an old beech tree close to the path where she'd be able to watch everyone coming and going, and climbed high into its dense, leafy crown.

Serlo was the first to come out of the manor, leading a group of villeins. Judging by their yawns and dragging steps, they had been woken early and given little time to fill their bellies before commencing their search. Janna kept a careful eye on them as they crossed the river and came on into the forest. She froze into stillness as they passed close to her hiding place, hardly daring even to blink in case someone caught a flicker of movement. As they disappeared along the path, she wondered if they were searching for her as well as Hamo. If Serlo had bothered to send some bread and ale to the barn, or even taken the victuals to her himself, he would know by now that she was gone. Everyone would have been warned to keep a lookout for her, and for Edwin.

The sun rose higher, warming the chill from the air and brightening the sky with its rosy rays. Janna's eyes felt heavy with sleep after her wakeful night. She lay along the length of a branch to rest, and felt her eyes close in the drowsy summer heat. A swarm of gnats found her. She flapped an irritable hand at them but they continued to bite and tease her until she found herself thoroughly wide awake again. She listened for sounds of the search but heard only the discordant clanging of the bell. After tolling for a time, it lapsed into silence.

To keep herself awake, she cast her mind back to what Eadgyth had told her about beeches. The tree had many healing properties, but of more importance to Janna right now was something else Eadgyth had said. "*The beech protects lost travelers. The old ones especially revered it because they believed the ancient gods wrote upon its bark and so the tree received their knowledge and wisdom. Even today, if you write a wish on a beech tree, it will be granted.*" After a moment's reflection, Janna pulled out her knife and laboriously began to inscribe her father's name on the smooth gray bark: J O H N. "Please let me find him," she whispered, as she cut into the hard wood.

The long morning wore on, and Janna was almost asleep again when the thudding of a horse's hooves jerked her upright. Hugh! She peered through the leaves to make sure, and recognized the green cloak coming toward her. He was riding the reddish brown steed he'd been on before, and he was moving fast. There was no time to lose if she wanted to keep him in sight. She slithered down through the lofty branches, grabbing hasty handholds along the way, until she missed her footing and fell. She crashed down into thick leaf litter below the beech, almost in the path of the speeding horse. Startled by her sudden appearance, it reared and whinnied in fright. Its hooves lashed out and pounded the air. Hugh clung tight to the reins. As he fought to stay in the saddle, he began to gentle the horse into stillness with his voice.

"Whoa there, easy up. Easy now." He kept on talking until at last his mount stood calm. Then he looked at Janna, and frowned with displeasure. "What on earth do you think you're doing?" he asked. "You could have killed us both!"

"I-I'm sorry, sire." Janna jumped up and bent her knees in a hasty curtsy, tried to correct it to a bob, remembered that Hugh knew she wasn't a boy, got her feet tangled up, and fell over. Scarlet faced, she scrambled up again, cursing her clumsiness and the ill-luck that had precipitated her descent right into his path. She had planned to follow behind Hugh without being seen; she hadn't expected to confront him like this.

"Why were you hiding up a tree?"

From the determined set of Hugh's jaw, Janna knew he would not leave without an explanation. She struggled to find something convincing to tell him, but nothing came into her mind. Eventually, she decided to stick to a version of the truth.

"I'm hiding from Master Serlo," she explained.

Hugh was still gentling and patting his horse. As the bell tolled out once more, his frown deepened. "There is no sign of Hamo, then?"

"No, sire." Janna shook her head, almost convinced that Hugh's concern sounded genuine. "The search has gone on through most of the night, but he has still not been found."

Hugh's lips tightened. There was a look of real distress in his eyes. "I must find Serlo," he told Janna. "But before I do, tell me why you are hiding from him."

"Master Serlo believes that Edwin and I stole some goods from a storage chest in the undercroft, but I swear to you, sire, that we did not."

"If Master Serlo accuses you of theft, I am sure it is for a good reason. No!" Hugh held up a hand to stay Janna's outraged retort. "I hold you in good faith, Johanna, and so I am sure he is mistaken in his belief. But what about Edwin? Your *brother*?" There was a wealth of sarcasm in the word.

Janna sighed. His question was fair, but she was unsure how to answer. "I have spoken to Edwin and I swear he knows nothing of it either." Janna hesitated, but decided to continue with the truth, partly because Hugh already knew it. "He has gone into hiding, sire, because he recognized the travelers who are staying at the manor. They come from his lord's own manor near Tantone, and Edwin was afraid they would return him there if he was seen. He's trying to stay hidden for a year and a day so that his lord can no longer lay claim to him."

"That's what I suspected." Hugh dismounted then, but kept tight hold of the horse's reins. "And is there any good reason why I should not hand Edwin over to Master Siward so that his lord can make his own decision about him?"

"His lord is a violent man, sire. Cruel and vengeful. Edwin told me he was beaten regularly, and I have seen proof of it in the scars on his back—and on his face. The other villeins were also beaten. Even the lord's own family were victims of his rage."

Hugh nodded thoughtfully. "That accords with what Master Siward hinted at, but you haven't told me everything, Johanna.

Or has Edwin not disclosed that when he ran away, he took his lord's favorite steed with him?"

"Yes, Edwin told me what he was accused of, but no, sire, he did not take the steed. He denied knowing anything about its theft, and I believe him. But he knew no-one else would, and so he ran away." Janna hesitated. "Certes, there was no sign of any horse when I encountered him in the forest, sire."

"Hmph." Hugh was silent for a few moments. "And what is Edwin to you, that you defend him so vigorously, Johanna?" There was a slight edge to his voice.

Janna smiled, rather flattered by Hugh's interest. Should she tell him he had nothing to fear, that Edwin was already in love with Bertha? A quick check with the reality of her situation wiped the smile from her face. She must never forget, for one moment, the reason behind her interest in Hugh. "Edwin was hiding in the forest, just as I was, sire." Better not mention her stolen purse. "We decided it would be safer for both of us if we traveled together, and that's why we made up the story about being part-Welsh and everything." She faced Hugh, willing him to believe her, to believe them both.

"You seem to tell lies so readily, Johanna, that I wonder how far I can trust you now?" Hugh's eyes rested on her with a steady gaze. She blushed under his scrutiny.

Whatever Hugh found on his inspection seemed to satisfy some of his doubts, however. "Very well," he said curtly. "I shall speak to Serlo. I shall make sure he knows you are innocent and must be left free. But for all your faith in Edwin, I wish to speak to him myself. And trust me, I will find out the truth." He hoisted himself back into the saddle. "Bring him to me tonight, Johanna, in secret, if you wish. There is no need for the travelers to see him. But you must make him come or I shall believe the worst of him and then not only the travelers but the whole shire will be looking for him. Tell him that he will be caught, he will be tried in my manorial court and, if necessary, I shall have him hanged."

Janna gulped, knowing from Hugh's tone that he meant every word of his threat. "There's something else you should know, sire," she said, in a small voice.

"What?"

"Master Serlo locked me up in a barn, but I...I managed to escape."

"And how did you manage that?" In spite of Hugh's grave expression, Janna thought she detected the hint of a reluctant smile quirking his mouth.

"I cut through the thatch at the top of a wall. There's a bit of a hole there now."

Hugh clicked his tongue in disapproval. "I've underestimated you in the past, Johanna," he said, "but believe me, I won't make the same mistake again. And I'll make sure that Serlo doesn't either." He dug his heels into the horse's flank and it took off across the water meadows. Janna watched the horse and its rider ford the river and fly on toward the manor house. She had no chance of keeping up with Hugh, but for all that, she must follow after him in case he led her to Hamo. The idea that he might have had a hand in his cousin's disappearance disgusted and repelled her. She so desperately wanted to trust him, yet she could not get past the thought that, with Hamo out of the way, Hugh would be Dame Alice's sole heir. He would be free to marry anyone then—including the luscious Gytha!

Janna grimaced at the thought. Her mood, as she followed him across the water meadows, was not improved by the memory of Hugh's last command. How was she going to persuade Edwin to come out of hiding and face him? He would think she had betrayed him, and in truth, Janna felt as though she had, although Hugh had given her no choice in the matter. With a heavy heart, she wondered what she could say that might make Edwin trust Hugh, and change his mind about staying hidden.

Trust Hugh? She almost laughed at the bitter irony of it. It seemed disaster awaited them, whichever way she looked.

She was nearing the manor house when she heard the sound of hoofbeats. She craned over her shoulder to see who was coming, and her heart began a painful thumping when she recognized Godric. She had not known that he could ride. She waited, hardly daring to hope. He noticed her as he rode closer, and his face set cold and hard. A wave of desolation washed over Janna—she was still not forgiven.

She looked beyond, to the party riding behind him and caught her breath in a gasp of dismay. In front were Robert of Babestoche, with Dame Alice beside him. The dame had a kerchief to her eyes; they were scrubbed red and raw from crying. At once Janna looked down to hide her face and stepped quickly off the path, hoping to escape their notice. But her heart went out to the mother of the missing child, knowing how frightened she must feel, and how bitter her grief would be if her only son had come to harm. Silently, desperately, she prayed that Hamo would be found alive. She also prayed that Godric would not blurt out her secret.

To her relief, and also to her shame, Godric ignored her. He rode past, escorting Dame Alice, Robert, their small entourage of servants and the laden sumpter horses to the manor. None of them spared a second glance at Janna, but she was shaking with fright as she stared after them. Robert of Babestoche here at the manor! She could hardly believe that the man who had wished her dead, who had incited the villagers against her and stopped at nothing to bring his wish to fruition, was now within reach. She groaned aloud as she recalled all those who could bear witness against her, if they had the mind to do so.

Cecily would hold her tongue, she was sure of that, but would Godric? Or Hugh? Or even Hamo, if he was found? She was in greater danger than ever before, and must hurry to those who might, albeit unwittingly, spell her doom with a careless word. She must warn them, for her sake, to be silent. And she would start with Hugh, who didn't understand why he must not speak her name aloud to his aunt. She would start with Hugh, in the hope that he would also lead her to Hamo.

Chapter 11

The groom was leading away the mounts ridden by Godric and his party, but there was no sign of them, or of Hugh, when Janna finally came to the manor gate. Trying to stay invisible, she sidled across the yard and up the stairs to the hall. Greatly daring, she pushed the door open a crack and peeped through.

Alarm took her breath away. Hugh was in there already, along with his guests. Cecily was also in attendance, red-eyed and ashamed. Only Gytha seemed to be enjoying herself as she plied them all with refreshments. Janna scowled at the young woman before turning to Cecily. How could she catch the tiring woman's eye, and ask her to pass on the warning to Hugh not to divulge her identity to his family? Impatient and perturbed, she jiggled and bobbed about in an effort to attract Cecily's attention. At last Cecily looked her way. Her eyes widened in surprise. Janna beckoned to her, then stepped hastily back out of sight.

"Janna! What are you doing here? How did you persuade Serlo to let you go free?"

"Never mind that now. You have to warn the lord Hugh not to tell Dame Alice or Lord Robert that I've survived the fire."

Cecily frowned. "But what reason should I give him?"

Janna was silenced by the question. Cecily's secret couldn't be told, but without that truth and what had led from it, there was no reason for her to be in hiding. "I've already told him that there are some who wish me harm, and sworn him to keep my secret," she said at last. "Will you remind him of his promise, and in particular ask him not to reveal the truth to any in his family? You can say I'm too ashamed to face them, if you wish."

"Very well." Cecily gave a reluctant nod. To Janna's relief, she set off at once and, without ado, bobbed a curtsy to the dame and drew Hugh aside. Janna shut the door and escaped down the stairs and into the yard.

Bertha ran over to her. "You shouldn't be here, Janna," she said breathlessly. "Serlo's told everyone you're a thief on the run. And Edwin too. People are out looking for both of you now, as well as Hamo." In her agitation, she'd grasped hold of Janna's sleeve. Her face was tight with distress.

"Don't fret, mistress. And don't make a scene and attract attention our way." Janna gently disengaged Bertha's fingers. "I've spoken to the lord Hugh. He knows I am innocent, and he also knows all about Edwin, but he wants to talk to him. He's told me to bring Edwin to him tonight, in secret if necessary. So if Edwin wants to stay here at the manor, you'll have to persuade him to come out of hiding. Do you understand?"

To Janna's relief, Bertha nodded. It was one hurdle out of the way. "Have you been watching Gytha? What have you seen?"

Bertha drew a quivering breath. Janna knew her fear and distress were on Edwin's account, not her own. She waited for Bertha to compose herself.

"Gytha spent part of the morning out with a search party. She stayed with them all the time and only came back to the manor when she saw the lord return. She's upstairs with him now." Bertha's eyes brightened with sudden amusement, her good humor almost restored as she continued, "I was following Gytha as you told me, and I heard my lord tell her to make herself useful for once, and fetch some refreshment for his family. I must say he didn't sound very loving, or even very friendly."

Janna smiled to herself as she absorbed Bertha's inform-ation. "You've done well," she said slowly. "Will you keep on watching?" She was fairly sure Bertha was wasting her time, but it was best to keep the young woman's suspicions centered around Gytha rather than Hugh. And it was always possible she'd misjudged Gytha, underestimated her pride and her ambition. The thought of Gytha's guilt was some consol-ation to Janna, even if she couldn't quite believe in it.

Bertha nodded, and walked back to keep watch on the stairs leading up to the hall. She flicked a hand in farewell, and Janna returned the gesture. She wondered what she should do while Hugh was engaged with his guests. Every instinct prompted her to join in the search for Hamo, but she was sure there was no point to it, for if the child was going to be found, he would have been found already. Rather than rush around pointlessly, Janna decided instead to follow the leads she'd come up with, in the hope that Hamo's whereabouts might become clear to her.

She could start by looking for Hamo's ball just in case its location could tell her anything. Although wondering if she was wasting time, she began a careful search of the yard. The ball could still be in Hamo's possession, she reasoned, or have been picked up by one of the young searchers she'd previously encountered. It was a prize worth having, being made of leather stuffed with dried beans, rather than the straw-filled pig's bladder that was the usual plaything of urchins. Without much hope, she poked and pried about bush and barn, and came at last to the reluctant conclusion that it was nowhere to be found. But there was still one place left for her to search, which might also help solve the mystery of the disappearing dog.

She hurried across to the kitchen garden, and peered behind the barrel where she'd found Bones hiding. She chided herself for being fanciful as her keen eyes scoured the area and found nothing. Disconsolate, she looked around the neat garden with its rows of herbs and vegetables, an abundance of food which brought juices seeping into her mouth when she remembered the few mushrooms and berries that had broken her fast. She approached a large bush of rue, and stopped to search for signs of footprints or anything else that might tell her who'd been picking posies from it. A round shape within the foliage caught her eye, and she plunged her hand into the bush to investigate. "Yes!" She seized Hamo's prized treasure with a shout of triumph. As she held the ball aloft, her spirits plummeted for it was clear now, beyond any doubt, that Hamo's disappearance was linked to what had gone before. This was a deliberate act by someone who wished him harm.

Hugh, she thought, with an ache of sadness that wrenched her heart. She resolved anew to stick by him, tight as resin to a tree. Sooner or later, he must lead her to his cousin. She left the kitchen garden and positioned herself at the side of the barn where she could see but not be seen. There was nothing for it now but to watch and wait until Hugh emerged from the hall.

Her feet were aching and her spirit weary when Hugh finally clattered down the stairs. He was accompanied by Godric. They stood together, conferring, while Janna fumed impatiently. She desperately wanted to tell Godric what was on her mind, and enlist his help in trying to track Hamo, but she could not while Hugh was present. Of course it was quite possible, she conceded as she watched them part, that Godric would not speak to her. She could waste time following him instead of going after her prime suspect. What, then, should she do?

Caution won. As she followed Hugh, she suspected Godric might have caught sight of her. If he thought she was hoping to rival Gytha for Hugh's attention, it would turn him even further against her. She longed to speak to him, to try to explain all that had happened in the past, but she could not. Not when Hugh might be on his way to check up on Hamo even now. So she skulked about watching Hugh, ducking for cover behind walls and trees every time he stopped for any reason.

He seemed in no hurry to join the search for Hamo, going first to the kitchen where he spent some time. When he came out, he was followed by Serlo. They spoke a few moments longer, and then Serlo strode off, while Hugh went into the kitchen garden. Janna sidled after him, and watched as he pulled an apple from the tree. The apples were still not quite ripe and she suspected he was about to give himself a bellyache, but he made no attempt to eat it, walking instead toward the stable. Janna felt a sudden leap of hope. Could Hamo be hidden somewhere inside? She broke cover to creep after Hugh, and took shelter in a stall while she waited for her eyes to become accustomed to the dim light.

"Johanna. Why are you following me about the manor?" Hugh's voice sounded weary and impatient.

Heat flamed Janna's cheeks as she hastily dropped Hamo's ball and stumbled reluctantly from her hiding place. "I—I—" She could think of no excuse that might explain her actions.

He stroked the horse's nose while he waited. The silence between them lengthened to snapping point. It was Hugh who gave in first.

"Was there something you wanted to say to me?"

Yes! But Janna was afraid to ask the questions that tumbled through her mind, for Hugh would realize that she suspected him of abducting Hamo. "I-I just wanted to see how Arrow's hoof was healing," she muttered.

At once, Hugh lifted the horse's hoof so that she could inspect it, gentling the horse all the while. Watching him, Janna found it impossible to believe him responsible for deliberately injuring the animal, or for carrying out any of the other acts that had plagued the manor. He loved Arrow—just as Janna was sure he loved his cousin Hamo, as well as the manor that had been entrusted to his care. Janna knew Hugh to be kind, and she had thought that he was honorable. Gytha might not be quite so honorable, but Janna doubted she had either the resourcefulness or the will to snatch Hamo or bring about the "accidents" that had gone before. And would she have the wit, or the knowledge, to think of leaving posies of rue to mark what she was doing?

But if not Hugh, or Gytha, then who? Once again, something niggled at the back of her mind. Something she'd overlooked, or something someone had said; something that might shed new light on the people who lived and worked here? What could it be?

Rue for repentance, rue for regret. But Eadgyth had said it could also be used to curse an enemy. As she tended the horse, Janna put aside her preconceptions and, instead, focused on the "accidents" and their outcomes. The significance of everything that had happened began to shift and change, forming a different pattern altogether. And with the new pattern came an unexpected name.

Perplexed, wishing she had time to make some sense of her thoughts, Janna began to bind up Arrow's hoof once more. "The wound is healing well, my lord," she said, "but you should not ride Arrow for a while yet."

Hugh nodded. He produced the apple and held it out to Arrow. "Don't forget, I want to see Edwin tonight," he said, over the sound of the horse's happy crunching. "I've told Master Serlo that you are not to be locked up again, but I want some answers from you both. Too many accidents have been happening lately, seemingly without any explanation. I'm told everything was going smoothly until you and Edwin arrived at the manor."

"We arrived at the manor before you did, sire. There were no accidents until you came home from Babestoche Manor."

Janna knew she was taking a risk, but perhaps it might provoke Hugh to deal honestly if he thought others suspected that he was behind the incidents. And if he was innocent, as she was beginning to suspect he might be, then the more he could tell her, the closer they might come to understanding the reason for Hamo's disappearance. Feeling a little fearful, she finished rebinding Arrow's hoof while she waited for Hugh's reaction.

He went very still. "What do you mean by that?"

Janna stood her ground, not allowing herself to be intimidated by him. "I mean nothing by it, sire," she said, in as respectful a tone as she could muster. "You and Master Serlo seem to hold Edwin and me responsible for the troubles here. I'm only pointing out a fact in our defense."

"Hmm." Hugh inspected her closely. Janna flushed more deeply under his scrutiny, all too conscious of the rough smock and breeches that she wore. Automatically, her hand went to her hair, to smooth and tidy it. It was a shock to feel only short wisps once more.

Hugh lifted a sardonic eyebrow. "Do you know anything about these accidents, Johanna, anything at all?" he asked in a more conciliatory tone.

Janna hesitated, then made up her mind. If she was going to defend herself and Edwin, and test him at the same time, she might as well do it properly, she thought. "I know that a posy of rue has been left at the site of every mishap."

"Rue?" She could have sworn his surprise was genuine, along with his question: "What do you mean, rue? That's a herb, isn't it?"

"I mean that a posy of rue was left at the henhouse at the time the fox got in, and another was found beside the lamb that was slaughtered. I found a posy of rue near the byre after the animals escaped and destroyed the new wheat, and there was also a posy attached to the haystack next to the one that was fired. I found rue at the stable door on the day Arrow's shoe worked loose and the nail went into his hoof and—and I saw a posy of rue at the door of the undercroft, from where the woolen cloth and silver goblets were stolen."

"And where are they now, these posies of rue?" Hugh sounded thoroughly bewildered.

"I-I was afraid that Edwin and I would be blamed for all that was going wrong, and so I destroyed them," Janna confessed.

"You've told me lies in the past, Johanna. Why should I believe you now?"

And why should I believe you know nothing about what I'm telling you, Janna thought in turn. "Because it's the truth, sire," she said instead. "I told lies in the past because I had to protect myself, but I have no need to tell lies about what's been happening here. Neither does Edwin. He *likes* it here, he wants to stay, he's told me so himself. Why should he try to destroy something when it is the means to his escape from his lord as well as providing his future livelihood?"

Hugh nodded thoughtfully. "And Hamo?" he said carefully, going to the heart of the matter. "Is his disappearance part of this same puzzle?"

Janna looked at him. Was he testing her, seeing how much she knew, or suspected, or did he really want to know? His face was gaunt, lined with worry and fatigue. She was almost sure his concern was genuine. "A posy of rue was left outside the undercroft where he was playing with his ball," she said carefully.

"And goods have been stolen from the undercroft," Hugh rejoined swiftly.

Janna nodded. "And by someone who has a key to the chests, for they were all locked, sire."

"And how do you know that?"

"I searched the undercroft when I found the posy of rue, just in case Hamo was hidden there."

"Was he?" Hugh seized her arm. He sounded truly fearful as he begged, "For God's sake, tell me if you know where he is, Johanna!"

"I do not know, sire. I wish I did." Baffled, Janna shook her head as the last of her carefully constructed suspicions fell apart in the face of Hugh's anguish.

Hugh let go of her arm and began to curse under his breath. Then he turned to Janna. "I must go out and search for the boy. You have given relief to my aunt in the past, Johanna. Will you see her again? Perhaps mix up some posset to ease her mind, for she is in great distress."

"I can't!"

"Why not?" Now Hugh sounded cold and hard as he continued: "I will pay you for your ministrations, if that is what is on your mind?"

"No! No, sire, it isn't that at all!"

"Then why will you not go to my aunt? Cecily said you felt too shamed to face her, but I'm sure you can make my aunt understand, and I know she'll be discreet if you tell her of your belief that people wish you harm."

"But that's the problem, sire. I fear everyone." Janna stopped to consider what she should say next. Hugh had already commented on his aunt's marriage. Would he be sympathetic if she told him something of what she knew about Robert?

"I especially fear the lord Robert," she said carefully. Hugh frowned. Janna knew she had come too far to back out now. She must go on, although she would not tell him everything. She wouldn't betray Cecily. "I asked you once before to keep my identity a secret," she said. "It was because I feared him. I believe it was he who incited the villagers to set fire to my cottage, even though they knew that I was inside. In fact, I suspect that was part of the plan, for Lord Robert wanted me either dead or run away. I want him to think he has succeeded in this. Indeed, my safety depends on it."

"Why should Robert want your death? What do you know about him?" It was a fair question, but Janna was not prepared to answer, at least not without Cecily's permission. She stayed silent while Hugh waited. At last, when he saw she would say nothing more, he heaved a sigh and said softly, "My aunt married unwisely when she chose Robert but, by calling in the priest to marry them at the church door, she now has the sanction of the church on her marriage and therefore cannot undo the union, no matter how much she might have come to regret it. That is why she summoned me for the birth of her baby, and that is why I stayed on at the manor afterward. She suspects that Robert has turned his affection elsewhere. How am I doing so far, Johanna? Do you know what I'm talking about?"

His question caught Janna by surprise. She gave a reluctant nod.

"And I suspect you know a lot more than you're telling me?" Hugh waited for Janna's reply, but she stayed silent. Although her mother had died because Robert tried to silence Cecily, Janna couldn't accuse the lord of anything without proof. The fact that he'd tried to silence Janna with the willing aid of the villagers, and failed, meant that he would try again if he realized his secret hadn't died with her.

"Perhaps you're not prepared to betray any confidences?" Hugh ventured. Janna nodded again, relieved that he seemed to understand her position. "Then tell me!" He grasped her once more by the arm, and thrust his face close to hers. "Does any of this have anything to do with Hamo's disappearance now?"

"No. At least, I don't think so." Janna looked up at Hugh, conscious of how closely they stood together. She could see the stubble of his beard, and smell the sweat on him after his hard ride through the forest. She closed her eyes, feeling suddenly faint with longing.

"Johanna." His voice was gentle. "I keep saying that I won't underestimate you, and then I go and do it all over again." He gave a rueful laugh. "But you still haven't told me why you've been following me about the manor, when you could have come straight to the stable if you really wanted to check up on Arrow."

His question brought Janna back to the reality of her position. She blinked, and stepped hastily away from him. How far could she trust him with the truth? "I'm looking for Hamo, my lord. I wondered if you…" She could not go on.

"If I…know where he is? If I can lead you to him? Is that it? Do you think I have him hidden somewhere?" There was a hard edge of anger behind the question. Janna tilted her chin, assuming a bravery she did not feel. Hugh gave a short, hard laugh. "I can assure you I don't know where Hamo is, and I'm every bit as concerned for his safety as you are. If you have any thoughts about where he might have strayed, or what might have happened to him, please tell me so that we don't waste any more time."

"I don't think he has strayed, sire. I believe he's been taken on purpose, and that was why the rue was left in the undercroft. I believe the thefts came after."

"Hamo's been taken? But why? And by whom?" Hugh looked stunned as the full import of Janna's words struck home.

Was her new understanding of the situation correct? A name was on the tip of Janna's tongue, but she found she could not utter it. Not yet, not without further thought. Not without proof. "I don't know, sire," she said instead.

"But you thought I was responsible?" Hugh nodded before Janna could answer the question. "Yes, I can see why you might think it in my interest to have Hamo out of the way, although I am sorry you should think so ill of me." He grasped Janna's shoulders and held her tight. "You must believe me, I know nothing of any of this," he said earnestly. "But by God, you can be sure I'll get to the bottom of it. No-one will be safe from my questions, no-one." He let her go and took a step back. "Not even Edwin," he added. "Go and fetch him now. I will question him along with everyone else." And before Janna could protest, he strode out of the stable.

Chapter 12

Janna picked up Hamo's ball and followed Hugh. All her fine theories about his guilt had been blown away, and she was more than glad of it, for she'd thought of someone else to take his place. She still needed to piece together what she'd seen and heard, to see if they added up, but she thought she'd discovered a possible motive behind the incidents. Even Hamo's disappearance was beginning to make sense.

She must start by asking questions, and finding proof. Fetching Edwin would have to wait for she had far more urgent things to do than go looking for him. As a first step, she went in search of Cecily. She didn't have to look far. The young woman was moping about the kitchen garden once more. Bones was with her, still tied with the old piece of rope. Even as Janna watched, the dog lifted a leg and sent a liberal spray over a patch of parsley. Janna hoped that the cook was as punctilious as her own mother had been when it came to washing herbs before using them.

"Cecily," she called, to prevent her from hurrying away now that her charge had done its duty. She tucked Hamo's ball behind her back as she approached. Bones barked and wagged his tail, and she bent to give him a pat, pleased that he stood four-square on his paws, apparently without too much discomfort.

Cecily gave her a woebegone smile. "I'm glad Serlo has seen sense and that you are free, Janna."

Janna grinned in return. "The lord Hugh has had a word with him, and knows about the missing goods. He knows I am not to blame, and he has spoken to Serlo about it." Surprised, the tiring woman opened her mouth to question Janna further. "Will you tell me again about the last time you saw Hamo?" Janna hurried on, unwilling to waste time on less important matters.

Cecily's eyes filled with tears. "I left him over there." She flung out her hand toward the staircase which led up to the hall.

"And he was playing with his ball?" Janna confirmed. Cecily nodded. "This one?" Janna pulled it out from behind her back and showed it to the tiring woman.

Cecily gasped. "Where did you find it?" She took it from Janna and peered at it as if it might reveal the secret of Hamo's whereabouts.

"It was here in the kitchen garden, where I also found the dog. I suspect Bones had been beaten. He seemed really frightened."

"But—who? Why?"

"I'm working on it." Janna took Cecily's hand. "Try not to worry," she said gently. "I think I'm close to finding an answer. If I'm right, none of the blame for Hamo's disappearance will fall on you."

"Do you know where he is? Is he still alive?"

"I hope so." It was as far as Janna was prepared to go right now. She released Cecily's hand, frowning as she noticed a patch of tiny blisters on her own hand. They were itchy and sore. Janna scratched them absent-mindedly as she continued to probe for the truth. "You said you went to speak to the cook about Hamo's meals. What prompted you to do that?"

"I'd been talking to Master Serlo," Cecily answered readily. "I asked his advice about Hamo. I wanted to know how I might keep the boy occupied during his visit here. He is so bright and merry, I knew he would not be content to stay by my side all the time. I thought Master Serlo might arrange for him to go riding, or become more proficient with his swordplay, for I know he loves to pretend to fight just like his cousin Hugh. Serlo gave me a few suggestions, and then advised me to speak to the cook about providing good fresh food for Hamo, including more meat, fish and fowl, for he is growing apace and is always hungry. Was hungry. Oh, Janna. How can he still be alive after all this time?" She began to cry.

"Shh. You mustn't give up hope. Not yet." Janna patted Cecily's shoulder, her mind wholly taken with what she'd just learned. Serlo! No-one had been more assiduous in the search for Hamo than the reeve. And no-one was more proud of the manor farm than the reeve. In Hugh's absence, he had taken charge of it as if it was his own. He had nothing to gain from setting a fox among the hens, or killing a lamb, setting fire to a haystack, destroying the new wheat or laming Hugh's horse. He had nothing to gain but the destruction of Hugh's reputation. But snatching a child...Janna's heart plummeted to her boots. Serlo might have started out with the intention of discrediting Hugh in the eyes of his aunt, hoping that it would further his own interests. But snatching Hamo meant a larger purpose altogether, a purpose Janna was beginning to understand.

If there was anything in Serlo's past to shed light on his actions now, the cook would surely know of it, Janna thought. The woman delighted in finding out what was happening around the manor and passing on the information, the more salacious or derogatory the better. She must be made to talk.

Conscious that precious time was passing, Janna turned to Cecily. "I'm going to make up a posset for Dame Alice, for I believe the lady is in sore distress," she said. "Will you come to the kitchen and fetch it by and by? I beg you, if you value my life, please don't tell my lady, or Robert, who prepared it."

Cecily nodded, and swiped her sleeve across her eyes to dry them. "I have kept your secret, as I vowed I would," she assured Janna.

"But will you also please tell my lord Hugh that I made up the posset as he asked?"

Cecily nodded. "I must go up to my lady." She thrust the end of the rope into Janna's hand. "Please take the dog. It upsets Dame Alice to have it nearby, while my lord Robert gives it a kick every time it comes close to his boots."

Janna could well believe it. The man was a bully, afraid of no-one save his wife. And the thought of anything that might jeopardize his comfortable life, Janna amended. She tugged on the rope to lead Bones to the herbs she wanted to pick for Dame Alice's posset. Wild lettuce and valerian would help to calm and soothe her, banish nightmares and help her to sleep, while motherwort, sweet marjoram or any of several other herbs would build her strength and lift her spirits. She glanced at the dog as she picked the roots, leaves and flowers she needed. He'd been washed, his coat was clean and shining. In fact, the dog was starting to look almost handsome. "Where were you when Hamo was taken?" she asked, sure in her own mind that Bones had been used as bait to trap Hamo, and that the dog had then been dumped, along with Hamo's ball, once the child was safely out of sight. Or dead. She hurriedly pushed the thought away. She could not afford to give in to despair, not while there was the slightest chance that Hamo might still be alive.

"Did you see Hamo?" she asked Bones. "Do you know where he is now?" The dog looked at her with bright, intelligent eyes, and whined softly. Janna gave him a pat and straightened, clutching her handful of plants. She sped to the kitchen, with Bones trotting willingly beside her. He'd obviously decided that the kitchen was his favorite place, and he strained on his lead to get there, setting up a frantic sniffing and barking once inside.

"Get that mongrel out of here," Mistress Tova said savagely, as she swiped a piece of bacon away from the dog's quivering nose. Janna set down the fragrant herbs she carried. She surreptitiously slid her hand over the piece of fat bacon before dragging Bones outside. While he was busy gulping down the titbit, she tied him to a post, leaving him in view of the door so that she could keep watch. She went inside, determined to put the cook's gossip to good use for once.

The cook glanced sideways at Janna. "Master Serlo was in here looking for you—and your brother. You're in a lot of trouble, both of you. He says there are some goods missing from the undercroft."

"My lord Hugh knows that we are both innocent," Janna said quickly.

Mistress Tova gave a suspicious sniff, as if to smell out the truth. "Doesn't do to get on the wrong side of Serlo," she muttered darkly.

It was the opening Janna was waiting for. "Tell me about Master Serlo, mistress," she said. She hooked a pot of water over the fire to boil, and began to prepare and chop the herbs she'd picked. "How is it that he lives in such a substantial house and is allowed to keep all those fields for his own?"

"This manor once belonged to Serlo's family." Unable to resist the chance of a good gossip, the cook came over and settled her bony backside onto a stool. "The land was confiscated by William the Bastard after the great battle at Hastings. The king gave this estate as well as several others to Dame Alice's grandfather, who had fought with him, as a reward for his service. Serlo's family lost their land and their livelihood, and were reduced to the status of villeins on a manor they had owned for centuries before that."

Janna was silent as she absorbed the cook's information. This was the link that completed the puzzle. It was also a familiar story. Many Saxon thegns had been dispossessed of their lands after the Norman invasion. She'd heard that King William had even taken an inventory of everything he'd conquered, right down to the last hide and plow, cow and pig, mill and fishery, and had kept a record in what people sneeringly referred to as "the Domesday Book", for it seemed like a final reckoning of their lives. But the commissioners had many arguments to settle first, so it was said, for the thegns did not give up their land and possessions lightly, while the Norman barons were always greedy to claim more than their entitlement. It had caused great hardship, anger and misery at the time. And now it seemed that the memory of past greatness and great wrongs did not die easily.

"My lady inherited the property through her own family, but Serlo still takes great pride in the estate," Mistress Tova continued, confirming the direction in which Janna's thoughts now lay. "It was to reward him for his good offices that my lord Hugh granted him the right to live in a cottage that had once belonged to his family, and gave him the gore acres as his own, on the understanding that the work was done in Serlo's own time and that it would not take anything away from his attention to the rest of the manor."

She hesitated, torn between loyalty to her daughter and confiding her innermost fears. "In truth, John," she said finally, "I have urged Gytha to encourage Serlo's attention, for I know he is keen—more than keen—to wed her. In faith, the reeve is besotted with her, he is sick with love, but Gytha will have none of him for she means to marry my lord and no other."

Janna nodded. She'd seen how Serlo looked at Gytha, and how disdainfully the young woman treated him in turn.

Serlo must know that he had a rival for her affections, and who that rival was. How he must hate being subservient to Hugh, especially as the whole estate had once belonged to his own family!

"Does the lord encourage your daughter's affection; has he spoken of marriage?" Janna asked, not sure if she really wanted to hear the answer.

Mistress Tova sighed. "He has not," she admitted sadly. "But my lord is lonely, and my daughter is beautiful. While he breathes, there is hope for her." She brightened slightly. "And if Gytha's ambition comes to nothing after all, Serlo will still have her and she must have him. She will see that he has much to offer and that she could do a lot worse than take him for a husband."

Indeed, Serlo had much to offer, Janna thought. No wonder he worked so hard about the manor, if Gytha was his intended prize. If he could take Hugh down at the same time, that would make his prize even sweeter. She recalled her first meeting with Serlo. "See how well my flock is doing," Serlo had boasted to the forester while she and Edwin were in hiding. His words had led Janna to believe that they were taking refuge on Serlo's own property, yet the fields he'd shown the forester belonged to Hugh's aunt.

Janna nodded thoughtfully. Serlo's slip of the tongue should have alerted her to his real purpose right from the start. Having already reclaimed a substantial property for himself, the reeve meant to have it all. By discrediting Hugh, he hoped to drive him off the manor farm and out of Dame Alice's good graces, leaving himself in charge. But he must have known that, even if his plan succeeded, his power would only last until Hamo came of age.

Janna's hand stilled on the knife she was using to cut the herbs. With a cold feeling of dread, she finally acknowledged the unthinkable. Hamo's visit to the manor was unexpected, as was his ducking in the river, but Serlo had wasted no time using those events to his own advantage. Hamo's death would also be attributed to Hugh's carelessness, and with the two of them out of the way, the path would be cleared for Serlo to petition Dame Alice for the right to reclaim what had once belonged to his family. She might well agree, for by then the manor would hold only the worst of memories for her.

Janna felt sick. Her hands began to tremble so badly she set down the knife lest she cut herself. Serlo. He had been left in charge of searching the manor grounds and forest in Hugh's absence. How easy for him to lead the search away from Hamo. How easy for him to ensure that Hamo—or Hamo's body—would never be found. Was Hamo alive, or dead? A hot tide of rage swept over Janna. She clenched her hands. If Hamo was dead, perhaps buried in the forest somewhere, they might search forever and never find him. I can't allow that to happen, Janna vowed. Alive or dead, he *must* be found.

A sudden thought lifted Janna's spirits slightly, and gave her a thread of hope on which to cling. Dame Alice would never relinquish the manor to Serlo while there was the possibility that Hamo might one day be found. Only his dead body would be enough to convince her either to sell or give the manor farm to Serlo—and so far, there was no dead body. Could that mean Hamo was still alive? Could Serlo be waiting for the hunt to be called off before causing the "accident" that would bring about the boy's death?

If that was the truth of it, then Serlo must be keeping Hamo captive somewhere. In his own cottage? It seemed the most likely place, but it was also the most dangerous. Serlo was the villeins' reeve, the first person they would call on if they had a grudge or a grievance to air. And for the same reason he was also the first person Hugh would call on. Anyone entering Serlo's cottage in search of him would find Hamo. It was surely too big a risk, even if Urk's mother had mentioned that Serlo discouraged visitors. But if not the cottage, then where? The fields round about? Janna considered the possibility, but only for a moment. There was no shelter out there to hide a child, not for this length of time. The forest? If Serlo had managed to take Hamo there without being seen, it would make the best hiding place of all, Janna concluded. He could choose a spot, somewhere wild and undisturbed, knowing that the boy would never be found until it was safe to produce his body.

Janna sighed. This was all thought and supposition; she had no proof to accuse Serlo of anything, nor would she unless Hamo could be found to bear witness against him. A sudden pang of doubt shook Janna as she remembered how Serlo had hidden them from the forester. He had given them shelter for he had recognized that they, too, were of Saxon stock, and his instinct had been to protect them from the terrible injustice of the forest law instituted by Norman kings. Even though they'd been expected to work hard in repayment for Serlo's kindness, she and Edwin had been grateful, so grateful. And now here she was, ready to suspect him of the worst deeds imaginable: kidnap and murder.

"Gytha was always proud. Of course she has many talents as well as being beautiful." Mistress Tova was still talking.

"Has Gytha spent any time with the young lord, with Hamo?" Janna interrupted, her certainty in Serlo's guilt suddenly shaken. No matter how unlikely it might be that Gytha was guilty, she couldn't afford a false accusation against someone as powerful as the reeve.

"Goodness me, no. She dislikes the child. Oh!" Mistress Tova put her hand to her mouth, too late to take back the words she obviously wished she'd never said. "I didn't mean it quite like that," she said nervously. "Gytha's very good with children, but she resents the fact that the young lord will inherit this manor when he is of age. Even so, she's very upset by his disappearance. She spends every free moment out searching for him. Poor little lad. He must have run off in a great hurry, for Mistress Cecily left him alone only while she talked to me, and she raised the alarm just as soon as she realized he had run away again."

Janna hastily finished chopping up the herbs and threw them into the simmering water. A growing sense of urgency possessed her. The cook had given her much to think about and she was anxious to get moving. "This is a posset for Dame Alice, to help her rest," she said. "Let it boil for as long as it would take to pluck a fowl, then take it off the fire and let it cool. Mistress Cecily will be along presently to fetch it for my lady."

Not giving the cook any time to argue, she rushed out of the door, pausing only to untie Bones. Delighted, the dog yipped and ran around in circles, almost tripping Janna as she set off across the yard. "Behave yourself!" She nudged Bones out of the way with a not-too-gentle foot, and hurried on. She had to find Hamo—and for that, she had to find Serlo.

Her hand was smarting quite badly now. Janna looked down at the rash, remembering how she'd plunged her hand into the bush of rue to retrieve Hamo's ball. She should have taken more care, wrapped something around her hand to protect it, she thought, recalling that rue was harmless enough except when the sun shone on it and brought oil to the surface of its leaves, the oil that had caused her skin to blister.

The elusive memory flickered once more, and in a moment Janna had it, the last proof she needed of Serlo's guilt. He, too, had once had a rash on his hand, the same rash that came from picking rue. She remembered that she'd offered to make up an ointment for it, hoping to deflect his accusations about the straying cows—and the fox in the hencoop and the slaughter of the lamb. If only she'd thought of this before, so much harm could have been avoided! Now, when it might be too late, she understood the posies of rue and what they signified. Rue to curse Dame Alice, and to mark his revenge against her for taking his land. She would repent that theft, and suffer the consequences.

Janna remembered how quick Serlo had been to correct her when she'd hinted that Hamo might have been taken on purpose; how he'd called Hamo "silly" for wandering away and getting lost again. Janna closed her eyes and groaned aloud at her own stupidity as she realized something else. Serlo had seen her with the posy of rue. No wonder he'd been so quick to act against her. He would have had a key to the chests in the undercroft and could easily have taken the missing goods. Perhaps his aim was to throw Janna off his trail if he suspected that she understood his purpose, but it was more likely that he meant to use the theft of the goods as an excuse to banish her and Edwin from the manor. He had certainly used it to discredit her. He'd made quite sure that, if she voiced her suspicions, she would not be believed.

More convinced than ever, now, of Serlo's guilt, and with a corresponding lightness of heart that Hugh was innocent of every charge, Janna thought of someone else who might help in her quest to find Hamo. Someone she could trust. Someone who was skilled at tracking, and who knew the forest better than anyone else, better even than the forester himself: Godric. If Hamo was hidden or buried somewhere in the forest, Godric would be able to follow the passage of whoever had taken the child.

Hamo must be alive. He *must* be! Her imagination tortured her with images of the boy's bright face, his open, trusting nature. She wondered if he could hear the bell tolling to bring him home. He would not understand what was happening to him, why he was being held captive. He would be so frightened. Janna's hands clenched in impotent rage.

She would have battered the truth out of Serlo with her bare fists if she thought it would help her cause. But punishment could come later, once Hugh found out the full extent of his reeve's treachery. In the meantime, Janna was sure that their best hope of finding Hamo alive rested with Godric.

Taking care to keep out of Serlo's way, for he was everywhere about the manor supervising the search parties, Janna walked quickly to the gate with Bones yapping at her heels. She was about to pass through when Bertha pounced on her once more, and drew her into the shelter of a barn.

"You must be careful, Janna," she said in a low voice. "I heard the lord tell Serlo that you're innocent of all crimes and he's not to lock you up again, but the hunt is still on for Edwin. Serlo means to have you followed in the hope you'll betray Edwin's hiding place. Promise me you won't go anywhere near him."

"Of course I won't." There was no doubt in Janna's mind now that Serlo meant to make Edwin the scapegoat for all that had happened. She couldn't allow that. "You don't have to watch Gytha anymore," she said. "I know she's innocent, and I also know who's guilty of these crimes, although I have no way of proving it unless I can find Hamo."

"Is Hamo still alive then?" Bertha's eyes shone with hope.

"Pray God that he is, otherwise we are all doomed," Janna said grimly. "You must go to Edwin as soon as you can, when it's safe, and tell him he's not to show himself on any account until we find Hamo."

She walked to the door of the barn and peered out. Serlo was nowhere in sight. "Have you seen Godric anywhere?" she asked.

"I saw a stranger go through the gate a little while ago. He came with my lady's party." Bertha answered. "Well built and with the fair hair of the Saxons. Was that Godric?" Janna nodded. "He walked down to the ford. It looked like he was planning to search in the forest."

"Good. Thank you, Bertha." Pulling Bones behind her, Janna left the barn and hurried off to the river. At the same time, she kept a sharp lookout for Serlo. To her relief, there was no sign of him or of Hugh. As she came to the ford, she caught sight of Godric. He was about to vanish into the thick green barrier beyond that marked the edge of the forest.

"Ho! Godric, wait for me!" she shouted, and put on a burst of speed to catch up with him. He'd paused, so Janna knew that he'd heard her cry out. It was too far for her to see his face, but she could imagine him scowling as he made up his mind whether or not to obey her command.

He stayed where he was, and she was grateful for it. "Godric!" she panted, as soon as she was within earshot. Although he'd waited, he'd turned his back on her and seemed absorbed in studying the myriad hues of green in the foliage ahead.

"What do you want?"

Janna bent over, holding tight to her aching side. "You have to help me," she gasped.

Godric took a step away from her. "I have more important things to do with my time, Janna," he said distantly. "I'm looking for Hamo."

"So am I," Janna said impatiently. She straightened. "I think I know what's happened to him. Please, listen to me." She poured out the whole story then, including her suspicions about Hugh, trusting that once he knew the truth, he would help her. "I know how good you are at following signs," she finished breathlessly. "If Hamo's hidden somewhere in the forest, I know you'll be able to find him, Godric."

He shook his head, looking dubious. "People have been searching through the forest for days, trampling tracks everywhere. How will I know whether I'm on Serlo's trail or someone else's?"

"Oh." Janna's hopes deflated instantly. "I hadn't thought of that." She took some comfort from the fact that at least Godric had listened to her, and that he was taking her opinion seriously. But his objection was sound. "Then we'll have to follow Serlo after all," she declared, adding honestly: "You'll have to follow him, Godric. He's watching out for me, he thinks I'm going to lead him to Edwin—which I'm not. Bertha's gone to warn Edwin. She loves him, and she'll make sure he stays hidden until it's safe for him to come out."

Godric nodded thoughtfully. He seemed a little more friendly as he said, "I doubt Serlo will make any move toward Hamo in the daylight. If he's making a show of searching for him, he'll continue while people are around to watch him. I suspect we'll have to wait until it's dark."

"So you do believe me? You'll help me?" Janna smiled up at him, delighting in the fact that they were friends once more.

He caught his breath, and turned quickly away. "I'll help you," he said gruffly. "But I suggest we also keep looking for Hamo." He hesitated. "It would be easier for Serlo to keep him hidden if he was already dead, you know that, don't you?"

"I refuse to even consider that possibility." Bones had started to bark and Janna cuffed him gently with her foot. "Shh!"

Godric turned on Bones. "We mustn't attract Serlo's attention. Can't you shut him up?"

But Janna was no longer listening. "No-one's searched Serlo's cottage, of course. It's over there." She pointed to show Godric where she meant. "It seems unlikely that he'd risk hiding Hamo there, but we should probably search there if we can."

She became aware that Godric wasn't paying attention, and waved a hand in front of his eyes. "Godric!"

Suddenly, and taking Janna completely by surprise, he pulled her into his arms and kissed her hard.

"Umph—ssfflk." It was too hard to protest with Godric's lips pressed against her own, but Janna did her best.

"Serlo's coming our way," Godric muttered, before kissing her thoroughly once more.

"But he thinks I'm a boy!" Janna protested, when she could speak once more.

"No, he doesn't." Godric kept his arms around Janna, and his mouth close to her ear as he whispered, "Cecily tells me she made a mistake one time, and called you 'she.' He's been asking questions about you ever since, including asking Cecily why she thought you were a girl."

Too alarmed by Godric's observations to think straight, Janna melted into his embrace. They stood locked together in a long and lingering kiss. To Janna's surprise, she found she was rather enjoying herself. "That's enough," she said at last, and pulled out of Godric's embrace.

Godric's eyes were bright and his face was flushed as he looked at her. Janna's own heart was thumping like the mill race. She found it hard to meet his gaze. "We've done enough kissing to convince the reeve."

Godric shook his head. "He's still coming toward us," he whispered. "But he might think twice about having you followed if he believes your affection lies with me and not with Edwin."

"Is that what you also believed?"

Godric smiled. "Not anymore," he whispered, and swept her into his arms again.

"You! John—or whatever your real name is. I want a word with you!" Reluctantly, Janna freed herself from Godric's embrace and braced herself to face Serlo. He came striding up to them with a thunderous expression. In spite of her resolve, Janna found herself shrinking back against Godric, badly needing his support. Bones pressed himself close to Janna and continued to bark.

"If it were left to me, you'd be gone from this manor by now, and with a beating to send you on your way, you and your so-called brother!" Serlo stood over Janna, glowering at her. Godric placed an arm around Janna's shoulders, and scowled right back at the reeve.

"You may have the ear of the lord Hugh, but I know how many lies you've told," Serlo blustered. "Unless you tell me where your brother is hiding, I'll make sure my lord finds out the truth about you, about who and what you really are."

Several comments came to Janna's mind, not least the fact that while Hugh already knew the truth about her, he certainly didn't know the truth about his reeve. But she held her tongue, knowing that she must not, under any circumstances, put Serlo on his guard.

"Where is your brother?" Serlo thrust his face close to hers, and Janna took an involuntary step backward.

"She doesn't know where he is." Godric pulled Janna into the crook of his arm and held her tight.

"This is no time for courting," Serlo growled. "You get back to wherever you came from, and leave the girl to me."

"I'm staying right here to help look for the young lord."

Serlo glared at them both. "Very well, then. I believe the boy may have tried to find his way home to his own manor but strayed off the track and is lost somewhere in the forest," he snapped. "You two can go and look for him."

It was too good an opportunity to miss, and Janna moved off with alacrity, tugging the furiously barking Bones behind her. But the reeve's next words stopped her dead.

"And get rid of the dog. If Hamo calls out, I want to be able to hear him." Noticing Janna's surprise, the reeve continued, "I'm coming with you. And so are they." He raised a hand and beckoned several villeins forward.

Were she and Godric being enticed into a trap? If so, there was little they could do about it. She spotted Urk and his mother watching from a distance, and dragged Bones over to them.

"Will you look after Hamo's dog for me please, Gabriel?" she asked, including Mistress Wulfrun in her friendly smile.

"Ooh, yes!" The boy fell to his knees and began to pat Bones with great enthusiasm. The dog wagged its tail, but kept on barking.

"I'm sorry, mistress. I don't know what's got into him," Janna apologized. "Do you think Gabriel could play with him for a bit, and keep him quiet?"

"Gabriel has a way with animals, 'tis true," his fond mother agreed. She nodded. "Go on, then. We'll look after the dog for you."

"Thank you." Janna wasn't sure who would take priority where Mistress Wulfrun was concerned, Urk or the dog, but she knew she could trust the woman to do her best.

Keeping close to Godric, Janna followed the villeins and Serlo into the forest. "I really am sorry about your mother, sorry that I wasn't there to physick her," she apologized, thinking Godric must listen to her now after what had just passed between them. The memory brought a blush to her cheeks, and a quivering to her limbs.

"I'm sorry too," he said soberly. "It's true what I told you before. No matter what some of the villagers might have said to you—and I know Mistress Hilde was one of them—they regret it now, and repent the action they took against you. Especially Mistress Hilde. There is no-one to make up the cream that your mother once provided, and her skin is red raw with scratching."

Janna felt a moment of fierce satisfaction. "She saw us together, and mistook you for her husband. So she killed my cat and tied it to a tree, as a warning to me, she said, not to lie with him again."

"She lives to regret it. She says now that your cat walks with her wherever she goes. She is in mortal fear that it will smother her baby. But no-one else can see the cat; it's just her sick fancy."

"'Tis Hilde's guilt that torments her now, guilt for crucifying my cat!"

Godric's face darkened in remembered anger. "I don't know how you could have held me responsible for that, Janna, not even for a moment. You should know I would never do anything to harm you. Why, I—" He clamped his lips together, and marched on.

"I know that now." Janna hurried after him. "I'm sorry, Godric, truly. I know I should have trusted you. Instead, I haven't been kind, or fair, to you at all. I've misunderstood everything you've done for me, and I regret it with all my heart." She felt the heavy burden on her conscience ease somewhat. She'd thought she'd never see Godric again; it was a huge relief to have the chance to apologize.

"Will you forgive me? Please?" She gave him a tentative smile. When he flashed a reluctant grin in return, her spirits soared. Then she remembered the task that lay before them, and her joy evaporated immediately. At once she looked for Serlo. He was watching them closely, seeming more interested in keeping them in sight than pretending to search for the missing boy.

Fear threaded through Janna and tightened into a knot of anxiety in her stomach. Serlo had already shown himself to be quick and resourceful, and utterly without mercy. Soon enough he would make a move against them. What did he have in mind?

One thought brought Janna a little consolation. While Serlo was watching them, he was unable to act against Hamo. She only hoped that, when the time came, she and Godric would be able to outwit the reeve and find Hamo in time to save the boy's life. If he still lived.

Chapter 13

The bell continued to toll at intervals through the weary day, the sound growing fainter as they moved further away from the manor until, at last, they could no longer hear it. Suspecting they were wasting time, Janna grew increasingly frustrated and impatient, but knew they couldn't start their own search under Serlo's watchful eye. The sun burned fiercely, its heat penetrating even the dim forest, parching her mouth and throat. She wished she'd thought to bring something to drink, and something to eat too.

At Serlo's signal, the villeins came together late in the afternoon to eat their dinner. Janna realized their steps had taken them close to the path again as she watched the villeins settle deep in the shade on either side of it, and unstopper leather bottles of ale to slake their thirst. She swallowed hard, trying to bring some moisture into her mouth. They must be moving back toward the manor; she could hear the faint sounds of the bell tolling mournfully through the silent forest once more.

Serlo turned to Janna and Godric. "You will continue the search. The rest of you can follow this track home after you've eaten your dinner."

"What's he playing at?" Janna whispered. Godric shrugged, and produced his own leather bottle, which he offered to her. She took it gratefully, and swallowed several mouthfuls of ale. It was warm from the heat of the day, and tasted somewhat of leather, but it ran down her dry throat like liquid gold.

"Thank you." She handed back the bottle, and accepted a piece of bread and cheese from Godric. "You're saving my life."

"Again." His smile took the sting from the word. With a weary sigh, Janna sat down, her back propped against a tree. Godric collapsed beside her, and they sipped and chewed together in companionable silence for a time. Looking around, Janna read the despair on everyone's faces. They've given up hope of finding Hamo alive, she thought, and Serlo knows it. Her suspicions were confirmed when Serlo dismissed the rest of the search party.

"You two come with me." He beckoned them up to follow him.

It was the trap Janna had suspected, the trap that could only lead to death. But she was the one Serlo wanted, not Godric. His life would not be in danger if he accompanied the reeve.

"Distract him while I double back to his cottage and look for Hamo," she hissed.

"It's you he's interested in, not me, so he won't go anywhere unless you're there too." Godric grasped her arm and hauled her along with him after the reeve. "If Hamo is hidden somewhere in the forest, you can protect him while I take care of Serlo. We can search the cottage later."

Janna saw the wisdom of Godric's reasoning and stopped resisting him. In single file, they tramped after Serlo, moving from light to deep shadow, and never in a straight line. "Did he do it? Did he do it?" a song thrush called, answering its own question: "Come out! Come out!" There was a rustle and flutter of wings as it flew off.

Serlo stopped for a moment to check on their progress, then began to push his way through the forest once more.

"I wonder where he thinks he's going?" Godric stopped and looked at Janna. Janna wondered if either of them knew, for she herself was lost, and had been lost for most of the day. "We've already been this way once before. He's taking us where we've already searched."

"He obviously doesn't realize you know the forest better than he does!"

Godric shrugged, and set off after Serlo once more, keeping a careful lookout for any signs of Hamo. Janna marveled at how silently he walked.

"Argh!" She gave a muffled scream as a sticky spider web suddenly wrapped around her face. Frantically, she clawed it off, sure that she could feel the tickle of spider legs across her scalp, down her neck, against her skin inside her smock. She beat at herself with both hands, hoping to squash the insect dead. Distracted by the spider, not looking where she was going, her foot sank into a hole, wrenching her ankle. She stifled a cry, but tears came into her eyes with the pain of it. She limped toward Godric, who was waiting for her. Serlo had vanished. "It's as I thought," Godric said, as she came up to him. "Serlo's been leading us around in circles, and now he thinks we're lost. He's done it on purpose."

"What about Hamo? Where is he?"

"Nowhere Serlo's been leading us, that's for sure."

"Could Serlo have hidden him in his cottage after all?"

Godric lifted his shoulders and spread his hands in a helpless gesture.

"We must find Hamo. We *must*!" Janna was frantic. "Let's go back and look, Godric. Quickly, while Serlo is still in the forest." A horrible thought stopped her. "Do you know where we are? Can you find your way out of here?"

To her great relief, Godric nodded. "Let's play Serlo at his own game first and buy us some time. Follow me, Janna, close as you can, and walk quietly."

To Janna's immense surprise Godric cut away at an angle from where they'd come, and silently began to make his way through a grove of trees. At once, she went after him, hoping he knew where he was going. Without warning, he jumped onto a fallen branch. The sudden crack sent her heart leaping in fear. She frowned, bewildered by his antics. "What—?" He pressed his finger against her lips. They waited a few moments. Nothing happened. Janna listened intently, but she couldn't hear anything, nor was there any sign of the reeve. Godric picked up the fallen branch and hit it against a tree. The dull thud echoed through the forest.

"Janna! Over here," he called. "Look what I've found! I doubt Master Serlo will be able to explain this away." Again, he cautioned her to silence. Above their heads, birds began to twitter and sing, serenading the closing of the day. But Janna knew Godric wasn't listening for birds. She strained her ears to hear if his ruse had worked, and became aware of a furtive rustling. Animal or human? Evidently Godric knew the difference for he grabbed her hand and swept her around a patch of holly, then pushed through a thicket of hazel, snapping twigs and swishing branches as he passed. He was making more noise than a charging boar. Putting his finger to his lips once more, he stopped and looked behind, waiting. This time Janna could hear the faint rustle of Serlo's boots on dry leaves. Satisfied that he'd taken the bait, Godric drew Janna off in a different direction, cutting silently through a long stand of tall beeches and oaks then scooting across a patch of open grassland. He gave another raucous call.

"Follow me, Janna! I think I know where to find Serlo." Janna had worked out by now what he was up to, and she grinned up at him. She couldn't see the reeve, but she could hear him. He was still coming their way. Godric set off again, this time moving deep into a grove of yew, an impenetrable maze of knitted branches and leaves. "Call my name," he whispered, and Janna did. The note of desperation in her voice wasn't all pretence. She was terrified, as much for Hamo's sake as their own, by this deadly game of hide and seek in the forest. Serlo knew, now, that they were on to him, and that they would betray him if they could. He couldn't afford to let them leave the forest alive.

"Call again," Godric prompted, and Janna obeyed. She listened, heart thumping and nerves quivering at the thought of what might happen. There was a smothered cough, and a faint rustling that told them Serlo was coming closer.

Godric nodded his head, satisfied. "Come," he whispered. "Quiet as you can." He took her hand and led the way, slipping silently through the dense growth. Once out of the copse, he kept on moving in a straight line through trees and weedy clearings, picking up speed all the way. To Janna's amazement, they emerged from the forest almost directly in line with Serlo's cottage.

"Hurry!" Godric urged, and began to race down to the water meadows. But Janna had noticed the shed where she and Edwin had once sheltered. If it came to defending themselves against the reeve, a weapon would be handy. She hurried inside to retrieve the sword, relieved to find it still in its hiding place. Ignoring the dull ache of her wrenched ankle, she sped after Godric, following him down through the water meadows and across the river. But the door of the reeve's cottage was barred against them.

"The devil take him," Janna cursed, although this confirmed their suspicion that Serlo had something to hide. "Hamo!" she called, and beat on the door with her fist. "Are you in there?"

Silence. Godric peered through a shuttered window, trying to see inside. "Hamo!" he bellowed, not caring now who might see or hear them. "Hamo!" They both stopped and listened.

Nothing moved. There was no sound in answer to their calls. Janna knew a bleak despair. If Hamo was in there, he had been silenced—perhaps permanently. Godric pulled out his hunting knife. Large and very sharp, it was the knife he used for protection when walking through the forest. Not caring about the noise he was making or the damage to Serlo's property, he hacked into a wooden shutter, tearing and splintering it. Wordlessly, Janna handed him the sword. At once he sliced through the shutter, making a large enough space for Janna to crawl through. She put her foot into Godric's cupped hands and launched herself through and into the cottage.

"Hamo!" she yelled, as she hit the ground. She rolled over and sprang to her feet. In spite of the heat, a fire smoldered in the hearth, and Janna waited a moment for her eyes to adjust to the dim light. There was no sign of anyone. She went to the door and unbarred it. She shook her head in answer to Godric's unspoken question, and stepped aside to let him enter. Together they unlatched the remaining shutters to let in the light before beginning a systematic search.

Janna's gaze fell on two wooden trenchers lying on the table, ready for food to be placed on them for the evening meal. Two trenchers? Janna felt a sudden surge of hope. "Hamo?" she yelled. "It's Janna and Godric. There's nothing to be afraid of, we're here to help you." She listened intently, felt her heart double thump as she heard a noise, but then realized it was the faint yapping of a barking dog.

"Hamo's here somewhere, I'm sure of it," she told Godric, "and he's alive! Look!" She pointed at the second trencher.

"So where is Serlo keeping him?" With renewed vigor, they burrowed into unlocked chests and investigated cupboards, and even checked under the covers and frame of a finely carved wooden bed hidden behind soft drapes in a small alcove off the main room. With increasing desperation, they searched even those places too small to hide a little boy, just in case there was some clue to Hamo's whereabouts, anything at all.

The sound of barking grew louder. A dog was coming this way. Bones? There was a furious scratching at the door, accompanied by a series of short, sharp yips. Desperate to stop the noise before it attracted anyone's attention, Janna hurried to open it. Bones shot in. Janna could swear that the dog was surprised to see her. He wagged his tail but kept on moving, sniffing at the ground until he stopped and sat as if keeping guard. The floor of beaten earth was covered with rushes. By the look of them, they'd been down for some time and needed changing. Janna frowned and looked more closely. The rushes near Bones seemed unevenly distributed, as if they'd been recently disturbed. Bones was still barking, but not so ferociously now. He looked up at Janna with bright eyes. Janna thought he was trying to tell her something.

"You were here before, weren't you, Bones?" she said softly. "Where is Hamo? Do you know?" The dog whined, and scratched at the rushes, scattering them. Janna looked at Godric. "I think there's something buried down there." She felt sick as an image of Hamo's small body interred in the earth came into her mind. "Careful!" She flung out a hand as Godric's knife flashed out and he knelt to dig. "You don't know what's down there," she breathed.

Janna knelt beside him and they began to dig into the soft earth with their bare hands. The earth shifted easily, testament to the fact that it was the gateway to something below. With a feeling of dread, Janna plunged her hands deeper into the soil. Her fingers jabbed against something hard. She began to throw handfuls of earth to one side, fearing what she might uncover. A small wooden panel came into view. Janna frowned at it. "Why would anyone want to bury this?" She lifted it, and the answer was instantly revealed in the dark hole beneath.

"It's a trapdoor." Godric crawled forward and peered down the hole. "Hamo?" he called softly.

Janna listened intently. She thought she could hear something, but even as she strained to identify the sound, it ceased. She must have imagined it."I guess this must be a storeroom?" She squashed next to Godric and they both peered down into the darkness.

"I'll go and have a look," he offered.

"No, I'll go." Janna looked about the room for something to light her way. Her eyes widened as she noticed a fat beeswax candle rather than the rush light she would have expected to find. A fine bed. A beeswax candle. Serlo must be saving them to impress Gytha—if only he could lure her to his cottage as he must have lured Hamo.

The thought stiffened her resolution to find the missing child. "Can you light that candle so I can see what's down here?" she asked Godric.

He shook his head. "Let me go. You don't know what you might find."

An image of Hamo's dead body came into Janna's mind. No! She would not, could not think the worst. "Hamo might think you're Serlo," she said, her voice wobbling slightly with the effort to be brave. "He'll be much less frightened if he sees me."

Godric gave a reluctant nod. As he stood up to light the candle from the fire in the hearth, Bones pushed in front of Janna and jumped down the hole. He started barking once more, short furious yips that echoed the urgency they all shared. Wasting no more time, Janna grabbed the candle from Godric, picked up the sword and dropped down after the dog, ducking her head under the low ceiling.

A thin shaft of light shone down through the trapdoor. The rest of the cellar was in darkness. The air was stale and smelt of damp earth. Janna held the candle out so that its light could be shed more widely. A quick glance confirmed the cellar's purpose. It was crammed with barrels and chests and newly combed fleeces, the latter piled high and ready for market. Truly this was a treasure trove, and not all gained by the honest toil of Serlo's hands either—Janna was willing to stake her life on it. How long had he been planning to take over the manor, deceiving Hugh and amassing wealth at his lord's expense so that, when the time was right, he would be in a position to make a worthy offer to the dame for the property?

Banishing Serlo's dishonesty from her thoughts, for there would be time enough for Hugh to take revenge on his trusted reeve, Janna looked about for Bones. She could hear him barking still, but the dog seemed to have disappeared.

"Janna," Godric's anxious voice called out. "Are you all right?"

"Yes, but there's no sign of Hamo. Come down and help me look." Janna dripped a little hot wax onto one of the barrels, and secured the candle to it. With the small light to see by, she and Godric began a thorough search of the cellar. Almost the first things she found were the silver goblets and the length of woolen cloth supposedly stolen from the undercroft. "Look!" She snatched them up with a cry of triumph, pleased that she would be able to prove her innocence beyond question now.

Everything else was sealed tight. From their weight, Janna knew that the chests and barrels were not empty. She also knew that if Hamo was concealed in one of them, he must surely be dead, for there would be no air inside to sustain him. Despairing, she thumped hard on their sides, calling Hamo's name. She didn't think he'd be able to hear her above the cacophony of barking, but even that might comfort

Hamo, if he was alive to hear it. Where was the boy? And where was Bones?

She listened for the direction of the dog's frantic barking, then followed the sound toward a row of barrels shoved against the earthen wall at the far side of the cellar. The barks came from behind them. Janna realized that there was a narrow gap between the barrels and the wall. She hoisted herself half up onto one of them in order to peer over and down into the gap between—and drew in a painful breath, and then another. The dog was wedged there, standing guard over a small, still body.

"Hamo!" Janna's cry echoed through the low chamber as she shoved at the heavy barrel barring her way, leaning all her weight against it so that she could get to the boy. Godric rushed to help her and, as soon as there was enough space, Janna darted in and crouched down. Hamo lay unmoving, but his eyes, wide and staring, gleamed in the faint light from the candle. Janna put her hand on his forehead, dreading to feel the chillness of death against her fingers. But his skin felt warm, although he did not move. "Are you all right?" He did not answer her frantic question. Then she saw why: Hamo's feet and hands were tightly bound, and so was his mouth.

A great fury shook Janna. "He's alive!" she shouted, as she crouched down beside the child and, with shaking hands, unfastened the gag that covered his mouth.

Hamo moistened his lips with his tongue. "Are you Janna?" he whispered.

"Yes, I am." Janna swallowed over a huge lump that had somehow got wedged in her throat. Godric shoved her aside. He whipped out his knife and slashed through Hamo's bonds. Janna reached out to take him in her arms. The child shrank back, moving as far from Janna as he could go. He cowered against a barrel. Bones began to lick Hamo's face. Hamo pushed him away.

Janna knew rage and a grief beyond anything she'd ever experienced. Serlo had done this. He'd destroyed Hamo's open, trusting nature. He had stolen his innocence.

"It's all right, Hamo." Janna kept her hand outstretched, but made no further effort to touch him. "You're safe now. Master Serlo can't harm you anymore."

"We have to get out of here," Godric said urgently.

"Just wait a few moments." Janna inched closer to Hamo, willing him to take her hand.

"I'll go for help." Godric stood up. "I'll let my lord Hugh know that Hamo is safe. I'll tell his mother too. And I'll suggest the lord brings men-at-arms with him when he comes."

"No, don't go." Janna tugged on his tunic to stop him leaving. "If Serlo comes back, we'll need you to defend us. But we can't go just yet. Hamo's too weak and stiff to walk after being tied up for so long. Just give him a little more time to recover."

Godric nodded. He squatted down beside Janna, and gave Hamo an awkward pat on the shoulder. The boy gulped, and pressed himself harder against the barrel. Godric cast a helpless glance at Janna.

"Bones found you," she said, with determined cheerfulness. "Do you know, he kept on barking and barking at Serlo. He knew what the reeve had done. And he came straight here as soon as he managed to escape. He showed us where to dig to find this cellar. He's a smart dog, is Bones."

"Bones was here before." Hamo's voice was so quiet they strained to hear it. "Serlo told me he had Bones. That's why I came away with him, even though Mistress Cecily told me not to go anywhere without her. But Bones was missing and I wanted to find him." His voice hardened as he said angrily, "Serlo kicked Bones, I saw him. He *hurt* Bones."

"I know. I know." Janna felt somewhat reassured by the fire that had come into Hamo's voice when he spoke of his beloved pet; his earlier silence and apathy had frightened her. She felt even more reassured as Hamo flung his arms around Bones. Miraculously, the dog had finally stopped barking.

"Look at all this!" Godric gave a silent whistle as he gestured at the riches that surrounded them. "I'll wager my life that the lord of the manor doesn't know about this secret storeroom!"

Janna nodded in agreement. "Serlo will be hanged for this. The lord Hugh will never forget or forgive what he has done." Her words brought home to her the danger of their position, and she stirred uneasily. Serlo wouldn't go willingly to face his punishment. In fact, he'd stop at nothing to prevent his secret being found out.

"We must go," Godric said again. "The sooner we get Hamo safely to the manor house, the better."

And the safer we'll be too, Janna thought. "Do you think you can walk?" she asked Hamo. He nodded, and climbed stiffly to his feet.

"Ow!" His face crumpled and he began to hop around as he felt the prick and sting of blood flowing freely through his cramped limbs once more.

Godric swung him up and carried him to the trapdoor. "Up you go," he said, and turned to Janna. "Your turn."

A muffled scream rent the air. Heart pounding in fright, Janna snatched up the candle to see what was wrong.

"I have the boy and this time I'll show no mercy." Serlo's face appeared briefly as he bent down to smile at them. "As for my cellar—no-one knows about it so no-one's going to come looking for you here. Its contents will keep...but you won't." His chuckle was cut off by the sound of the solid oak panel thudding into place, sealing them into the earth.

"No! *No!*" Janna screamed the words in defiance, while beside her Bones began to howl. She pushed against the panel, but Serlo held it down. Godric sprang to her aid and, together, they strained to shift it. Scraping sounds above told them that Serlo was pushing something over the trapdoor to secure it. They were trapped, sealed tight into an earthen tomb. Serlo had spoken the truth. No-one knew they were down here, no-one would come looking for them. Soon enough their air would run out. The candle would flicker and die, and so would they.

Janna looked at Godric in despair. "What are we going to do now?" Her voice was almost inaudible against the noise being made by Bones.

But Godric had already seized up the sword. Arm raised above his head, he began to saw at the wooden panel.

"Wait!" Janna stayed his arm as a thought occurred to her. "The trapdoor was in place when we found it, but there was still air enough for Hamo to breathe while he was trapped here. We should look for an air vent somewhere."

Godric thought for a moment. "The air seemed a little fresher where Hamo was lying. We should start by looking there." He laid down the sword and followed Janna. She squeezed into the cramped space behind the barrels, gave the candle to Godric, and began to run her hands over the rough earthen roof. "I can feel a small hole!" She poked an exploratory finger through. "Give me your knife!"

She thrust the blade into the hole and jiggled it around, enlarging the space. "It's blocked at the top," she said finally. "Serlo must have shoved something over here as well to make sure we'll suffocate and die here."

"Then we'll just have to try to saw through the trapdoor," Godric said. "We're not going to give up, not yet, and not without a fight."

He walked back to the trapdoor, and began a determined sawing once more. Using Godric's knife, Janna began to attack the panel from the other side. Silently, desperately, they sawed through the wood, neither of them voicing their fear that their air would run out before they could cut a hole big enough to escape through.

"Help!" she shouted, just in case there was anyone around to hear her. She put her full voice into the cry. "Help! Somebody, please help us!"

Time slowed to a crawl. Terrifying images ran through Janna's mind as she realized that Serlo would have to carry out his threat now that events had forced his hand. It was a miracle the child had survived as long as he had but from now on his life could only be measured in minutes, if he wasn't already dead. She had promised Hamo that he was safe, that Serlo could never harm him again, and she had failed him. The knowledge was shattering; she felt almost paralyzed with grief and fear.

"Hurry!" she begged, although she knew Godric was as frantic as she was to escape. She fancied that the air in the small crammed cellar was already becoming foul with their breath. She could hear Godric panting, or perhaps it was her own gasps for air. She put her hand over her nose and mouth to see if it would help to filter the stink, but instantly felt as if she was suffocating.

She quickly snatched her hand away and took in several deep breaths. It was not enough to satisfy her need. She looked about for Bones. He'd collapsed on the ground nearby. Janna could see the rapid rise and fall of his tiny stomach. Beside her, Godric sawed on with grim determination.

The candle, burnt down to a stub, guttered and died, leaving them in darkness. Somehow, their fate seemed even more horrible now they could no longer see each other. Janna stopped cutting for a moment, and reached out to touch Godric. She needed to connect with someone. She needed to feel that she was not alone. He took her hand, and kissed it, his lips warm and comforting. Neither of them said anything as he released her and began sawing at the wooden slab once more.

They worked on in silence and with growing despair, until there was a crack and part of the wooden lid fell down into the cellar.

"We're through!" Godric shouted. Janna sensed movement beside her as he reached up to feel the opening. Why was no light shining through?

Her question was answered by Godric. "Serlo must have pulled something really heavy over the trapdoor to make sure we can't escape. Help me try to shift it, Janna."

Together they reached up and pushed, trying to slide the blockage aside. But the angle was too awkward, and the object too heavy to budge. They strained until their arms ached, until they had to stop and rest, and acknowledge that whatever was obstructing them had not moved by so much as an inch.

Janna closed her eyes, swept by a wave of fierce anger that this was to be their fate. "Help!" she screamed again. "We're trapped inside Serlo's cottage. Somebody, help us please! For the love of God, save us!"

Chapter 14

"Bones! Bones, where are you?"

The voice sounded muffled, far away. Janna wondered if she was imagining things. She put a hand on Godric's arm. "Shh." She listened intently, sure she'd heard a voice.

"Bones? Where are you?" The voice was louder now.

"Here!" Janna shouted frantically. "We're here under the ground of Serlo's cottage! Bones is here too!"

Silence. Janna wondered if she was hallucinating, conjuring up what wasn't really there. "Did you hear anything, Godric?" she asked at last, reluctant to give up this tiny fragment of hope.

"Something. I don't know. Maybe." He raised his voice. "Help!" he bellowed. "We're trapped in a cellar underneath Serlo's cottage. There's a trapdoor with a chest or something on top of it." He stopped, and they listened intently.

Silence.

Janna heard a faint creaking above her head. Her heart leaped high with elation. "We're down here!" she shouted. "Hurry! Please, please hurry!"

A scraping noise was followed by a sudden waft of smoky air. Janna sucked it gratefully into her lungs. A faint beam of light from the fire slanted down the hatch, the light blocked suddenly as their savior peered down at them with a worried expression. Urk. The boy was as welcome as the angel after whom he was named.

"Gabriel!" She bent to scoop up Bones, and thrust the dog through the hatch into Urk's arms. "Thank God you're here. You're just in time to save us! And Bones too." She turned to Godric. He cupped his hands together and Janna put her foot in the cradle. He heaved her up while, from above, Urk grasped her arms and hauled her through. Then it was Godric's turn. Snatching up the sword, he pushed it through the trapdoor then pulled himself up after it.

"Thank you," he said. "Thank you for saving us."

"I heard you shouting." Urk smiled his big smile at them both, and turned aside to pick up Bones once more. The dog had recovered somewhat, and licked his hand. Godric took only a moment to catch his breath before seizing hold of Urk and Janna and hustling them out of the cottage and into the darkening night.

"Go and fetch my lord Hugh," he told Urk urgently. "Tell him he must come at once. Tell him Serlo has taken Hamo. Tell him to bring men-at-arms to hunt Serlo down."

Urk looked bewildered. He clutched Bones tighter to his chest. "Bones ran away," he said slowly. "I looked all over for him. And then I heard you shouting."

"I'm so glad you did, Gabriel. But now we have to hurry and find Serlo and Hamo. And you must take my message to my lord Hugh. Do you remember what I told you?"

"Go and fetch the lord Hugh," the boy repeated obediently. "Tell him Serlo has taken Hamo. Tell him to come at once. He must bring men-at-arms to hunt Serlo down."

"Good boy." Godric patted his shoulder. "Hurry, it's almost dark. There's no time to lose."

Still the boy hesitated. "Go!" Godric gave him a shove.

"You can take Bones with you. Look after him," said Janna, understanding at last what was delaying their messenger. "And thank you for finding us, Gabriel. You're a hero, just like the lord Hugh."

Urk's face split into a smile. He set off at speed, straight as an arrow toward the manor house. Janna prayed that he would remember their message, and that Hugh would believe the boy. Although impatient to be on the move, she forced herself to stand quietly while she peered across the fields, carefully scanning the landscape in the lambent light of the evening sky. They had no way of knowing where Serlo had taken Hamo, for there was no sign of him now. If he hadn't risked dumping the boy in the forest before, he certainly wouldn't risk going there now, not while bands of villeins might still be roaming about the water meadows in search of Hamo. Where else might he go?

"I can't see them anywhere," Godric muttered, sounding discouraged. "You realize, don't you, Janna, that Serlo can't afford to leave the boy alive, not now. We may already be too late."

"No!" Janna said fiercely. "I'm not giving up, not yet. It's not quite dark. People may still be out searching for Hamo, so Serlo will take him somewhere that's already been searched, and where he knows they won't be seen."

"Like this copse?" Godric flung out a hand to indicate the grove that stood guard over Serlo's cottage.

Janna thought for a moment. She swallowed hard. "Even if Serlo has silenced Hamo forever, I don't think he'd bury him here. It's too close to his cottage. Besides, the villeins might be allowed to forage through here for kindling, while the pigs will soon be let loose to hunt for acorns and beechmast. Serlo would know that the grave would be found sooner or later."

An idea flashed into her mind. "What about the river?" She turned to Godric, her eyes full of hope. "The banks have already been searched thoroughly, but no-one will question another drowning, not when Hamo so nearly drowned that first time. Come on!"

"While we're here, we must search the copse, just in case he's hiding Hamo here until it's properly dark." Godric sheathed his knife and uncoiled his slingshot as he ran toward the bushy cover.

Janna ran after him. "Please, God, let us find Hamo before it's too late." She repeated the prayer under her breath as they hastily inspected the small copse. In spite of their fears, there was no sign of a small body or the reeve among the bracken and weeds that grew rank beneath the trees.

"He's not here." Janna wiped her sweating face on the sleeve of her smock. Godric nodded in agreement. Together, they left the shelter of the grove and hurried down toward the river. It spread before them like a long silver ribbon in the dim evening light. Finally Janna stopped for a moment, and bent over, clutching hold of her aching sides. "He'll probably hide among the trees until it's dark," she gasped. "But where do we start looking?"

While Janna caught her breath, Godric searched the ground for a handful of flints. Finally he straightened and looked toward the river, narrowing his eyes to see more clearly, watching for any movement that might betray the reeve's whereabouts.

"We can't waste any more time," Janna said. "Let's split up. You go downriver and I'll go upstream."

"No." Godric stood his ground. "You can't face Serlo alone. We must stay together. You can hold the sword."

Janna stuck out her jaw, looking stubborn.

"I mean it," Godric warned. "I'm following you, whichever way you choose to go."

Janna clicked her tongue. "Look," she said impatiently. "The closest cover of trees is over there. Maybe that's where he's taken Hamo? He can't risk the boy being seen, not while there are people about." She began to run once more, with Godric keeping a steady pace beside her.

As they came closer, Janna slowed and tried to quieten her panting breaths. Godric crept forward; she followed close behind. It was dark in the thicket of young alders that crowded beside the river bank, and they heard Serlo stumbling through the trees before they could creep close enough to actually see him. Janna felt an unutterable relief when she spied the small boy clasped tight in his arms, being dragged along against his will.

Alive! Hamo was still alive. He was silent, and Janna's fists clenched as she imagined what Serlo must have done to keep him quiet. Truly the reeve would pay dearly for his treatment of the boy.

Godric crept stealthily forward, slingshot at the ready. He was gaining on Serlo, who was encumbered by the struggling child. Janna knew how accurate a shot Godric was, but even so her heart thumped in fear at the thought that he might miss and bring Hamo down instead. She stopped, hardly daring to breathe, frightened that she might make a noise and alert Serlo to their presence.

"Be careful," she whispered, knowing that Serlo wouldn't hesitate to use Hamo as a shield against any attack. She couldn't bear it if, in the end, it was Godric who brought the boy to harm. He was busy fitting a flint into his weapon. Janna prayed that the flint would find its mark in Serlo's back and bring him down.

Godric took another step forward. A twig cracked and snapped. Serlo whirled and saw them. At once, he pulled Hamo close in front of him. Janna saw that he held a knife at the ready. No wonder Hamo had been so silent, she thought, as she understood that they were powerless now to save him. She reached out a hand to Godric, to stop him from doing anything that might jeopardize Hamo's safety. But she was too late. Godric's arm swung around. As Serlo whipped the knife up to the boy's throat, Godric loosed the flint.

Time stood still. Janna stood motionless, listening to the fearful silence. Then, with a grunting sigh, Serlo fell to the ground, taking Hamo with him. Janna forced her legs to move. She ran to Hamo, dreading what she might find: that Serlo had slit the boy's throat and Hamo might be dying or already dead. She became aware that Godric was beside her as she fell to her knees beside the reeve. There was blood everywhere. Neither Hamo nor Serlo was moving. She reached out to Hamo with a trembling hand.

"Ohhh." It was a long, drawn-out sigh of relief as she saw that the blood soaking Hamo's tunic had come from the reeve. The flint had hit Serlo's forehead. It was bleeding profusely, and so was a long cut in his arm where his knife had sliced through his sleeve as he'd fallen.

Ignoring Serlo, Godric snatched Hamo from the reeve's limp hands and carried him to safety, while Janna bent over Serlo to inspect his wounds and determine if he was dead or merely stunned. She wanted the reeve alive to face Hugh, to know public humiliation and disgrace before the hangman put an end to his pathetic, miserable life. As she leaned closer, his hand shot out and grabbed her. She cried out, but it was too late. Serlo had her firmly in his grasp. She lunged sideways for his fallen knife, but he was too fast for her. He snatched it up and staggered to his feet, holding her in front of him as a shield.

"Drop the sword." She felt the prick of his knife against her throat.

Frightened into silence, she obeyed his command. Godric put Hamo down. He rose to his feet, knife in hand, and faced the reeve. Janna stared at him in despair. He could do nothing to save her without risking her life at the same time. The reeve pulled Janna closer. He pressed himself against her; his arms trapped her tight. She couldn't move; there was nothing she could do to free herself. Fighting panic, she waited numbly for death.

"Give me my life, or I'll take hers." Serlo's voice rumbled behind her. Godric nodded acceptance. He dropped his slingshot and slowly sheathed his knife.

"No!" Janna's mind cleared as she remembered how she'd been trapped like this once before. Before Serlo could move, she raised her foot and stamped down with all her strength onto his instep. He stumbled, loosening his hold as he struggled to keep his balance.

Janna wrenched herself free and ran to Godric. With a wide gesture, he swept her out of his way while, with his other hand, he pulled his knife out of its sheath and, in one fluid movement, sent it flying toward Serlo. Silver glinted in the dim light, and Janna heard a thud.

Serlo lay on his back on the ground, with Godric's knife embedded up to its hilt in his chest. "Your life, Serlo, instead of hers." Godric walked to the reeve, gave the knife a twist and pulled it out. Serlo's fingers plucked feebly at the air, then fell nervelessly to his side. He gave a faint groan and his body went limp.

Knowing that the danger was over, Janna rushed to Hamo. He was curled up in a ball. His eyes were wide with terror; his whole body was shaking. Not giving him any chance to retreat this time, she scooped him into her arms and held him close. For one long, agonizing moment, he fought her, but she held on. "Shh," she murmured. "Serlo's dead. You really are safe now."

With a strangled yelp, Hamo burrowed into her and began to cry.

"It's all right, Hamo," she comforted him. "Serlo will never harm you again." She glanced sideways as a faint drumming came to her ears. Horses! She caught a glimpse of torches.

"We're here!" Godric shouted. "We're down by the river!"

The drumming sounded louder. "Is the boy safe?" Janna recognized Hugh's voice, and felt an overwhelming relief.

"Yes!" she shouted. "Your cousin Hugh has come to fetch you," she said to Hamo more quietly. "He'll take you back to the manor, Hamo. Your mother and father are there, waiting for you. They'll be so glad to see you. So glad." A sudden thought brought fear to Janna's heart. "Don't tell them my name," she said urgently. "Please just call me 'John.'"

"John," Hamo echoed. There was a moment's silence, and then came the question: "Where's Bones?"

Janna didn't know whether to laugh or cry. She hugged Hamo tighter. "Bones is safe too," she said. "Urk has him, he's looking after him for you. Urk saved Bones, Hamo, and he also saved us. He let us out of the cellar so we could chase after you and Serlo. You're safe now, Hamo, I promise you. Everything's going to be all right. Everything."

The nightmare was over. The knowledge filled Janna's mind and heart, and left her overflowing with joy and relief.

Chapter 15

The moment of peace and thanksgiving was quickly over as Hugh leaped off his destrier and hurried over to check for himself that Hamo was alive and safe. Not wasting any more time, he pulled Hamo up onto Arrow and galloped back to the manor house with him. Soon enough, a joyful pealing of bells told of their safe return. Meanwhile Hugh's men fashioned a litter and carried Serlo's body home, stashing it in a barn to await burial. He had escaped justice on earth, he'd cheated the gallows, but he would have to account for his actions in the highest court of all. Janna hoped that he would be condemned to hellfire and damnation forever.

Leaving Hamo in the tender care of his mother and father, Hugh summoned Janna and Godric to the solar. They sat in comfort, with a hot bowl of pottage and a meat pie to bring new warmth and life to their tired bodies, and a jug of ale to wash the food down. After Hugh expressed his thanks, as well as the gratitude of Dame Alice, he set to questioning them about the night's events and all that had gone before. Between them, Janna and Godric gave him a full account of all that had led up to this moment. But Hugh had still more questions for them.

"What made you suspect Serlo in the first place?" He looked to Janna to answer his question.

Janna paused mid-chew. "Lots of little things," she said indistinctly, and swallowed her mouthful. "When we first came here, when he saved Edwin and me from the forester, he talked about 'my sheep.'"

"Saved you from the forester?" Hugh quirked an eyebrow.

"It's a long story," Janna said hastily. "I thought, from Master Serlo's words, that the manor belonged to him." She gazed up at Hugh, feeling a tide of color wash over her face and hating herself for it. "I didn't know it belonged to you. I wouldn't have stopped here if I'd known that."

Hugh's eyebrow rose higher.

"I also saw the way Serlo looked at Mistress Gytha, wanting her for his wife, although all she could think about was you."

"Me?" Hugh spluttered. "But Gytha is a child still!"

"She's old enough to wed—and she has a certain amount of ambition in your direction," Janna commented dryly.

Hugh shook his head in wonder. "I had no idea her thoughts lay with me. Although I must confess I...er... noticed lately that she was...er..."

He could hardly have failed to notice what Gytha had been so determined to display. Janna hid a sly smile.

"...but I thought, when the time came, that Gytha might make a match of it with Serlo," Hugh stammered on.

Janna interrupted his musing. "And Serlo was desperate to have her. But he understood her ambition only too well. He knew he had to improve his station if he was to have a chance with her, and it was to be done at your expense."

"Hence the spate of so-called 'accidents?'" Hugh ventured.

Janna nodded. "But it went further than that. He's been stockpiling goods to sell at St Edith's fair at Wiltune, or per-haps even at Winchestre. Mistress Tova told me he takes several cartloads to the fair every year, your produce as well as his own. You'll find a great quantity of chests, barrels and fleeces in his cellar. There's far more than he could have come by through honest toil."

"I certainly knew nothing about them," Hugh said grimly, "but I should have suspected something, and questioned Serlo earlier. Although we've had fair seasons for some time now, the manor farm has not been as productive as I'd expected. I had no idea Serlo was robbing me blind." His expression was thunderous as he contemplated his reeve's dishonesty.

No wonder you were so keen to visit your aunt and make yourself agreeable, Janna thought. She wondered if the dame had questioned Hugh's management, if she'd been having second thoughts about leaving him in charge of what should be a profitable manor.

"It's a hard lesson to learn, but I will be less trusting, and I'll take more of the reeve's duties on my shoulders in the future," Hugh continued.

"The woolen cloth and the silver goblets Serlo accused us of stealing are also down in the cellar," Janna added, anxious to clear both her and Edwin's names. "My guess is that Serlo planned to sell them as well, while using them as a device to rid himself of both of us. I'd become a threat to his safety, you see. He knew that I didn't believe the incidents were accidents; he might have thought I knew the truth even earlier than I did."

"I can see how his mind worked," said Hugh. "With Hamo gone and me discredited, my aunt would have been anxious to cast off this manor with all its unhappy memories and he would have had the means to make her a generous offer."

Janna nodded in agreement. "Serlo couldn't have known that Hamo would visit you, but once Hamo vanished the first time he saw how a second disappearance might work in his favor. I think he snatched Hamo with the intention of drowning him, but he was unable to carry out the deed because Mistress Cecily was so quick to raise the alarm. With so many villeins out searching, he knew he'd be noticed. Instead, he had to keep Hamo alive for a little while longer. My guess is that he planned to take him away in one of the carts with all his goods for sale, and drown him somewhere along the journey, past where anyone might have searched the river for him before. Once Hamo's body was found, he could then approach my lady with his offer."

Hugh's lips tightened. He muttered a savage oath against his once-trusted reeve.

"I'm sorry Serlo is dead and that you cannot bring him to an accounting for his deeds," Godric ventured. "I would not have thrown my knife at him by choice, but I knew that if I let him get away with Janna, he would have killed her rather than let her go free to speak the truth about him. I have never killed a man before, but if I had to, I would make that choice again."

"You made the right decision. I am glad that you were there," Hugh reassured him. "I only wish it had never come to this. If I'd read the signs right from the start, all this might have been avoided." He looked at Janna. "Why did Serlo leave rue at the scenes of his crimes? What was he thinking?"

"I didn't understand, until the cook told me how Serlo's family had once owned this manor. It seems they were forced into servitude after the Conquest. The rue was both his curse and his private message to your family to repent that theft." Janna didn't add that she felt a sneaking sympathy with the reeve's grievance, although she could never condone what he'd done in revenge.

Hugh nodded thoughtfully. "You have all my gratitude for finding Hamo and opening my eyes to Serlo's true nature."

"Don't forget Gabriel—Urk," Janna said. "But for him, we would have died in that cellar. If he hadn't come in search of Bones, and then faithfully conveyed Godric's message to you…" She shuddered, marveling at how narrowly they had all escaped death.

"Urk will be rewarded, as will his family. But for my part, I am indebted to you for rescuing Hamo not once but twice, and bringing him home alive." His warm smile encompassed both Janna and Godric. "Please be assured that you have a home here for as long as you like, and forever if you wish it."

Janna's mouth went dry. She couldn't find the words to answer him. But Godric spoke up. "I thank you, my lord. Indeed I would like to stay here and serve you." He shot a quick glance at Janna, and continued hurriedly, "But I am tied to Dame Alice's manor. I cannot leave without her permission."

"You can leave my aunt to me," Hugh said confidently. "I have lost my most trusted reeve and must replace him. Although the villagers will elect a new man, I'd like to have an honest man by my side, if you'll agree to it, Godric?" A mischievous smile tugged at the corners of his mouth. "I venture to suggest that you would be far more to young Gytha's taste than Master Serlo ever was."

Speechless, Godric and Janna exchanged glances. Godric found his voice first. "I have my own cot and land at Babestoche, sire," he said. "If I came to you—"

"You would not lose by it." Hugh cut him off. "Master Serlo's cottage and lands lie vacant now. They are yours, as my reward to you for saving Hamo's life."

"That…that is very generous of you, my lord." As Godric absorbed the full extent of Hugh's generosity, his face blazed alight with hope. He turned to Janna, but before he could say anything, Hugh addressed her directly.

"And Edwin?" he queried. "What has become of him? Has he had a hand in any of this business with Serlo?"

"No, sire! He planned to stay in hiding until your visitors left the manor and it was safe for him to come out again. But if you wish to speak to him, you'll find him sheltering with Bertha, the carpenter's daughter."

Hugh tilted his head to study Janna. "And will he want to stay here with you, do you think?"

"Not with me, my lord. He wants to stay here with Bertha."

"And so he shall." Hugh's mouth curved into a wide grin. "But what about you, Johanna? How can I reward you for your deeds this day?"

Janna gazed up at him, at a loss for words. A reward? It was something she hadn't looked for, didn't want. Unless Hugh could help her find her father? Could she ask him to do that?

"I must confess, I would like you to stay on at the manor, but in a lady's attire if you please," Hugh continued. "I cannot get used to you in the guise of a man." His gaze narrowed slightly as he looked more closely at Janna's smock and breeches. "Where did you find those clothes you wear?"

Janna was thrown by the unexpected question. She blushed as she wrestled with her conscience. "I–I stole them, sire," she confessed.

"From the barn that burned down so suddenly on my aunt's demesne?"

Janna pondered what to say. It had been an act of defiance, intended to pay back Robert of Babestoche for his evil deeds, and also to hide her theft of the garments. She could explain some of it to Hugh, but would he understand? Worse, would he tell his aunt? If she was charged in a manorial court for her misdeed, the penalty would be heavy indeed.

She was saved from having to answer as the door from Hugh's bedchamber was flung open. Dame Alice bustled into the solar, closely followed by her husband. At the sight of Robert, Janna quickly turned aside. She bowed her head as she hastily rose to make her obeisance.

"Please, sit down and finish your supper." In spite of her red eyes and obvious exhaustion, Dame Alice's face was radiant with relief. She took a handful of silver coins from her purse and set them down on the table in front of Janna and Godric. "This is your reward for bringing my son home safely," she said, her voice trembling with emotion. "But no silver, or words, or anything I can do or say, can ever convey to you my most heartfelt gratitude." She took Janna's and Godric's hands in her own, and held them tight. "Thank you," she said huskily.

"It was a pleasure to serve you, my lady." Godric spoke for both of them, while Janna desperately tried to come up with an excuse to flee the room. Had Hamo spoken her name? Did they already know who she was, or had Hamo remembered to keep her secret?

"I know you, of course, Godric, but I don't know your companion. John, is it?" Unexpectedly, the dame reached out and took Janna's chin, raising her face toward the soft candlelight that bathed the solar. Janna had no choice but to look at her, and also at Robert, who was standing behind his wife.

The dame sucked in her breath in a sudden hiss. "Could it be...?" she asked, in a tone of wonder.

"His name's John," Hugh interrupted, suddenly awake to the danger Janna faced. "And if you've finished your supper, John, you can go now."

But Hugh's words had come too late to save Janna. As she'd looked up, she'd seen recognition flash across Robert's face: a moment of fear, followed by an expression of fierce resolve that told Janna he would not be thwarted; that he would kill her rather than risk his affair with Cecily and his role in her own mother's death being found out. Once more she was in mortal danger.

"Come, John. Come with me." Hugh grasped Janna's arm and marched her out of the solar and into the hall. Godric snatched up the silver coins and followed them.

"I'm so sorry," Hugh said, once they were safely out of hearing. "I didn't tell them you were here. I thought they would stay in my bedchamber with Hamo."

"Lord Robert knows who I am. He recognized me," Janna whispered. She was shaking with fright. She had never before encountered such vicious hatred. Now that Robert knew she was alive, he would have to act to silence her. She was filled with dread.

"They'll be going home soon, and probably taking Hamo with them," Hugh said thoughtfully. "They'll be no danger to you after that, Johanna. In the meantime, Godric and I will keep you safe."

Godric stiffened. "I can look after Janna perfectly well on my own, sire," he muttered.

"But I don't want to be looked after by anyone!" Janna retorted angrily. "How can I live any sort of life if I'm constantly watching over my shoulder in case the lord Robert returns on a visit?"

"You would be safe with me if we were wed," Godric said eagerly. "I have a cottage and land of my own here now. I have more than enough to support a wife."

Hugh's glance swiveled quickly from Janna to Godric. He seemed suddenly unsure of himself.

Janna took a moment to consider. She'd hurt Godric's feelings once before on this matter; she must not do so again. Marrying him would not answer her problem, but how could she explain that to him? How could she explain to both of them the idea that had been forming in her mind ever since Hugh had told her of the abbess's knowledge of her mother, the idea that now seemed absolutely perfect? It would keep her safe from Robert's wrath. It was the answer to everything.

"You asked how you could reward me, my lord," she addressed Hugh. "You can reward me by letting me go." She turned to Godric, and took his hand. "While I live, I am a threat to the lord Robert, and he knows it. I had thought to keep myself safe by pretending my death and changing my identity, but my strategy has come to naught. All that's left for me now is to find refuge, a place of safety where no-one can touch me. And so I have decided to seek shelter at the abbey at Wiltune."

"You're planning to take the veil?" Hugh exclaimed, thunderstruck.

Godric said nothing, but Janna saw his face crumple. He looked absolutely shattered.

"No! No, but I will stay there for a time, and give everyone a chance to forget about me." Janna raised her hand to touch the purse at her waist, felt the outline of the precious parchment, the letter from her father. She needed to talk to the abbess, but she also had another reason for going to the abbey. She smiled at the thought of it. If she was allowed, she would stay there long enough to learn to read and write. If she could only read her father's letter, she was sure it would help her find him; help her solve the secrets of the past. Her heart felt lighter; new courage flowed through her as at last she saw the way ahead.

"I thank you for your offer, my lord, and for yours too, Godric." Impulsively, she reached for his hand and kissed it. "You are very dear to me, but my mind is made up," she told him. "I shall leave tonight."

"No!" Godric exclaimed. "Janna, please—"

"This is something I have to do." Janna looked into his eyes, begging for his understanding.

Godric was silenced. Finally, he spoke. "With your leave, sire, may I escort Janna to Wiltune?"

"Of course." Hugh looked every bit as unhappy as Godric about Janna's sudden decision. "But are you quite sure?"

"Yes, my lord," Janna said. "I am quite, quite sure."

*

The iron gates of the abbey clanged shut behind Janna. She looked at Godric, and a great wave of desolation swept over her.

"Goodbye, Janna," he said quietly. "God go with you."

"And with you, Godric." On impulse, Janna stretched her hand through the gate and drew him closer. She puckered up her lips to blow him a final kiss, then smiled ruefully as she heard the tut-tutting disapproval of the nun waiting behind her to take her to the abbess. She would miss Godric dreadfully; she would miss them all. After living alone with her mother for so long, she'd found a home within the small community of Hugh's manor. It had given her new confidence to know that she was liked and valued there, and that she could make a life for herself even without her mother's guidance. It was hard, now, to walk away from everyone she had come to know. It was especially hard to walk away from Godric—and from Hugh.

She'd escaped Robert, but not her own heart, she realized. Perhaps time away from the world outside would give her a chance to order her emotions, as well as giving her the opportunity to learn the skills she needed for the journey she must make if ever she was to find her father.

Perhaps time away would also give her the chance to forget about both Godric *and* Hugh? She would do well to succeed in that, for while she was locked in here, Gytha would have the run of the manor and be free to choose whoever might make her an offer. Looking closely into her own lonely, aching heart, Janna knew that in Gytha's shoes, she'd find it hard to make a choice between Godric and Hugh. Better perhaps to be in her own shoes here at the abbey, with no choices left to her at all.

"Come," said the nun. She beckoned, and Janna followed, turning her back on Godric, and on the outside world. In an effort to scrape up some courage, she set her shoulders square and tilted her chin. One thought gave her comfort. She was Johanna, daughter of John. Wherever she went, and whatever she did, she would make her father proud of her. Finding him was her goal now. For the time being, romance would just have to wait.

Glossary

Aelfshot: A belief that illness or a sudden pain (like rheumatism, arthritis or a "stitch") was caused by elves who shot darts at humans or livestock.

Ague: Fever and chills.

Breeches: Trousers held up by a cord running through the hem at the waist.

Boon work: At busy times in the farming year (such as haymaking and harvest) villeins were required to work extra days in the lord's fields. In return, they were given food and ale.

Canonical hours: The medieval day was governed by sunrise and sunset and divided into eight canonical hours. Times of prayer were marked by bells rung in abbeys and monasteries beginning with matins followed by lauds at sunrise; then prime, terce, sext, none and vespers at sunset; followed by compline before going to bed.

Carol: A medieval 'singing dance'.

Caught red-handed: Literally with blood on your hands, evidence that you had been poaching in the king's forest.

Coney: Rabbit.

Cot: Small cottage.

Cottar: A medieval villein (serf) who occupied a cottage and a small piece of land on his lord's demesne, in return for his labor.

Demesne: Manors/land owned by a feudal lord for his own use.

Forest law: From William the Conqueror's time, royal forests were the preserve of kings and the "vert" (living wood) and the "venison" (the creatures of the forest) were protected and managed. The laws caused great hardship to the peasants, who needed timber for building and kindling, while hunger tempted many to go poaching—but they faced punishment, and sometimes even death, if caught by the forester with blood on their hands.

Gore acres: The odd corners of fields too awkward to plow.

Gorget: A cape with a hood, worn by the lower classes.

Hayward: Manorial official in charge of haymaking and harvest, and the repair and upkeep of hedges and ditches.

Heriot: A death duty to the lord of the manor, usually comprising the best beast, and sometimes also some household goods such as metal utensils or uncut cloth. This constituted "payment" for the loss of a worker.

Hue and cry: With no practicing police force other than a town sergeant to enforce the law, anyone discovering a crime was expected to "raise a hue and cry"—shouting aloud to alert the community to the fact that a crime had been committed, after which all those within earshot must commence pursuit of the criminal.

Kirtle: Long dress worn over a short tunic.

Medale: A drinking festivity after the lord's meadows have been mown.

Mortuary: Death duty paid by a villein to the parish priest—usually the second-best beast.

Plowshare: Along with the coulter, the iron cutting parts of a plow. The coulter is a blade or wheel that makes the preliminary cut through the soil; the share is the cutting blade of the plow.

Posset: A hot drink with curative properties.

Pottage: A vegetable soup or stew.

Reeve: The reeve (steward) was usually appointed by the villagers, and was responsible for the management of the manor. Shire reeves (sheriffs) were appointed by the king to administer law and justice in the shires (counties).

Rush light: A peeled rush dipped in hot animal fat, which made a primitive candle.

Strip fields: A system of farming practiced in medieval time, whereby two fields were plowed and sewn for harvest in summer and winter, while a third field lay fallow.

Sumpter horse: A packhorse used to transport goods.

Thegn: An Anglo-Saxon man, second in status to a nobleman or ealdorman, who holds land from the king in return for military service.

Tiring woman: A female attendant on a lady of high birth and importance.

Tocsin: A bell rung to sound an alarm.

Villein: Peasant or serf tied to a manor and to an overlord, and given land in return for labor and a fee—either money or produce.

Water meadows: The farmland on either side of a river that floods regularly.

Week work: Two or three days' compulsory labor in the lord's fields.

Wortwyf: A herb wife, a wise woman and healer.

Author's Note

The Janna Chronicles are set in the 1140s, at a turbulent time in England's history. After Henry I's son, William, drowned in the *White Ship* disaster, Henry was left with only one legitimate heir, his daughter, Matilda (sometimes known as Maude). Matilda had a difficult childhood. At the age of eight, she was betrothed to a much older man, Heinrich, Emperor of Germany, and she was sent to live in that country until, aged twelve, she was considered old enough to marry him. Evidently she was beloved by the Germans, who begged her to stay on after the Emperor died, but at the age of twenty-four, and childless, Matilda was summoned back to England by her father. For political reasons, and despite Matilda's vehement protests, Henry insisted that she marry Count Geoffrey of Anjou, a boy some ten years her junior. They married in 1128, and the first of their three sons, Henry (later to become Henry II of England), was born in 1133.

Henry I announced Matilda his heir and twice demanded that his barons, including her cousin, Stephen of Blois, all swear an oath of allegiance to her. This they did, but when Henry died, Matilda went to in Normandy while Stephen went straight to London to gather support, and then on to Winchester, where he claimed the Treasury and was crowned King of England.

Not one to be denied her rights, Matilda gathered her own supporters, including her illegitimate half-brother, Robert of Gloucester, and in 1139 she landed at Arundel Castle in England, prepared to fight for the crown. She left her children with Geoffrey, who thereafter stayed in Anjou and in Normandy, pursuing his own interests. Civil war between Stephen and Matilda raged in England for nineteen years, creating such hardship and misery that the *Peterborough Chronicle* reported: "Never before had there been greater wretchedness in the country ... They said openly that Christ and His saints slept."

I became interested in this period of English history while researching the Shalott trilogy. As this new series began to fall into place, I realized that this time of shifting allegiances and treachery, of fierce battles and daring escapes, of great danger and cruelty, formed a perfect setting with many plot possibilities. Janna's travels will bring her into the company of nobles, peasants and pilgrims, jongleurs and nuns, spies and assassins, and even King Stephen and the Empress Matilda. With England in the grip of civil war, secrets abound, loyalties change and passions run high. Janna will encounter the darkest side of human nature: the jealousy, greed, ambition, deceit and fear which so often lead to betrayal and murder. As well as solving the mystery of her past, and of her heart, Janna's mission is to find out the truth and bring the guilty to judgment. But she will need great courage, intelligence and insight to escape danger, and also to solve the many crimes she encounters along her journey.

For those interested in learning more about the civil war between Stephen and Matilda, there are numerous biographies on both of them, while Sharon Penman's *When Christ and His Saints Slept* is an excellent account of that period. On a lighter note, I have much enjoyed the Brother Cadfael Chronicles by Ellis Peters, which are also set at that time. While Janna's loyalty lies in a different direction from Ellis Peters' characters, her skill with herbs was inspired by these wonderful stories of the herbalist at Shrewsbury Abbey.

The Janna Chronicles begin in Wiltshire, England. Janna's quest for truth and justice will take her from the forest of Gravelinges (now known as Grovely Wood) to royal Winchestre, seat of power where the Treasury was housed. I've kept to the place names listed in the *Domesday Book* compiled by William the Conqueror in 1086, but the contemporary names of some of the sites are: Berford—Barford St Martin; Babestoche—Baverstock; Bredecumbe—Burcombe; Wiltune—Wilton; Sarisberie—Sarum (later relocated and named Salisbury); Oxeneford—Oxford, and Winchestre—Winchester.

The royal forest of Gravelinges was the only forest in Wiltshire mentioned in the *Domesday Book*. While it has diminished in size since medieval time, I have experienced at first hand how very easy it is to get utterly lost once you stray off the path! Wilton was the ancient capital of Wessex. The abbey was established in Saxon times and became one of the most prosperous in England, ranked with the houses of Shaftesbury, Barking and Winchester as a nunnery of the first importance.

Following the dissolution of the monasteries during the reign of Henry VIII, ownership of the abbey's lands passed to William Herbert, Firstst Earl of Pembroke. Some 450 years later, the 18th Earl of Pembroke now owns this vast estate. A magnificent stately home, Wilton House, stands in place of the abbey and is open to visitors.

While writing medieval England from Australia is a difficult and hazardous enterprise, I have been fortunate in the support and encouragement I've received along the way. So many people have helped make this series possible, and in particular I'd like to thank the following: Nick and Wendy Combes of Burcombe Manor, for taking me into their family, giving me a home away from home and teaching me about life on a farm, both now and in medieval time. Mike Boniface, warden of Grovely, who guided me through the forest by day and ensured that I also saw it (and the badgers and glowworms!) at night. Pat Sweetman from the USA, who warned me about rue, and who shared her knowledge of herbal medicine with me. Gillian Polack, mentor and friend, whose knowledge of medieval life helped shape the series and gave it veracity. Finally, my thanks to all at Momentum for their thought, care and expertise, and for enabling me to introduce the Janna Chronicles to a whole new audience.